VILLAGE
with BLUE DOORS

Books by Meredith Steinbach

NOVELS:

Village with Blue Doors

Beata Rustica: The Tale of the Would-Be Saint

*The Charmed Life of Flowers:
Field Notes from Provence*

The Birth of the World as We Know It; or, Teiresias

Zara

Here Lies the Water

SHORT FICTION COLLECTION:

Reliable Light

VILLAGE
with BLUE DOORS

A Novel by
MEREDITH STEINBACH

HOUSE OF REMINGTON

PUBLISHING

Book Design by Mary Tiegreen
Author Photograph by Zach S. Hartman

With gratitude to Mary Tiegreen for her continued artistic grace and acumen in the designing of this book and its cover; and to Sally McHenry for her keen eye and discerning editorial powers.

SENTRY *in a* YELLOW BOAT

ON THE MORNING OF THE FLOOD, having abandoned his small, yellow *van de poste*, and having then soared through our village in his swollen, emergency, inflatable, also yellow boat on the incoming overland tide—after the unnatural current had finally dwindled out from under him on the vineyard plateau that lies between St. X and St. G—Monsieur Pereault *de Poste* was able to telephone the news: if only our mayor Henri Béranger, The Beloved as we called him then, would go around—careful of the deluge, *bien sur!*—to the *Place* where the lower boules court still coincides with the descending garden of the church, The Beloved would there note his closest friend Père Martin's most peculiar whereabouts.

SALUTATIONS

FOR MANY REASONS, PÈRE MARTIN HAD BEGUN THAT DAY in a splendid mood. An azure sky dangled above the undulating orange-tiled roofs of St. X, doctored by a firmament of burning, candle-shaped clouds. A burst of springtime purple iris blooms escorted his stocky body along the narrow lane and back toward Rue de Versailles where Ferdinand the Baker sold his essential morning beignets-café. Up and around his favorite little blue lanes, our priest stumped, ever in his dark clerical robes, crisscrossing Rue Vivienne, reliving the celebrations of the preceding night and chortling to himself.

What a *fête* that had been! What a day. And, what a night! Yes, indeed. Finally he had successfully counseled marriage for that most recalcitrant of bachelors, Ambrose le Beau, the one-eyed embezzler of many feminine sympathies, owner of the St. G Music Shop, and conductor of the regional children's symphony. Père Martin had persuaded him to marry his latest fixation, that lovely little albino foreigner, Pearl Queneau, with whom coincidentally le Beau had been living for nearly two years. That in itself was a sort of miracle.

Père Martin did not need to brag to any villagers, least of all to Doctor Christian Malaplate—who had had the privilege of tranquilizing several disenchanted ladies in his clinics next to the bakeries in Sts. Z & G—nor to Mayor Henri Béranger who was himself surrogate father to The Colossus, as Ambrose le Beau had insisted on calling himself even before his size as a pre-adolescent had far surpassed that of the other boys, even before Ambrose le Beau had lost sight in his one eye in the famous boyhood river incident.

On the Eve of The Flashflood Unforeseeable, Père Martin set the date of the wedding for late autumn, immediately following the grape harvest. Hopefully this would be just far enough away to give opportunity for preparation and not long enough to allow the eruption of debilitating bachelor qualms.

The blissful couple hurried home to invite several continents of relatives, traveling band members, and Pearl's old school chums from her days at the international lycée and from her university in Paris. Then they bounded off to rejoice at Café Rousseau where Père Martin had already proudly propped himself against his usual gold-fringed pillow in his customary chair beside the *chimenée* and was knocking back small milky glasses of his favorite licorice-flavored aperitif.

Père Martin tallied up at least seventeen times that the lithe, chalky-skinned, translucent-haired, popular teacher Mademoiselle Queneau was hoisted like a stem of St. Bernard's lily onto the well-polished limestone bar. Pearl sang and swayed as she was compared good-naturedly to a vanilla treat in extemporaneous verse and song. Beside Ambrose' stand-up bass, the pair's musician friends were in good form in jazz and rock. Tomás and Mimi Gibain arrived from Sète bearing, respectively, clarinet and flute. Ebert, the mad drummer of St. G, drove over around midnight with a full set of traps and twin toddlers in tow.

Père Martin nestled a child beneath each arm and kept time with fork and spoon, cutting excessive volume from the amplifiers with the corners of two flowered napkins screwed into his ears.

Le proprietor, Georges Menard, too, caroled repeatedly from behind his bar, plugging the jukebox with francs from his cash register, playing Johnny Hallyday and Edith Piaf discs on demand, then Edgar and Johnny Winter's "Good Morning Little School Girl" as a particular tribute to the bride during interludes taken by the bands. Creative invective streamed steadily from the neighboring room, accompanying the knocking together of the cues and balls.

Around three a.m. in a blue-and-yellow frock and matching party apron with her hair tied back in a ponytail, Madame Menard popped out of the kitchen and presented the after-hours version of her *coq au vin*. In turn, Jean-Luc Redon, who had already studied with the bride-to-be for several weeks in her Wednesday evening English class, was so reduced to tears that he launched a gravelly, quasi-English toast, "To cheers, Ambrose *et* Pearl. Many the happy weddings for you!" And then, his formerly sonorous voice erupted from his skinny form and paralyzed the room.

It was the first song Jean-Luc Redon had emitted from his axe-like face since the night two winters before when he had broken with his Adam's apple the motion of his steering wheel against the bridge abutment between St. X and St. Z, permanently converting even his spoken voice from tenor to lower bass.

After the luxurious meal, dancing resumed on the floor and on the bar itself as a pink morning sun projected its orange tentacles through the budding vineyards playing king of the mountain with the well-used cars in the parking lot. Once again, Georges Menard tapped a glass on the bar and reminded amiably, "Stockings only, if you please. Stockings only on the bar!"

The FLASH FLOOD UNFORESEEABLE

 **SOON ENOUGH, THE DAY OF THE FLASHFLOOD UNFORESEEABLE HAD BEGUN.** Under azure skies, in the haze of the slightest hangover, Père Martin turned again to reminiscing about his early manhood days before the priesthood and in the war. Who knew how much time had passed before the elderly priest began to realize that several persons were raising a commotion, if not at him, then toward someone very near to him. Was someone calling his name? he asked himself. A flurry of telephones jangled out from the linked stone domiciles; and then came the hurried machine-gun fire of blue shutters slamming, as if in preparation for a grand mistral. Soon enough all the time-inscribed lanes of St. Xavier seemed to Père Martin far too deserted for a forenoon in late spring.

Quickly Père Martin veered toward the distant side entrance of his church, ducking down Rue du Lion, when suddenly the foremost rim of the run-away mountain current lay above him like a massive, green, descending exit ramp off the auto-route. Everything came to a stop for him then, including any movement in his normally agile limbs; and he could not help thinking how the sight was not all that different, except in color, of course, from that slaying blade of surf that had been pursuing him since early youth in his nightmares of the famous Red Sea incident. In those dreams he had tried, well into middle age, repeatedly and most unsuccessfully, to play the liberating leading role, only to find the force of abundant red water crashing down on him.

All too real then, the immensely expanded Emerald River asserted itself through the Place where the seven principal way-fares meet, until Père Martin found himself striding up to his waist in runaway water and holding over his head his remaining café-flavored beignet.

From their attic window, Hubert Hauberk the Butcher and his wife hailed him all too briefly as he saw himself split by multiple reflections of toy propellers from the wooden flying machines he had so often admired in the butcher's window display. Lifted out of the water and dashed back down, in a near faint with buzzing in his ears, he had been carried completely around the block, only to be pressed entirely under the madly careening, green, liquid bombardment. Among the rapidly jettisoned fragments of debris, Père Martin tripped and gasped and bobbed as he clamored to give himself higher perch.

Weighed down by his heavy robe, even the patina on his newly polished shoes seemed too cumbersome, until finally he found himself entirely subsumed. His eyes opened under the floodwaters with little reassurance. For a long time, Père Martin thought himself to have been struck blind. Or, even dead perhaps. He could not be sure. In a series of hallucinatory moments brought on by the stinging cold and damp, and then, too, as the growing asphyxiation had its effect, he was compelled to believe that in some strange way he was being hand-laundered by none other than God himself against the ribs of that all too familiar stone staircase, the one that to this day cascades down through Père Martin's own crimson creation, his plush red rose garden, the one without thorns.

IN TIME *and* INFINITE SPACE

Monsieur le Maire **Henri Béranger**—The Beloved, as we called him then—responded quickly to Pereault de Poste's hysterical call from that singular telephone box that still protrudes from the minor crossroads on the Plateau of Vines between St. X and St. G, where his yellow, inflatable, emergency boat had finally come to rest. Along with every villager *le Maire* could gather to help him on that day, he came to elevate Hubert Hauberk's aluminum extension ladder toward that point in time and infinite space where our benevolent Père Martin, glowing red in the eyeballs and mottled as a piece of steak, lay in the blue arms of the newly painted statue of the Sacred Mother. There, miraculously, he proceeded to squeak a few too-blue words from his temporary roost and cast them down upon the multitudes of St. Xavier:

"Until this day, of you eight hundred or so souls gathered here who have been consecrated by me, not one of you has ever truly understood the agony or humiliation of any other human being residing along side you here in St. X, or in St. G, or for that matter in St. Z. Just this once, if you please, at least pretend to care about another living being! And, stop pointing and ogling me, when all I want to do is get down from here and let Malaplate have a look at my legs!"

The yet pontificating priest was none too soon disentangled from the sacred arms of the Blue Mother and was trundled on the hunched back of the crowd to the rectory where Doctor Malaplate, after several hours of hard work, posted a sign on the door of the priest's ginger-colored residence:

If ever you,
who read these words,
are planning to need aid—
be it from Doctor, God, or Government—
take this warning. Heed:
Do NOT disturb the door
of this rectory or Père Martin
who rests gravely ill within.

—C'est moi, none other than
the One that's written this:
Monsieur Christian Malaplate,
Médicin de Médicine Générale
for the locales of Stes. X, G, & Z
and all surrounding vicinities.

Also earnestly decreed,
by Monsieur Henri Béranger,
Honorable Mayor
Of this Village Formidable,
St. X.

DETAILS *from the* RECTORY

THE YARN BEGAN TO UNFOLD ITSELF as details sifted down from Père Martin's room. Doctor Christian Malaplate reported some of them, and also Mayor Henri Béranger who, upon returning home, immediately conveyed the information to his lovely elder sister, Brigitte, who had taken care of the mayor since that other terrible river incident just twenty years before.

Before long, an intimate portrayal of the history of Père Martin's accident was all over town: it was that final underwater dash of his hip against his favorite stone pediment that the abbot claimed had saved his life. He swore on oath that he had heard a sound like a cracking plank when he sustained that most unfortunate of the multitudinous injuries—his hip fracture—the pain of which had sent him bolting upward as though squirted from a fish, there to land on the newly painted outstretched arms of the Blessed Blue Mother in his famous belly flop.

By midday of the very next day, the details of the doctoring session were already legendary in Café Rousseau. A thoroughly shaken Doctor Christian Malaplate had daubed and plastered Père Martin from the salt and pepper strings of his armpits down, applying the hardening paste over and around the turtle-shaped paunch, saying, as he always said in the direst circumstance, "Pas de problème!"

"Not a problem, Père Martin!" he exaggerated, leaving the head of the priest's cowering sea turtle a place to pop out and relieve itself. Even then, over the fractured hip and legs, the distraught doctor skimmed toward the hairy goat-like ankles, there to stop with a start at the priest's inexplicably too warm feet.

Le Maire, too, could not help but notice the heat rising off Père Martin's foot, as he placed his hands on the arch. "It is then one good thing, isn't it, Martin, that that rose garden of yours has no thorns," *le Maire's* awkward voice croaked, "or we would be plucking thorns from you still, and watching the water exuding from your sieve-like, hairy hide."

Our priest wheezed out then, from under Malaplate's hardening plaster encasement, "Can't you say something encouraging for once, Henri? And you, Malaplate, plaster Henri instead so he will shut up! Start with his head!"

"And," persisted the mayor, "what about that most excellent painting job, Martin, that old Monsieur Didi finessed up there, painting the Blue Mother already before the Bastille Day fête? What did you think of the craftsmanship once you got up so close?"

Their young friend the doctor coughed at both of them to stop, but just as always they went on, goading one another. Goading.

Unrestrained by the doctor, Béranger blabbed on: "And he only spilled the little dabs on his horse and cart, I admired that. You were so skeptical of him, Martin. Now, you have had a first-hand look, have you not? At the Blue Mother, I mean! Not the horse! Har har!"

At least Père Martin was still lucid, the doctor was thinking with increasing concern. As if in reply, the priest only moaned.

"Well, one good thing now anyway, Martin," the mayor declared. "Now at least you can't stage any more of your so-called religious protests at my town meetings for a while."

"Is that so, Henri?" Père Martin growled, his face already a-bristle with greying daily growth. "I can still do my worst against the likes of you, Henri. Get me something icy for my head, can't you! Please, Henri. It feels like my head has an axe in it. I must have struck my head on something, too. Ice please, Christian!"

"Tais-toi," the doctor warned. "Both of you. Can't you see I'm busy here? *Bien*, now lift him up on that side, *Monsieur le Maire*, please."

The priest gave out a wrenching groan as the two large men shifted him. Père Martin might have liked just this once to take a swing at either one of his closest friends, but his reflexes were too pained as his multiple contusions drained his strength.

"Malaplate, don't lift that leg again," he begged, grinding his teeth. "I don't want that cold goop on my skin. Put it on my head, I say. My head is breaking but I can hardly feel my feet. Cease frosting my legs, I say, Malaplate! What is wrong with my feet?"

His blocky teeth clattered away like cutlery at a village feast as our *maire* Henri Béranger left off for a moment with the chatter and jokes. Truly worried now, *le Maire* snatched the priest's nightcap from its hook, packed it with ice from the priest's half-size refrigerator, and gently pressed it over the pale, pink crown to nestle its edges against the grey fringe. He held tightly then to Père Martin's shaking fists as Doctor Malaplate hurried to finish the body cast. Then, all three of them began to fight back tears.

When a silence hovered over the room loud enough to terrify all three friends, Doctor Malaplate took a turn in trying to distract them from the predicament. "So, Martin—" He cleared his throat. "I would be interested to hear what the Blue Mother said to you when she held on to you so intimately like that." He broke off the glass tip of yet another glass vial and drew the medicament into his syringe. "Without her, I'm afraid you might have been lost to us."

"Not another pique! Malaplate! You know, I'm not keen on shots!"

"Now, Martin, you should answer Christian Malaplate when he asks you a fervent religious question in a moment of serious angst like this," *le Maire* intervened. "Besides, you don't often get such a good chance to lecture both of us at once."

The priest barely breathed as the needle went in. And then, a film of sweat beaded up like a crown of crystals around the edge of the icy hat. "Well, the Virgin did say something—"

"She did, Père? She said something?"

Henri Béranger stared into the priest's quickly spiraling eyes and wiped the terrified brow and placed a handkerchief into his friend's palm. "There, there there, the Blue Mother can't have been all that malevolent, can she, Père? After all, what's so terrible that she might have said to you, when in the same moment she decided to save your life like that?"

The priest's face turned sallow as creamed cauliflower. "The Virgin—" he sighed. He gathered the strength to speak. "She scolded me," he squeaked.

"She scolded you, mon Père?" Doctor Malaplate asked tenderly. "But why?" How he regretted then that he had ever brought the subject up. He was very nearly done now, but Père Martin had already begun to lose contact with time and place. Soon, he knew, Père Martin's clock toward Whatever Was the Inevitable would begin to tick on its own.

"The Virgin is disappointed in me," the suddenly aging man simpered. "She said, 'Can't you see, Martin? I am not your old used car!'"

"Not your old used car!" the two friends could not help blurting at the absurdity. Just as swiftly, they tried to take their outcry back, *"Pas de problème, pas de problème, Père Martin,"* the young, mustachioed Malaplate crooned. Together the two pals crooned it again and again to their old friend. *Le Maire* stroked the priest's hands while the doctor set loose another tranquilizer.

When finally the body cast had set, *le Maire* covered his life-long friend tenderly with warming sheets and blankets while Christian Malaplate delivered his directions for that day's Most Unfortunate of Unfortunates:

"There there, take your peaceful sleep, *mon* Père. The time will come when you will feel much better again. To be sure, one of us will be right here beside your bed to look after you when you again awake."

"Not your old used car,'" the priest moaned, drifting slowly toward an existential agony that seemed to surpass even the tortures of body, bone, and lung. "What She must think of me, my dear boys. What She must think."

"Such a very bad dream, dear Père," the doctor said, "caused by so much water down your throat. Sleep fast, mon Père. We look after you."

"Bonne nuit, Martin," the mayor whispered. "My sister will come around to tell you her little stories like she does. You know how comforting Brigitte can be. She is on her way right now. I remember how she took care of me when the river, too, got at me. One of us will be with you. *Bonne nuit."*

"That's right, Martin," Christian Malaplate said, hovering beside the bed. "Soon Brigitte will be here, stroking your brow and telling you again and again how wonderful you are. Especially for buying the contact lenses, Père, for the little goat herd girl so she wouldn't fall off the mountainside in the rain again, you know how Brigitte liked that."

"You know how she loves that story," the mayor whispered. "Brigitte has always been so appreciative of you."

"As are all of us, Martin!"

"Not your old used car!" Père Martin began to screech, trying to fling himself off the bed. He was then like a parrot on fire, until, after an agonizing time, eventually the tranquilizer bloomed into the lessening volume of his voice.

The doctor smoothed the top coverlet over him, the one with the red roses the village women had embroidered in honor of Père Martin's successful village beautification experiment. How lovely it was, they had said repeatedly, not to have to worry about the children falling off their bicycles into the vast expanse of new roses, they said. And also not to have to embroider all those thorns! With any other priest, there would have been thorns. No, they knew, Père Martin had never been able to stomach the finer details of the crucifixion.

"Not the used car!" he squawked again.

"One day soon, all of it will seem only a bad dream, Martin, if you can just give up now and rest yourself."

"Rest now please, Martin. Have sweet reveries!"

"Pas de problème…pas de problème," they chanted ever more softly from under mutually worried brows. *"Pas de problème…pas de problème,"* they crooned until finally Père Martin fell into his deep slumber, dreaming of a frightening deluge of used car salesmen in an inundation of red and green.

"What a mercy, what a trip," they said. "Finally, he sleeps." Then together they made their way down through the chaos that their village had become. They had gone but a few blocks or more before one of them exclaimed about the metamorphosis, for in addition to the mud and refuse lying everywhere and the overturned cars, there was a distinct difference in the color scheme. It would seem that the giant green wave that had overtaken the town had washed away all of the newer paint on all the doors, and left behind only the weather-worn blue from days of old.

Wolves' Teeth

Chunks of peasant bread, Ambrose le Beau slivered into dozens of elongated, slightly curved shapes. In a veil of butter and garlic, he sautéed them and carefully placed them in a ring. Pearl woke to find him crouching beside the bed, tugging at the hem of her nightgown like a child. He led her out. In the kitchen, he had built up the wood in the *cheminée* and arranged all the kindling and even the larger sticks into a teepee on the grate. A blaze of smoke and light shot through the morning chill.

He draped his leather jacket over her shoulders; around her legs he tucked her shawl to ward off any possibility of flu. So many months it would be before the warmer outdoor weather penetrated the thick walls; of this he felt he must remind her repeatedly. Yellow and azure paisley napkins flowered upon the tablecloth. He poured her coffee out, and for a moment he made her shut her eyes.

When she opened them, the breakfast plate seemed an abstract painting within its colorful cloth. *"Voilà! Les oeufs brouillées Argenteuil."* The yellow plate held silky eggs, perfectly poached and garnished with the palest green asparagus tips. A halo of slim orange slices mimicked its poached salmon center. A rain of delicate white sauce cloaked it all, dusted with the light green filaments from his indoor herb garden. And, what was this? A necklace of fifty hand-cut golden segments of toasted peasant bread, cashew-shaped, like an amphibian's claws, encircled the outer ridge of his offering.

"Investigate the little wolves' teeth, *la!*" he exclaimed.

Indeed, those little wolves' teeth were incomparable. So simple, yet she could not stop crunching them.

"But what about you? Aren't you going to eat the little teeth, too?"

"Oh no!" He pursed his lips, momentarily anticipating his own attempt at English syllables, but finally he kept silent.

"Oh, Beau," she said. "You are too cute for words."

"*Cute!*" he blustered as though he could really be angry with her. "*Cute?*" Peevishly, he buttoned his shirt's top buttons. "There will be no *l'amour à la papa* with Ambrose le Beau! There will be no watching the clock on the wrist with Ambrose!"

"Don't brag so," she said, engrossed in her salmon.

"*Brag?*" he said. "What means the *brag* to you?"

"Don't swagger so."

"*Swagger?*"

"This breakfast is magnificent!"

"*Wolves' teeth,*" he pronounced proudly, "*Mais non,* the teeth of the wolf are not *cute.* You know this word *succulent?* Knowing you, my first true love, I am not surprised if you *do* know it." He kissed the air for emphasis, bowed and swooped, making his awkward, overgrown gestures.

∞

When later in the week it was again his turn to cook, he prepared what he thought would appeal to her American nature, explaining, "*En Amerique,* you have the *hamburger.* And admit this, you have brought your victims here to the disgusting very hot dogs. I do not speak of the French or even the Italian *saucisse.* Or even the schnitzel of Wiener. You bring me the red shirt and the pin for the lapel with the hot dog on it, but not the baseball of Mickey Mantel. Ah well, what can we expect of priorities *Americaine?* Of French cuisine and in life of France, all is superior. Even the most insignificant of sausages."

She pleased him then with tales of the little island, the Isle of Man, from which her grandmother had come, and tales of the gigantic Viking king who'd been called The King of Man and the Isles, and of the Manx language as it had been supplanted by the English one, and—just as much to his liking—of the tailless cat, the Manx, which roamed everywhere on her great grandmother's small stony island.

But he, like most of the others she'd met at first in St. X, when they heard that she'd been raised there and had American relatives still living there, it was that which consumed their assumptions about her character. It was as though she had never mentioned that she had spent nearly half of her life in France.

∽

They continued under the influence of imported American television and its simple shows, badly chosen for their dynamics and for easy translation into French—mostly for the ever popular presence of cleavage and guns—and dubbed most hideously. Ambrose preferred watching the American-made conflicts of wealthy Texas oil barons, fast police cars and emergency rooms. His specialties, as he called them, were spy operations with heavily armed and particularly crafty sleuths. He was dumb-struck to hear that Pearl's American relatives did not watch such shows or even carry guns.

"Not even when at home asleep? Everyone knows *les Americaines* sleep with guns for the man who prowls."

"Not even when asleep."

"Your relatives must be so very brave," he said with concern. "Or, they are crazy." This worried him visibly for a moment. She watched him dismiss its possibility.

"My closest relatives come from the Isle of Man," she patiently told him yet again—this time in French. "There the houses of government are called the Council and the House of Keys. Don't you think that interesting? The House of Keys. I find it fascinating."

On the counter then, with aplomb, he laid out for himself one spongy grilled sandwich, the ham and cheese *croque-monsieur* that she had avoided so thoroughly during all her years in France. As far as she could determine, it was the only culinary catastrophe in the history of France, but a large one, she told herself, and rather soggy-looking at that.

"Patience, *mon petit chou-fleur*—" he murmured, dancing about with the iron pan in the air and the silver spatula flying.

As she dolefully edged into the chair, she pressed her napkin to her lap. His spatula slipped over her plate. Before her lay nearly the same horrific sandwich as the *croque-monsieur* on his platter, but her sandwich had a hole cut out of it. In a tortured and somewhat soppy slab of bread, and in addition to the steamed-to-death cheese and ham, nestled a large, watery egg—partially poached!

"Voilà! My invention: *croque-madame!* We must understand these Manx and *Americaines.*" She sat quite still, waiting for his pronouncement. "This is my answer to your relatives' hot crossed dog!"

The egg in the middle stared up at her. She felt something tiny cut loose in her lower abdomen, and threaten to come up. Perhaps the sight of his *croque-madame* had actually triggered an ovum, she laughed to herself. She controlled her thoughts, as she often did when her amusement threatened to race away with her. This she did by imagining that his one visible eye was purple as an early lavender sprig.

He tapped the butt of his knife on the tablecloth and pulled his plate toward himself. "*Ouais!* You now admit French superiority in the making of the sandwich!"

"Never. I have never claimed the hot dog you offend, my dearest Beau, not even for the sake of comedy. If you must poach and steam, give me the fresh poached bass! Give me the north Atlantic salmon! Do not give me these sandwiches! Give me the fruits of the greatest of Great Lakes, give me the Isle's, give me food from the Irish Sea! Give me anything French but these! Give me *le croque-mort,* the undertaker!"

Ambrose scowled, in a bleak mood now. "You women of all countries, you hate men these days; it is too apparent. Even when we cook! We can do nothing to please."

"So," she smiled, tepidly, "you assume women feel at home with eggs? You were right the first time. Besides, I know you didn't invent the *croque-madame,* Ambrose. Give me the teeth of wolves! Toasted, or plain. I much prefer the teeth of wolves. For that, I thank you! You can keep each and every one of these monstrous, stewed and staring things, but give me the wolves' teeth."

That she hoped would put an end to his dramatics.

∞

Anyway, light-heartedly, she was off to visit Père Martin, or at least pine for him at the base of his stairs if the way was barred. She would lean against his blue door and sing to him. Though she was no singer officially, or not much of one, she could carry a tune. Père Martin would understand the missed notes. He was like that. She would sit on his front step and influence her dreams for the better, she thought. It would be like him to appreciate that.

A Challenging
Décor

JULIETTE MENARD FLED THE HEAT OF THE KITCHEN at Café Rousseau to set a vase of irises and early red rose buds beside Père Martin's usual armchair, where he could see them from his bed.

How it pained the villagers to hear what she had seen. During the long night before, while Père Martin lay in the bedroom of his rectory encased in Doctor Christian Malaplate's infamous body concrete, someone had dared to creep in by night and desecrate the priest's cast! In bold capitals, in bright green, permanent, marker pen, it had been written and so improperly misspelled:

HERE LIES

PÈRE MARTINI

GUIDE TO OLD USED CARS

What a hideous insult to poor Père Martin, who might yet live or die. What did it mean? Only the Rabbit Catcher could have been so perverse, or so crafty, as to have stolen his way through locked and guarded doors. Stolen cars had been among the Rabbit Catcher's more youthful interests, before Père Martin had rehabilitated him, so it was recalled to one another in Café Rousseau; but no, never was it said directly into the Rabbit Catcher's big-boned, taunting face.

Mais non! Most certainly not. Yet the Rabbit Catcher's eyes were small, as though scratched into his face with a paper clip. It was better to ignore the oaf's so-called accomplishments, better not to encourage him in his disruptive ways. Who knew what might happen next with such an irreverent one as that one.

Still, the conversations went on in the café. And then ensued the debates, beginning and ending with the requisite defense: Perhaps the Rabbit Catcher had had a brief moment of tenderheartedness? queried the tenderhearted Madonna Meulemeester after her morning cherry juice.

Mais oui, offered Camille Desbordes. Perhaps he had placed his motto on Père Martin's cast as an act of kindness for his priest? After all, Père Martin had been the Rabbit Catcher's only defender in St. X since his earliest encounters with the police.

Ouais, ouais.

Everyone over a certain age could remember that.

No, that graffiti was the Rabbit Catcher's crow of triumph, no doubt about it, the frustrated little cock. That was his manner of signature! Breaking and entering another's domicile? That was nothing to him.

Report of the martini joke had caused a hush to fall over Café Rousseau the likes of which would not soon be heard again. They were all thinking of it now.

No, no, even the Rabbit Catcher could not be so cruel. Everyone knew that the Rabbit Catcher had spelling issues *extraordinaire*. They put the martini part of the affront down to spelling error, on that much finally they agreed.

After a suitable pause, the amiable Georges Menard could be heard squeaking his cloth along the surface of the marble bar. Then, in front of the lunch crowd, he ramped up the argument, moving on to even more sensitive issues. There was the matter of representation, or lack thereof, in the church.

In accepting the unctuous Septum as replacement for the stricken Père Martin, had the lovely village become the dumping ground for the lowliest of all the lowliest of available priests? That was the real question, wasn't it? There must have been quite a pecking order, even among the city priests.

Who were the most suspect of representatives available among those who were said to represent both the living and the dead, even Those Beyond, and Especially High Above This Earth?

The argument followed and soon enough became a din. Such treatment of the lovely St. X by higher authorities in the church seemed inconceivable at the beginning of the argument and far too plausible by the end!

There had been very good reasons, after all, that the church had been so desecrated, even priests drowned, during the Revolution, it was pointed out.

Day turned into night and the weekend left and the big doors closed behind the last paying dinner guests. By early Monday morning, only the last holdouts at the bar remained.

Georges Menard completed his polishing of the glorious panels of his antiquated crimson jukebox, the bulging translucent dome through which the records could be seen spinning into the brain of the machine and the music made, and all the black lettered and silver numbered buttons where anyone in the village might be represented by himself, or in times like these, by herself. Indeed.

He set about to make his stemware gleam. The brilliantly colored bottles once again seemed to effervesce in the mirror, showing off their contents, surrounded twice over by the splendidly carved wood frame. Once the perennially rising and falling after-dust and damp from the flood had once again been removed, Georges Menard poured out a fine St. X rosé, rather on the dry side, from an excellent former year.

Pastis was served to the arriving more hardened, sweet-toothed citizens, and another salute was raised to Père Martin.

In the kitchen Juliette Menard could be heard sniffing back her tears. And, who could blame her, after a whole day of trying to efface the writing on the cast, with typewriting correction fluid, paint to no avail, and even wallpaper and paste. "Everything bleeds!" was all she could say, as she delivered up the soup.

In Père Martin's usual corner by the fire, his lonely gold tasseled pillow seemed to accept accolades for him.

George Menard put forth a few last minute queries for consideration by the Café Rousseau philosophers: What did this cross section of the village think? Would the kindly Père Martin consider the presence of The Septum, Père Pepin, to be an act of divine vexation? Was it akin to the brush-up the goodly Père Martin had received in the rose garden, under the flood's murky element? Or, would Père Martin think it an inspiration toward divinely inspired tolerance?

Was Père Martin even at that moment lying in his bed, awaiting a frightening sequel to his celebrated rescue by the Blue Mother?

And, George Menard asked wistfully, would Père Martin himself eventually take the confused and rather distasteful younger priest under his, hopefully newly-mended, wing?

For that matter, it was interjected from a table near the window, would Père Martin be mended or would he be awarded wings?

In response, enough shocked words could not be cast. All questions about Père Pepin himself—respectfully stated, *bien sur*—surely had leaked into St. X out of his own ignoble past and were to be met with barely respectful disdain.

After assisting the nearly comatose Père Martin earlier that evening with his wash and feed, Juliette Menard had looked upon his ashen skin where it erupted in few enough places from his cast, put her head down on her forearms, and had a fit of sobbing that echoed down the street.

At Café Rousseau, questions arose without resolution. Life was too difficult. There was an end on it.

Straw, Cork, Rod, Staff

FOR THE OLD PRIEST, A LIFETIME OF DREAMS CAME BACK TO HIM: the red sea crashed down on him and on his multiple young saviors from all the old times ever after, and in each and every moment. He dreamed himself a piece of straw then, and again, and a cork then, and he had been a cork.

No rod, no holy staff, no meeting at the crossroads, no uplifting momentary image, or holding back of the floodgates occurred for him. He was his own whipping boy, after what She had said to him. Red was not his color, nor his friend, he told himself, without or within.

He had thought his life to be important, so many turns of phrase, of tenderness had been offered in his life to him, from him, to others, and in return. Whole towns had been affected by him and yet he could not in the moment now feel any part of it. He felt himself as nothing at the moment, nothing but an infinitesimal dead weight, a cork after all in the great sea, without contact.

And here he was now, again, stuck in, in plaster. A cork with a concussion, a plaster plug shot full of medicine and flooded with hatred. He was nothing like himself now! he told himself. Who was this wretched cork between fabrics? He tried to recall his name and could not. He tried to recall his profession. He tried to recall his past life, even days recently passed, and could not.

He tried to recall a moment, just one, any one, perhaps one at his mother's side. He could sense her, but he could not see her. He tried to recall a moment, any moment when he had found himself to be without the fracturing doubt. But it was the fracturing doubt now, and only the fracturing doubt. The fracturing doubt was upon him. It held sway now and would not give him up. He had seen it before, and the war was not even the worst of it. He knew that much. The depths of the fracturing doubt were unknowable. No more, no more! he thought. No Moses. What would he do about that?

Under Geraniums

FROM A NUMBER OF THE NEIGHBORING, flowering, wrought-iron balconies, it was easy to have a good look down upon the narrow cobbled rue that ran before the church, easy to see the two lovers waiting there just outside Père Martin's study. They were waiting to finalize the plans for their upcoming wedding ceremony, this time with Père Martin's substitute, Père Pepin, sent all the way out to St. X from Toulouse. Or, was it Lyon? From somewhere else it was, certainly not from here. Certainly they made a handsome pair on the street, tall and short, dark and light.

But then, the betrothed couple's good looks were nothing unusual in a country where everyone seemed to have about them some remarkable element of attractiveness and charm. There was something vivifying in the spring water and the wine. Even the most unlikely visiting foreigners were sometimes known, after a few good dousings in the St. X mud bath and super spa, to resemble models on the runway of a Parisian fashion institute.

⚮

So the villagers had yet another look at them: the lovely colorless woman, whose people came from the shore of some faraway lake, and the friendly St. X gargantuan lad. Under his thick dark curls, Ambrose's neck bore a strong resemblance to the trunk of that most marvelous chestnut tree at the center of St. X. Yes, after midnight many a woman on the way home from Café Rousseau had flipped her skirts about her knees and leaned to kiss that chestnut tree and called it Ambrose the Bountiful.

Ambrose's legs were large, the women said, shaped like that last tall pair of ancient plane trees that flanked the seventh road, the road that came in over the Pont du Diable from St. Y into St. X. Ambrose's shoulders were broad and meaty, too, they said; that much was obvious.

∞

Beside Ambrose stood his darling girl, the thin, exceedingly pale, straight-haired Mademoiselle Queneau, unapologetic *etranger*. If one looked closely, one could see the pink pupils of her eyes, shimmying ever so slightly in her head, as they always had. She could have been from any place, her French accent was that oddly lyrical. And so elusive was the origin of her complexion that she might as easily have been from England as from deepest Africa.

She said her people hailed from the Isle of Man long ago, and then from one Lake Michigan in America; and so said some of the return addresses on letters from people she said were her family. So they were noticed by Monsieur Pereault de Poste in the weeks after her arrival just seven years before. Perhaps it was true. Her acquired mannerisms passed almost well enough for her to be French, even for someone from America, they said.

There must have been some French in Pearl Queneau's ancestry—so said the afternoon revelers at Café Rousseau—or else, where did that albino girl get such keen intelligence and also her last name? She had been educated quite well enough, they admitted, having been to secondary school and university in Paris, after all.

Pearl Queneau was not a native of St. X. No, she was not. She was skillful enough to teach the St. X children English at school and a few adults, too, who took her Wednesday evening class.

The most striking point about her, of course, was never in dispute; it was obvious the moment the first villager turned to stare at her upon her arrival into town. This topic they brought up repeatedly at first, and still it filtered in after seven years of her being in their midst, and yet again it erupted in their endless discussions of the couple's upcoming nuptial merriment. They saw Pearl's hair as not white or platinum. It was flossy and clear as water, long-hanging, well below her waist. Her calves sprouted thin and shapely from the slight white knobbing of her knees.

Pearl Queneau had broad cheekbones, which she made even chalkier when she applied her scented face powder.

Concealment was so necessary, the herbalist Camille Desbordes explained at afternoon *pastis*, so necessary to protect the girl's disadvantaged skin from what would be, to her, a poisonous exposure to their luscious Mediterranean sun.

There, and just there, again, and over the bridge of her nose, and even into the delicate entrance to those eerily colorless nostrils, around the pale pink eyes, each day the sunscreen and then the dusty white powder puff intervened.

Yes, Pearl Queneau was sleek as a ferret, almost frightfully high-breasted. Pearl Queneau carried herself bolt upright, like someone who had been struck, fortunately or not, by two life-riveting thoughts at once.

But, of course, the customary carousers at Café Rousseau's bar agreed that Pearl Queneau was too sharp-witted for an outsider, but she was definitely too easy-going to be French.

Yes, that was an annoying trait, they said, nodding into the bottle-lined mirror of Café Rousseau at their dark selves.

There was always that hopeful note in Pearl, that weirdly joyful attitude.

Also, it could not be forgotten that Mademoiselle Pearl had chosen to waft sumptuously the scent of their local linden flower. The ladies of the village, and many men as well, admired her sensitivity to the St. X culture in that choice.

Camille Desbordes herself had concocted the perfume for her, as she was quick to point out. That intoxicating scent seemed to go well with the passionate, pinkish color of her eyes, Camille said.

Those pink eyes could be made to look almost violet, whenever Pearl Queneau troubled to put in her tinted plastic lenses, the ones that Enid the Goat Herd had so coveted.

No, they could never entirely disguise those red pupils and pink irises that marked her albino character, no, of course not. That would be absurd for the albino lady to wish, they said. Maybe that was why Pearl so rarely troubled to wear the things.

For a time, Mademoiselle Pearl lent her lenses to Enid the Goat Herd who had already streaked her glasses in the rain and fallen down a cliff pitifully several times. Once, Enid had even had to be rescued with an aluminum ladder, a length of rope, and a helicopter, from the Great Crevasse.

In the end, Pearl's gesture had not been sufficient since Pearl Queneau's eyes were not yet nearly so bad as Enid's were. Père Martin had come to the rescue then with his so-called *anonymous* donation to the optometrist in St. Z, for the exact amount of the cost of lenses for

Enid's eye correction—with Enid and her little son's safety in mind.

Yes, much can be seen from a balcony in St. X and remembered, even something as small as the slightest change in expression. Or, the lack of a pair of nearly transparent colored disks under the lids of someone's eyes.

The QUANDARY

 **MADEMOISELLE QUENEAU STOOD,** covered from head to the tip-toes of her gold shoes in her long, exquisitely sculpted jacket and tulip skirt, wearing a broad sunhat and white gloves to protect her hands, peering through ivory sunglasses at the window of the priest's study.

Any minute now, the happy couple thought, they would knock on the centuries of hardened layers of thick blue paint, and the heavy door would give way. In an instant they would be admitted to the vestibule and then to the office that had been known for many generations as the Quandary of Père Martin, and all their problems would be solved. Their marriage plans would again be underway, with the assistance of The Septum, as the unfortunate substitute priest had been called from the moment he crossed the bridge between St. X and St. G.

The enlistment of The Septum had finally been necessitated by Père Martin's yet wavering recovery. Soon, it continued to be said, Père Martin would be well. But, how soon? And, meanwhile, what was the young couple to do? Already the invitations had been sent out on the mayor's ever-hopeful advice and already so many preparations made. Already the seed pearl decorations cascaded down over the bodice of the wedding gown to the Cinderella princess waist, sewn on by Madame Meuelemeester, who was so often said to be Good Luck Herself in matters of fabrics and millinery.

"Look, Ambrose!" Pearl whispered in dismay, observing through the leaded window The Septum caught unawares. "Ambrose! That new *mec* Père Pepin—he looks like he's made of paraffin."

"Pearl!" Ambrose rolled his good eye with its brilliant mahogany-colored pupil around at her, clicking his tongue and pressing his cigarette into his thin lips, withdrawing and ejecting it, finally crushing it, unsmoked, into the cobblestones. "You can't call a priest a 'mec.' He's not just some '*guy*.' You *Anglais* have no respect!" He took a quick look through the window at The Septum who had flung himself into Père Martin's holm oak chair and propped his feet on the desk. On the other hand, Ambrose thought to himself, the man does look short.

Madame Menard passed just then beside the east entrance to the church in her pink polka-dotted, black dress. So *chic*, Pearl noticed, so red-belted, so like a little warbler.

The young couple appeared to Juliette Menard particularly ill-fated on this their pre-nuptial meeting day, as though a spotlight had picked them out in the stone corridor of the Street of the Lion. Madame Menard was just in time to wave them inside the church, when she saw them hesitate.

Madame Menard herself would have apologized repeatedly, if anyone had later asked her opinion about them publicly, saying only that she would no longer presume to tell anyone even exactly what day it was. She was lately that over-worked. Well, what was one to expect when one spent so much time cooking massive meals behind the scenes in the kitchen of Café Rousseau.

Her last child had gone off to university and returned to annoy his parents permanently in the restaurant. Now at their son's insistence, but without his help, just to be economical, she found herself ringing her own chickens' necks. Their dear friend, the butcher Hubert

Hauberk, as a consequence, grew annoyed that Café Rousseau was no longer requiring his helpful poultry-dressing services. So she was telling Madame Meulemeester as they met up and proceeded around the corner into the background noise of the auto-body shop.

EARLY IMPRESSIONS

"**WELL, IT DOES LOOK LIKE PARAFFIN,** Beau," Pearl complained rather too loudly on the street. "It's awful seeing him installed in Père Martin's study like this. If you ask me, he has a sickly sheen. Yesterday, Madame Laurent said he smelled ever so slightly of, well, you know—gas."

"Too—too—too—critical, little Pearl," Ambrose huffed as was his natural first inclination, to negate and deny. Yet, most kindly, he did not point out to his pale bride that The Septum was not the only one in the vicinity to have a peculiar-looking skin, although no, no, his fiancée did not have gas, no, indeed.

"But, Beau, do you think he looks okay?"

Ambrose le Beau came away from the heavy, dark blue door to stand beside her on the stretch of narrow passageway. From all the iron balconies of all the towering interlocked pastel houses, flowering drifts of replanted red and pink ivy geraniums seemed to cascade over them as they were peering into one of the smallest leaded windows ever to be cut into the side of a church. Indeed, a line of dried mud still swept four feet up, across all the walls in the village, where the top of the flood had passed by.

Pearl polished the mud from the pane with a tissue from her purse. "There is something truly odd about him, Ambrose."

Framed by the windowpane in the book-lined room, the scrutinized Père Pepin crossed and uncrossed his brief legs under his long robe, fluttering his pinched nostrils as he read. Then, before they could even blink, The Septum had leapt out of Père Martin's desk chair and fled the room. The door slammed hard behind him with a thud that could be heard clearly on the street.

Before the young couple could even sigh, the familiar study and the extensive library sat entirely void of human life and The Septum was plunging through the oaken door, shouting, onto the street.

To be sure, at the sight of his irate face, the young couple bolted as one, straight off the pavement, like a pair of conjoined hares surprised by hounds.

Both Madame Menard and Madame Meulemeester, just then returning with their morning baguettes, nearly laughed themselves into faint-headedness at the sight of the couple in the air and the priest red as tomato, shouting at them.

Quickly, quickly, the women turned and pretended to admire the enormous stand of pink *fleur de laurier*, the one that followed so rapidly the bend in the old stone wall and lead so very quickly down the Rue de l'Eglise on the other side of the church, and toward the handsome, oil-stained auto mechanic's garage.

"Oh, Ambrose!" Pearl whispered, mortified by the gaunt young priest glaring at her with his hands stuck to his brown-robed hips.

"What are you two spies doing there, staring in?" Père Pepin cried out in a haggard voice that one could not help noticing, even on a distant balcony. Perhaps the tiny priest had been nearly as mortified at the sight of them.

On the day before, he'd caught a glimpse of the bride-to-be in a long-sleeved dress and apricot-colored hat, but he had not seen her face. She had been hand in hand with her over-grown brute, or so The Septum thought of Ambrose.

"Entré! Entré! What do you think you're ogling? This is not your local sea aquarium. If you want to talk with me, come in!"

The Septum seemed rather like a gigantic death's head moth, Pearl thought, the way he flapped the sleeves of his robes at them. She couldn't help wondering, had he actually hissed?

HANDSTANDS

PARKED IN A LONG-AGO SILVER-FRAMED PHOTOGRAPH ON THE STUDY WALL, out from between two wartime field vehicles, the far younger, yet recognizable Père Martin tried to caution the couple. If only they had paid more attention to their elder's handstands and incessant waving from the photogravure.

Père Pepin reached across Père Martin's rosewood desk to switch on the radio. A distant tenor voice and then a saxophone crooned forth momentarily in a song that Ambrose had been learning recently. The couple's attention fixed briefly on it, only to be swallowed up by the new priest's grumbling. Pearl could not keep from staring at him as he crossed his little pipe-cleaner legs. Maybe he would not now make her feel so uncomfortable if his ear-length hair had been submitted down the street for a good wash at Coiffures d'Amalie, Pearl thought. Maybe that was it. Or perhaps he had added some ill-advised lotion to his hair; maybe the eerie sheen over him was intentional? A stunning thought!

"What a peculiar village you have," Père Pepin observed. "What an honor to have been called to elevate your poor element."

Already Ambrose's long hands drummed on the knees of his second best pants. "It will not be necessary to elevate us, Père Pepin. But, it is our indulgence to meet with you," Ambrose offered brusquely, in attempted polite return.

Pepin leaned back in his chair and went on as though Ambrose had not spoken. "Monsieur le Beau and Mademoiselle Queneau, yes, a troubling time soon leaves us, or so I trust. Soon I hope to be able to carry your story back to my own metropolitan rectory where I make my permanent home. The whole order is shaken and uplifted—and uplifted!—by what has happened here in your quaint St. X."

The Septum attempted to smile at them, but his visitors saw only his mouth. Can the man still have his milk teeth? Milk teeth! Pearl thought.

"We do not find a flashflood and the impairment of our priest uplifting, Père. Perhaps you are finding some entertainment here that we do not acknowledge."

The Septum waved Ambrose's thought back at him. "As my predecessor Père Martin found himself, we too are rescued."

"He is truly very great, our Père Martin," Ambrose offered. "Greatly revered in our village, a kinder more honest man or priest never lived in France."

"Yes, I can hardly imagine it. To be literally hoisted out of harm's way by a limestone statue of The Celestial Mother." He cocked his sallow head as though to shake unholy water out of it, and attempted pleasantries. He looped the bows of a pair of wire-rimmed spectacles around his ears and absent-mindedly began to sort the pile of mail on the desk while he spoke. "I myself have never had the privilege to see a flood and yet I am in your petite village because of one. This is the first flood like this since Père Napoleon, so they told me, supposedly to tempt me here. As if *that* could turn the tap on in me!"

The priest halted, blanched, and stared at the slender envelope that had lain unnoticed on his desk. Trembling, he ripped it open. Then his lower lip began to lose some of its rosiness.

It really was quite perplexing the way the rather young man then began to break up in front of them. To Pearl, Père Pepin seemed so like the rhinoceros beetle when annoyed by any of a number of known unseemly parasites. He reeled in and expelled his breath with a splutter from his upturned nose. Perhaps he had the schizoid personality, she was wondering. Just as soon as he seemed near to violence, in a fraction of a moment he was nearly overcome with tears.

"Père Pepin, we have come about our wedding, not about your visit here," she interjected. "Are you all right?" But he had begun to sputter and spew.

"People, this very moment I have the news… I had no idea it was here. Right here. They say they will not accept my petition—*indefinitely*! Look at me! To be here—in this locale so hideous. Here! Because your Père Martin had not the sense to come in out of a driving rain. It's a wonder the Blue Mother did not hold him under until he turned blue as death. Why did she not just dispense with him?"

The couple's gasp could surely be heard all the way to Café Rousseau.

The Septum caught his breath then and sat down, spine upright, red-faced in his chair. "But, alas, this significance is not important to you. Only you are important to you, that is very clear. Try to tell me what you think. Children, don't hold back! Tell me then, Monsieur, why you think this an appropriate time to marry this little, pale *etranger*?"

Coming from a civilized and rural community, Monsieur Ambrose le Beau had never heard such offenses spoken to his face from the clergy or, for that matter, from anyone respectable. That would, of course, exclude the Rabbit Catcher's running commentary; but then, almost everything and everyone excluded him. The pair sat together in shock for a moment, yet feeling quite alone on their individual chairs. They could not think how to meet his words. The substitute priest seemed more than the "bit deranged" that others had said of him.

Ambrose leaned forward, fingering Pearl's ring on her hand, bolstering himself until ready to point out to The Septum, and perhaps also to The Pearl, a few compensatory local facts that neither might have known, both having had the misfortune to have been born somewhere other than St. X.

Yes, both the priest and the Colossus' fiancée were *etranger*, but the priest was much more so, certainly, even though from France, than Pearl Queneau who had been in the village now for nearly seven years and who had become the sweetheart of the St. X school children. He looked around with his one good eye at his bride-to-be, toward her permanently inflamed eyes, and administered a little squeeze of her fingertips between his great broad palms, as if to say, Try a little pity, Pearl. Perhaps we've only startled him. *Calmé-toi*, Pearl. It is just as you might find it, anyplace where you might have ventured during those erratic journalism tours of yours—studying and reporting on the exotic colorings, flight patterns and mating habits of your world of bugs, flowers, beasts and birds. Give this new man a chance to regain himself. We admit: he has had the shock—rejection by his own.

While Ambrose preferred not to look so directly at a depressed human being as to actually see into demented eyes, he sat calmly in his chair watching Pepin planting his elbows on Père Martin's fine leather desk blotter, snaking out his wan neck, and shuddering and swallowing hard.

"Monsieur le Beau, you wish to be married after the vendange, *c'n'est pas vrais?* That's what I have heard. This is August, Monsieur le Beau—certainly you have noticed? I wonder why I haven't heard about such plans before, from you yourself. Is this the way you ignore and insult me, before the whole village, while the village plans for your day? Or perhaps it is endemic—a lack of manners here in the rustic reality? But then you probably wouldn't notice such rudeness, having lived here all your life."

The dead end of the priest's pen twirled in a small imaginary circle on one side of his shallow face, and then he went at it on the other side, ever absent-mindedly. Pearl considered rather uncharitably that The Septum recently might have lost a slender, though elongated, putty-brown mustache, perhaps with a tinge of green in it not unlike that of an Amazonian parrot—or, even more so, like the green of the miraculous local clay which was said to heal nearly anything, even deeply infected wounds.

Perhaps the imaginary mustache had been waxed to go with his pasty skin—skin that might have been made of oiled parchment, she thought, lifting her white eyebrows in surprise. That imaginary mustache surely would have matched the dense, muted hair flattened at the crown of his head. His was not the stick-on kind of hair, much as she now would have liked to have been the one to recognize and widely report the comical toupee. This was truly fortunate, she thought to herself, for she was not that kind of person, she knew. She would have had to keep it to herself, or to tell it only to Ambrose.

Certainly, Pearl thought, the man was in a terrible state of despair—homesick apparently for Lyon, or Toulouse, or from whence he had come to them, horrified at finding himself thrust into their Eden and so ignorant as to think of it as Hell.

Poor man. *Pauvre Père Pepin.*

PRIVATE LITTLE
LANGUAGE LESSONS

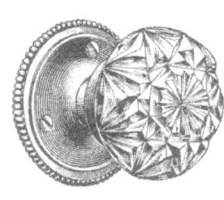 **As Camille Desbordes warned her,** repeatedly, "The first year of *le mariage,* now that will be the worst. So much worry and thinking: Who is this *mec* anyway? And, what do you mean—*toujours*? Who agreed to that anyway?

"Soon you will be married, Pearl, and you will see for yourself. I just hope after all this waiting you don't have to marry Ambrose twice, in the way that I have done everything. I can never get anything right the first time around. Do you think I am slow, or just a perfectionist?"

"Oh that," Pearl scoffed, "that dreadful weather business. You French persons are tantalizing, but you're a little demented, if you ask me."

Aside from the words *football, sports,* and *jazz,* Ambrose's early attempts at English, not so very oddly, were pointed toward describing eating utensils and food. Ambrose perched in their archaic kitchen on their mammoth hearthstone, forming without success those syllables approximating the English *fork, plate,* and *spoon,* beating two of them in frustration against the sides of his platter. "If I do not learn your English now, you and my children will tell histories about me right under my eyeball. Bring the English book, the book of idiots!"

"*Idioms,*" Pearl laughed. "You mean *idioms.*"

It soon became apparent that what he thought were her gross inadequacies in assuming his French language were almost as serious as his own difficulties in acquiring fluency in her tongue. Several weeks after a mistral cooking experiment, Ambrose appeared after work with twelve settings of antique silverware. First he indicated that these were the first installments in certain Bastille Day plans and that they were to go in a little basket he had on order. In French and then in attempted English, he presented the silver to her, piece by piece, commencing beside the fireplace and finishing at the table, starting and ending, repeatedly, with the fork, his favorite. He had prepared a speech.

"All courtiers must have speeches. I now present you, my little darling, with mine!" His act of courtly love included much information that would surely be of use to her some day, he said, such as the fork's presumed genesis in Italy; its previous ritualistic uses; its mistaken identity in Belgium as a weapon. (When first it was seen, no one was safe from being stabbed at the table. Here Ambrose made a brief and faulty demonstration (nearly emasculating himself) showing off the fork's subsequent use as a parlor game; (think darts with sharpened forks!); its increasing number of tines as time went on; (when it was a young fork with only two feet); and among other things, Ambrose's own tantalizing predictions of the arrival of another tine for the fork within their own lifetimes.

That bit of educational exuberance he performed in English to Pearl's subsequent applause while making her a surprise dinner, and without his ever once managing to pronounce the 'r' in any utensil's English name. His lecture was also sprinkled with his attempts at an acceptable English pronunciation of the various kitchen furnishings that she had previously tried to point out to him.

Bounding about the room in animated display, pointing at objects and checking repeatedly on the correctness of his elocution, he ended by reeling off a few juicy quotes in French, followed by any necessary translations, supposedly taken from Josephine, that most illustrious bride of Napoleon Bonaparte.

Yes, yes, she knew who Bonaparte was, she laughed. He needn't be so patronizing.

But, of course, Bonaparte was a much smaller man than he the Colossal Beau, so Ambrose unnecessarily reminded her. And, he had had many conquests.

∾

As ever, Pearl was careful not to hurt Ambrose's pride, which could be most severely injured as she that night once or twice found out while watching him tip up a glass of Pernod and weep quietly over his notes and pieces of graph paper. She grew most careful whenever he boldly attempted to forge ahead with the more difficult parts of her language. Failure always set him off; he was so very French in that.

If ever she lost her own humility during his attempts at learning a new language, she had only to bring herself back to earth with one memory. Blushingly, she would think how, a few days after her arrival in France, while opening a bank account, she, in the original quiet way of her grandmother on the Isle of Man, in her new and decidedly beautiful hat, had declared to the astonished bank officials in her softest voice, repeatedly and with increasing determination and then volume, that, as of yesterday, her new landlord was indeed and without doubt, completely *merde*. Yes, yes, she declared, he truly was and that was why she'd been two days late to her appointment and did not have his signature on the rental papers, all of which were requisite to her opening an account with them. She knew that. But surely they could see her problem?

Only too slowly did it dawn on her, far too slowly, as she stared into three bankers' blanched faces and a little crowd of onlookers, that she, a beautiful, well-intentioned, rather unusual if even albino, individual, yet a teenager, had made a terrible verbal gaff of some kind, and so she had tried to fix it all by repeating it. Over, and over, and over. She tried to explain herself with sign language, strangulation gestures, swan songs, until they thought her perhaps a murderer, or potentially so.

Yes, she insisted, he had dropped *merde* at her door and she would not, could not now, be able to turn in the papers of residency, so necessary for the opening of her bank account in this part of the European world, at least for the next few weeks until she was able to get things straightened out. Therefore, she definitely required their understanding and also the requisite bank account. And that was why, although she knew it had irritated them, she had not kept her first appointment with them. "O, pardon!" She gave them a hopeful little smile, her pink eyes wide and innocent. Why oh why, had she thought immersion the way to learn a language thoroughly?

Pearl the teenager stared back at them. The bankers went white. She *had* killed her landlord!

Suddenly, as if on a bolt from heaven, her heels took a little hop and it occurred to her. "No, no, no!" she cried out. "No, I see! He did not drop *merde* at my door! He dropped *mort* at my door! Stone cold dead. *C'est vrais*, my landlord of less than twenty-four hours! No, he was not *merde*! He dropped no *shit* at all! Please, oh please, he was, most unfortunately, completely dead! And, so I can not have the contract with him, a dead man, for you! It is completely impossible, I hope you see that now. Please, oh please. *Comprenez vous? Comprenez vous?*"

Perhaps it was a tribute to the French, or to bankers in general, that they did not laugh at her; but there was considerable smiling, followed almost immediately by their gleeful, explosive congratulations, and one even embraced her and gave her several little kisses on alternating cheeks. Then the account book was delivered into her hand, and she was left to limp emotionally back to her little car. There she laughed and hiccoughed herself into a frenzy until she had to put her forehead onto the steering wheel. After a while, still chortling in little bursts and gasps, she got the car onto the fast-moving round-about and was swept out into the absolute sea of French-speaking persons and their automobiles.

Truly, it did make one humble, still, to think of it.

STRANGE PRIORITIES

"*MON DIEU,* WHAT DID YOU THINK about Rabbit Catcher's graffiti then?" Camille Desbordes asked when they were alone.

"Breaking and entering?" Pearl's voice crackled. "Lack of respect?"

"*Mon Dieu!* They are for whores."

"The cars? Along the road? The old used cars are for *whores?*"

Camille Desbordes retrieved some palliative cheeses and sausage from the refrigerator as quickly as she could, all the better to change an inflammatory subject. But in the end they were talking about the same thing again anyway, age and beauty. Always, in her experience, lovers had always been just the same. That was the way in the thinking of Camille Desbordes.

UP *the* NOSE

DEFINITELY, THAT RIGID, RELIGIOUS NEWCOMER Père Pepin did not want to say that he had fasted several days before arriving, and had entered into fervent prayer and self-mortification ever since. The marriage of Monsieur le Beau and Mademoiselle Queneau would be the first he had ever performed alone; and, after all, he was used to a large city parish where everything was done in small ceremonial cliques, with the youngest the least responsible in his task. And, he had been the youngest! He sat up as straight as possible, burnished his cross on his sleeve, and started on the chain before proceeding with his planned pronouncement. Before he knew it, he was saying it:

"And then, Monsieur le Beau, there is this heat, this drought, the multiple effects of the flood, this unparalleled heat, I say it again! How can anyone bear the intensity of such heat in a landscape compromised like such? I have slept drenched in my underdrawers for at least six nights. The *Place* is besmirched with petrified muck and broken glass, even your vineyards, too, from your flood that was already months ago! Performing a wedding ceremony for you now would not be beautiful. I cannot start my tenure here with a performance that could only be the slapstick affair." He gazed over his nose at them sitting there like oddly paired performers at *la Cirque*, the gigantic one with the eye patch and his tiny translucent counterpart with the broad-brimmed sunhat and the parasol. "It would be—it would mean—the ridicule."

Ambrose shrugged, lacing his massive, if elegant, fingers together, looking up from his perch on the edge of the chair, and tried to set things right. "Perhaps someday, Père Pepin, just as you have said, that which seems inconceivable to us today will be known as the first day of The Great Drought That Was, The Most Incredible Drought in All History. If you wish to believe that, I am not one to stop anyone from his belief. We are a secular village with a profound belief, partially because of one good man who came to us willingly in my father's time, but who are we to say who will think what they will.

"It *is* a tiny bit hot for a wedding, as you say, although, truly Père, it is hardly a drought. We had quite the deluge recently, that is true; you say you have heard of our deluge. The water supply must be good because of it, wouldn't you say? Hardly a drought. Yes, the weather is very uncomfortable for you now, *ouais*—because you are not used to it; but there is no drought, certainly not. *Pas de problème.* Almost never does it rain in St. X in August and September. *C'est normale.*"

He shrugged up his significant shoulders in the tight grey sport coat and tried to look compassionate; but still he trained his eye intentionally on the wall instead, just behind the priest's head. This was not hard to do, he was well aware, as his one good eye was ever so slightly frosted anyway, and the priest merely thought he was seeing a further defect in him.

Ambrose drummed the rhythms of his favorite tune on the arm of the chair as he spoke. In this way, he controlled himself. Pearl heard him saying, "Our wedding would be a very good way for you to start. Pearl is much loved in the village, you know. She is hardly a stranger here. . . . And I have had the good fortune to have lived here since my birth."

But that had all been earlier in the week, and now Ambrose regained his presence of mind, for here he was yet again in The Septum's Quandary, with his little Pearl, and The Septum was sneering at them. Pearl leaned forward, staring back in return. Her knees edged coldly out like white cabbages from under the peonies printed on her skirt. She smiled her small, icy, powdered smile at him. Everything about her was tiny, and captivating, Ambrose thought, even when anger had gripped either one of the two of them, or both.

"Père Pepin," she began in a falsely silken tone, trying hard not to boil anything up in untoward emotion that her mate could see. Her true voice was a melody to him worthy of repetition in each of his pleasing days, he thought. "Père Martin is not yet receiving visitors, or certainly we would not have bothered you, Père Pepin." The priest, in return, fingered his pen at the tips of his mouth and seemed decidedly disinterested.

Who could not notice that her disquieting eyes seemed to glaze beneath her hardening brow as she spoke? "Last spring Père Martin himself convinced us to marry after the *vendange*. He would want us to continue as planned. He was adamant about the timing, and we agreed. School doesn't start here until the end of September, and he wanted our wedding to interfere as little as possible with our students' lessons, don't you see? Père Pepin, have you noticed our school children or their importance to us? This whole village seems aware that you feel us too difficult an assignment for you to undertake."

The groom-to-be leaned slightly forward over the central flower of Père Martin's Aubusson rug to press Pearl's neatly shaped, opalescent fingernails in a cautionary way. He couldn't help thinking how he had helped to bring the blue carpet down for Père Martin, a donation from the second story of Monsieur Premier's home when Madame P. had suddenly decided to redecorate all in white. About this color change, Pearl, who adored all things colorful, had curiously approved.

"Père Pepin—" Ambrose ventured, feeling as if he were balancing again on a youthful dare along the railing of the old Roman viaduct over the Pont du Diable. And, he had only fallen once, injuring his head only enough to have been in hospital for two months. "Perhaps it is not obvious—but our decision to marry is not precipitous. We have spent time in contemplation with one another. Mademoiselle Queneau and I have lived together for many months. In fact, over a year has passed. We do not mean to be disrespectful. We thought Père Martin would be well by now."

"Eighteen months," Pearl reported proudly, "and one week. We have lived together eighteen months and one week. And we knew each other before that, too."

"So one would hope." The priest lit another cigarette and sipped at its filtered end, studying it intermittently, his eyes crossing with pleasure only transitorily.

At this sight, le Beau could not help remembering what was being whispered in the Bar des Sports in St. G, perhaps incorrectly, one hoped! It was said that Père Pepin had left his last city church with his person in disarray, and quite hurriedly. His arrival in St. X had little to do with the flood, they said. An incendiary moment between Pepin and one of his male parishioners at the Saturday open market had escalated into a ludicrous display of fisticuffs during which a ruffian from a local fruit stand had flicked a cherry at Pepin, hitting him squarely in the eye, throwing him at a disadvantage in the scuffle and causing its own rather severe orbital bruise. It was a very noticeable, deep purple and moss green eye, which was, along with his shredded robes, rather difficult to explain to his senior colleagues and to the horrified, on-looking parishioners upon his return excursion to the church.

Père Pepin did have a sickly appearance, although perhaps a modern one. Ambrose could see that now, as eventually he himself trailed off into what he came to see as oratorical failure before The Septum. Perhaps the priest's blushing head had been pinched in the birthing tongs at his unfortunate naissance, Ambrose thought. He wondered at the misfortune of Pepin's mother upon first seeing him as an infant. Ambrose puffed himself up in his chair, patting the knees of his second best trousers, snorting smoothly through his elegant nostrils like one of Monsieur Gaston's white bulls when anyone approached the fence too swiftly without offering the formal greetings appropriate for bulls.

This one called Pepin, Pearl observed, could not be more than thirty-one to thirty-three. Ambrose himself too quickly neared his fortieth, although he tried not to think of it. He seemed so like a boy; indeed most of the villagers still thought of him as one, perhaps because he had remained unmarried for so long.

It would not be the first time, she surmised, that Ambrose had worried that marriage would instantly age him. Now here he was, pushing bravely forward into his belated coming of age, fiercely determined now to marry, increasingly now because of his own innate contrariness.

Let it never be said anywhere that Ambrose le Beau had backed down in the face of adversity, he thought.

∞

Coincidentally, Père Pepin, too, found himself spurred to the recollection of this self-same moment in his previous environment.

Perhaps it was because of the behemoth seated before him with the frosted eye and the cocked eye patch with the quarter note drawn onto it, and the whole thing strapped around his thick black-haired head. Pepin, too, was thinking of that unfortunate little embarrassment, and feeling grateful that at least here in the remote village of St. X no one was likely ever to have heard of it.

Divine Intervention, and Pepin's own good works to that date, no doubt, had slowed the horrid fruit man's pitch and delivered him from the fate he saw in both the Colossus' eye patch and the albino girl's permanently discolored eyes.

Inwardly, he laughed up his nose at them, if a little hysterically, thinking, Well, at least they have two things in common while heading toward their unspeakable marriage: eye trouble and their complete freakishness. Just think of the children that would be spawned from that! He shuddered and composed himself, fully upright then beside the exquisite desk that he himself had irreproachably polished that day.

Pepin stared at the would-be groom dwarfing one of the most dazzling Regency side chairs that he had ever seen, chairs that belonged yet to Père Martin, as much as any object could belong to a declining mortal anyway. His damp hands folded themselves decisively in front of his surplice, in fear that one of these peculiar petitioners might try to touch one of his hands as he unexpectedly stood and turned. He led them silently along the coolness of the hall, and then ever more rapidly through the heavy doors, delivering them into the blast furnace that was now the Street of the Lion.

This was that very same stone funnel of a lane that had carried a torrent, two meters high, roaring past these very same dark blue, plank doors, towing his predecessor, who, by all reports, had danced like a mad man both on top of the current and beneath, and was faltering still between eminence and merest humanity. At this thought, he could not help but sniff.

Père Pepin squeezed the door shut then on his visitors' astounded expressions as though on a very bad dream. In Pepin's mind, his predecessor could at least have had the good sense to expire in the Celestial Mother's arms or to rise up entirely invigorated by his odd experience. Pepin much preferred the latter, by all means, as it would have meant the certainty of a permanent escape for him.

HAUBERK'S BUTCHER SHOP

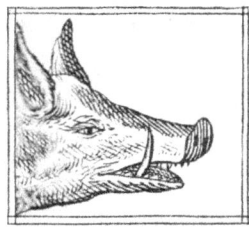 **AMBROSE LE BEAU STOOD IN LINE THAT DAY** as Hubert Hauberk, the tattooed butcher, reported again his personal sighting of Père Martin's sad, near-death accident. And, who would better know how long it took for someone to expire than a butcher, after all, he didn't need to ask, but asked aloud anyway. And, none-the-less, for a butcher, who with his wife had actually witnessed the tragedy, it had been the most horrifying incident!

"Fully half the hour Père Martin suffered an underwater death! *Mais oui!* From Arianna's attic sewing room, we saw the water rising around him in the street, and could do not one thing. He was up, bobbing, and then he was down under, long enough to suffocate any creature with the holy spirit spluttering in him. *Mon Dieu, quelle horreur.* How can he have any brains left in him? If he survives, only a miracle will give him thought."

With barely a pause, Hubert Hauberk offered Madame Menard a sampling of his new pâté on a piece of parchment paper, over the immaculate meat cabinet.

"Hubert, I'm so sorry about the poultry. My son has returned and insists. Now I must kill the chickens myself. He doesn't realize what it does to me. What with caring for Père Martin and killing chickens, I can not stop weeping from six o'clock a.m. to ten. And, Gerard will stay out of it, he won't say a thing, now that Estevan is home again."

The butcher shrugged up his broad shoulders. He leaned around the end of the counter to whisper sympathetically. Perhaps the beautiful Juliette might use a quantity of pâté in Café Rousseau? Or, perhaps he and Madame Hauberk might slip by and help her with the dreaded chickens before their other chores?

The door opened and a cluster of customers came in, among them the village's would-be groom.

"Try our pâté creation! I've laced it with my new cognac, Madame Menard. *Bonjour,* Ambrose, you might attempt to convey one of these pâtés through Doctor Malaplate's barricade, would you? Just the scent of this one pâté is sure to wake Père in time to deliver you to that long-awaited marital state."

The tiny Juliette Menard bounced on the balls of her feet, peering up through the glass cabinet. "How kind you are, Monsieur Hauberk! Why not also send one of your magical flying machines to Père Martin? I will pay, if you think it would cheer him on. That one, the flying bicycle, he loves. You have no idea how long Père has admired it. Why our Estevan wasn't seven when Père Martin first brought the two of us over to admire your handiwork."

Monsieur Hauberk tapped without self-consciousness on the crow's feet that were said to have been tattooed at the corners of his eyelids during a brief and drunken, very youthful bout, twenty years before in Sète. The lines were at first alien, but now Hauberk was old enough for the artifice to have settled into the natural lines he had developed on his own.

The butcher washed his hands, hung up his unremittingly white apron, and retrieved the wooden flying machine he had made, the first to leave the window after its initial inbound flight. With a studious contemplation, he placed his precious object deep within the paper sack, on top of the carefully packaged pâté, and insulated it from further shock with nine or ten mini-bags of the priest's favorite potato crisps.

"Ambrose," Hauberk inquired. "Would you mind conveying my encouragement over to The Beloved? Ask him to take this up to Père Martin. And please accept this pâté for yourself. I've dressed it in cognac, too, for your new adventures with Mademoiselle Queneau— to give you added strength."

Monsieur Hauberk laughed heartily then, accompanied by nearly all his customers, rocking back and forth in mirth from side to side, towering over everyone in the room except for le Beau. "No, you have never been lacking in strength, *mais non, Ambrose.*

"But, for your nuptials, *bien sur*, the man must become the force *formidable*, beyond the every day." Hubert Hauberk emitted a deep roar at this, accompanied again by all in the store. Juliette Menard, too, fell into her titillating peal at his words.

Yes, Ambrose did force himself to laugh along with them, although only very slightly. Inwardly incensed, he simply could not see the full humor that the already married saw in those approaching the state, particularly in this modern age of prenuptial live-in partnerships. He scoffed quietly as he took up the package and ambled quickly out of the shop, though he waved his hand toward the window glass in acknowledgement as he began to plummet down the street, hailing all. *Bonjour, madame. Bonjour, monsieur.* Left and right, on his way to the stricken priest's habitat.

〜

As always, once started, Ambrose continued to fume. Who would have thought that a simple downpour of feeling would have resulted in such travail, or that a decision to marry, so long awaited and avoided, might now turn out to be so difficult? Outside Père Martin's sky blue door, which had always been open to all, he heard that the mayor had already departed and no one else was allowed.

In the mayor's office then, he heard that the mayor had already left, this time for the very place from which he had just come, and was likely already ensconced beside Père Martin's sick bed. Retracing his steps and receiving yet again no answer to his appeals, Ambrose tied the butcher's package to Père Martin's doorknocker, where it was gladly retrieved a little later by Marthe the Potter's enthusiastic briard.

FROM *the*
ROSE GARDEN

 ***ET ALORS,*** Time, as He will, passed *tout de suite* through the village of St. X; and, perhaps, He did just the same in St. G and St. Z. It was hard to tell unless you had braved the record-breaking heat to venture across either bridge. In any case, gradually the villagers from St. X set about the reconstruction and cleanup efforts made so necessary by what was now called Père Martin's Deluge. Earnest groups of villagers, including the very youngest citizen of St. X, who was employed solely in the task of cooing encouragements from his perambulator, and the very oldest, who was set to sweeping the entrances to nave and residence, set out to reconstitute the partially demolished church and public gardens. Trellises were built anew and strung with wire for future growth; upturned and missing stones were fitted or replaced in the old walls and paths; newly purchased, seemingly dead roots and tubers were dug anew into the stony ground. The entire rose garden was replaced and the Blue Mother given still another coat of paint.

And so, too, *et alors*, many lesser offences committed by The Flashflood Immeasurable were written rather quickly into their places in the village archives. But, in far too many ways, the graver effects and the memories of the flood failed to disappear.

∞

Daily, the villagers encountered the all-too-silent reminder that Henri, the splendid blue coq that had presided above the blue indigo

62

door to Hauberk's Butcher Shop, too, had been lost in Père Martin's Deluge. The coq had shown himself to be the Patriarch of Time in St. X, after the custom of his father and his father's father's feathered fathers before him. Now time in town, even for the local bell-ringer, did not rightfully exist without the blue coq's reveille. Even the most punctual citizen now seemed to be heeding some kind of randomly set, interior, tinny, metronomic display.

Many shops and businesses were still signed up for the deluxe mildew treatment and remained closed. News arrived, with school about to start in another month, that the replacements for the children's desks could not yet be delivered through St. Z. And, of course, as was mentioned by everyone in Café Rousseau, no agreement had been reached about the wedding of Mademoiselle Queneau to Monsieur le Beau, which it was hoped might yet in some small way stimulate the tottering village economy with its promised influx of paying guests.

The sorely missed Père Martin lay yet firmly fixed to his recovery bed, muttering, declaring himself upon occasion to be Saint Catherine of Alexandria, so it was said, perhaps or perhaps not reliably, in the village café-bar. Perhaps the Rabbit Catcher had had a hand in creating that ruse.

All baptisms, confessions, catechism classes, visits to the sick and dying, and abatements of lover's quarrels were relegated to the inexperienced Père Pepin, who delayed at every turn, awaiting Père Martin's return, oddly enough to the villagers' delight. Perhaps Père Pepin was jockeying to be expelled from St. X on a rail and doing it well, but for one little point. He had not counted on the civility of the little hamlet. No, they would never eject their assigned priest. The man would have to leave of his very own accord.

In the interim, the decision was unanimously taken, within the informality of Café Rousseau, that no one would make use of The Septum's services until he would agree to marry the Colossus and the Pearl. But, The Septum remained oblivious, fully engaged as he was in his letter-writing campaign to bishop, archbishop, and Pope to regain his former post. So it was conjectured here, there, and everywhere by a puckish Monsieur Pereault de Poste. The little postman said: "Yes, just perhaps we will see it in our lives: The Septum will lose his equilibrium enough, after failing with the Pope, to post his appeals to the good Saint Nicholas."

It was sincerely hoped that no funerals would soon occasion a call for help to any of the like-suffering neighboring communities. The most elderly gentleman of the region, Monsieur de Graff, tottering on the edge of life and death, declared that he would sooner be frozen, salted, and/or stuffed by Hubert Hauberk, and even eaten at Café Rousseau, before he would have The Septum administering last rites and funereal words over him and levying enormous citified funeral rates over his estate. So his relatives dutifully reported it.

The Saturday street market, nearly devoid of local vendors, could only exhibit the produce and dry goods from nearby untouched neighboring towns. Water had to be imported by tank trucks from the spring two *départements* over, while the St. X Spring Water Extraordinaire Bottling Plant boiled and washed itself clean.

Slowly things seemed to be regaining bits of normality; however, it was the slow but steadily creeping appearance of moulder on hectare after hectare of grapes from St. G to St. X, and from St. Y to St. Z and beyond, along with the threatened delay of the *vendange* and the latest unrelenting heat, that set the teeth in St. X and surrounding vicinities onto their very thinly enameled rims.

Madame Meulemeester's Dress Shop

 **AT MADAME MEULEMEESTER'S EXOTIC DRESS SHOP,** to Madame's surprise, her friend Arianna Hauberk popped in to say that she had noticed a segment cracked out of the front window. When the small collection of glaziers had been able to release a pair of their own harried crew for the repair, they pointed out to her and perhaps to an overly omniscient crowd, that not only had the missing piece been in the exact same shape as the crescent moon that had seemed to linger over the town in the weeks before and after the flood, but that the missing arc of glass was actually resting intact, nearly invisible against the ankle of Madame Meulemeester's lady mannequin.

"Someone has been playing horseshoes with Madame's nude!" the elder glazier sang, balancing the new sheet of glass against the younger glazier's hip and setting them all to admiring the oddly cut anklet on the pert pink mannequin. After a rather escalating debate, the reluctant Madame Meulemeester was finally convinced by the reconstruction crew, and later by informal poll in Café Rousseau, to leave that interior portion of the window display permanently encased just as it was.

After all, she had had good fortune, hadn't she, coming out of it all with nothing but a nasty cold and all? Her most expensive dresses had been spared; and the season would all too soon be coming into autumn fashions again and, quickly thereafter, the winter woolens. It would be good to have a reminder of a few of the more whimsical aspects of the flood, wouldn't it? Well, wouldn't it? Regard: the loveliness of the nude dressed only in a crescent of glass anklet! Marvelous! *Très chic!*

Yes, she had seen their point all right. The crescent moon remained around the lady's ankle behind the new plate glass. Madame Meulemeester, however, politely but firmly drew the line and declined the Rabbit Catcher's suggestion that she rename her shop The Lucky Nude—even though secretly she entertained the notion whenever she took her shower and looked into the mirror, and then again each day, most particularly when she cleared her throat and entered her key into the azure door to enter her store and saw the unscathed mannequin still naked and dancing among the ever-changing frocks.

PHILOSOPHY *in* CAFÉ ROUSSEAU

 **IN ALL OF ST. X, ST. Y, ST. Z, AND EVEN IN ST. G,** no one could change the subject like Jean-Luc Redon, a notable blessing and a curse. As an antidote to pervading cynicism and gloom, he recited for them Père Martin's recent speech from on top of the Blue Mother's arms, delivering it in the depths of his resounding, even relished, new voice. His new voice sounded very much like a heavy chair being dragged over old cement. Then Jean-Luc Redon stroked both his chin and his recently assaulted Adam's apple, and pointed out something that drew the attention of all his drinking companions to his newly graveled voice. "For a reason unknown even to myself, *mes copains,* I have had the need, and satisfied it, to reread Voltaire."

"You don't say," Georges Menard saluted, relieved to be seemingly headed onto a quiet afternoon course. "But, Rousseau is the greatest philosopher, as you know."

"*Mais oui,*" the lean Jean-Luc admitted. "Truly we admire Rousseau, but you must admit Voltaire had a sense of humor quite unique while wading like the rest of us through the *merde* of life."

"Here here."

"A delight!"

"That bastard Voltaire," Jadot the Rabbit Catcher sneered, reminding everyone abruptly of his presence lingering still at the far end of the bar. Obnoxiously, he ground the bottom edge of his glass along the corner of the granite surface, releasing a shriek from all who heard. "That bastard Voltaire should have been beheaded in the best of all his possible worlds. At best he should never have been let out of our Bastille!"

Rouen the Wood Sculptor nudged his wife, indicating The Rabbit Catcher, whom he had vowed never again to look directly in the face. Cautiously, he kept an eye on him through the convenience of his wife's hand mirror, set at a slant in the open center pocket of her purse, and thereafter reflected via the mirror over the bar. "I'm with you, Jadot. Give me Rousseau instead."

"I second that," George Menard declared, lifting the glass he was polishing, "with a declaration of devotion to his ways and to this our café so clearly named after him! Although I, too, am devoted to Voltaire. Rousseau is our citizen, the Honorary Philosopher of St. X!"

"A salute to Café Rousseau! His very own namesake. If only he were here to join us now."

"And to the village what has the noble café!"

"To our own St. Xavier!"

"Salut to Rousseau! Salut to St. Xavier! Heroic men, heroic deeds! Salut to Martin!"

A surly female voice unreeled then from the corner of the room that truly shocked the crowd.

"Don't say that name in the same blink with Père Martin's! That disgusting Rousseau, I reverse my opinion about that *mec*." Camille Desbordes slammed down her glass, as she most certainly never, even on the most irritating occasions, had done. Camille jerked back her inebriated auburn head.

"Rousseau the Wretch," she shouted again, gathering steam. "I didn't know it myself until just last week. On the Internet, Monsieur Rousseau, our so-called Enlightened Father, Father of the Happy Romanticism, put his own five children, his own, note that, into an orphanage! I suspect, like I, you also did not know. He put them in an orphanage, I say! Five! While his wife was well and alive and begging him to think *encore!* Into the orphanage." Her voice petered into indecipherable streams of syllables delivered to the shiny surface of the bar.

"No, he did not! *Mais non*, Camille Desbordes, I did not realize you had drunk so much." Georges Menard patted her hand with alarm, as he had done for so many of his patrons. "He couldn't have. Not Jean Jacques."

"Certainly not!" the Rabbit Catcher chimed in, ready to break his glass and defend. "*Impossible!*" he decried to all at the bar and even to the empty dinner tables in the adjoining rooms.

"What about an orphanage?" Juliette Menard stuck her head in from the kitchen, looking horrified.

"*C'est vrais?*"

"It can not be true."

"Have you ever known me to give you, Juliette, or anyone, an untruth?" Camille confirmed, her head bobbing onto her arms and bouncing up again.

"I'll bring the espresso for you, Camille. *Vite!* This can't be true."

But the proprietor of Café Rousseau had begun to moan aloud, and absent-mindedly to rub his own arms with his polishing towel. "That would be the crime extreme against humanity. We would never, never, never give our children up. Nor would anyone from St. X or even St. Z or G, or Y or Z. *Mais non!* It can not have been Rousseau."

"The too truthful *histoire*, my poor Juliette, my poor companions," Camille Desbordes confirmed. "My heart is ravaged like yours."

At this, Juliette buried her hands in the sides of her hair and looked soon to begin whimpering. "Never!" she moaned. Her curls, which had been so carefully piled on top in Coiffure d'Amelie that very morning, sprang flat as Roman spit curls against her head. "Never in a millennium would I ever have guessed that this, too, in such as this most horrible of horrible years, would come to us."

"*Mon Dieu,*" George Menard and most of the gathered villagers cried with a true sense of tragedy. "Is his act not treasonous, in retrospect? Is it enlightened? Is it even romantic? No! Where's the reason in that?"

"Perhaps it is elsewhere well-known that the great Rousseau spat five times, in spite of his good sense, and gave his issue up."

"He spat in spite of his good sense? What does that mean?"

"That passes all my cognitive powers!"

"*Au secours!* It was on our honeymoon we thought of it. And then we had our five children. Just like him, we joked. We thought it so romantic, too. Now it is imperative! We must change the name of the bar!"

The gathered devotees circled around and began the query yet again in lowered tones, winding down toward the last call.

"Not Rousseau."

"*C'est tragique!*"

"Madame Desbordes she jokes with us."

"Impossible."

"That's the top and the bottom of bad humor!"

"Can it be true?"

"We will search the internet when we are home."

"*Ouais*, hopefully we will find it a ruse."

"Camille Desbordes has been bitten temporarily by the mistral madness, to be sure."

"But the mistral is no where to be seen. This is very serious."

"Madame Desbordes never lies or jokes about something so serious when children are involved. Look at her. She is under the vine."

"That is true indeed."

"Tonight, again, there is no mistral."

"Perhaps a mistake in your source."

"Yes, that must be it. No need to change your banner, Menard."

"*Oui*, an innocent mistake of the internet."

"*O pardon bien*," Camille broke in, lifting her head. "The weather is usually the last to bother me, but perhaps the *humidité* has boiled my head. I meant to keep that news to myself. Please forgive me, most beloved of friends." Her head sank back onto the bar.

Georges Menard regained his floor, scolding aimlessly as he never did. "I wish you had, Madame Desbordes. *Quelle horreure!* Could it be already a *blague* on me and my café. Me just a joke circulating around the globe.

"We didn't know the great Rousseau was bizarre in his secret history," Juliette put in and began to cry. "My heart is in fragments now. Poor Rousseau."

Ambrose's enormous head erupted like a cabbage rose thrown from the adjoining room, followed by his shoulders and then the rest of him trying to right itself, his pool cue ready for the joust. "I mean to try out for fatherhood!" he cried, stopping short to find himself in such unusual atmosphere. "Did I miss the point, Menard? Anything? What goes on here?"

"Ambrose, would you give your children up for adoption?" Ferdinand the Baker asked.

"Monsieur le Blé, you should not drink so much *pastis*," Ambrose replied boisterously. "Fatherhood, I mean to try it! Just as soon as possible! Who said I, Ambrose le Beau, would abandon children? Orphanage? *Jamais!* Not five, or twenty-five of them. You can count on it."

Pierre Jadot hunched over his glass of Pernod, tapping his grizzled rabbit's foot on the magnificent countertop of the bar. "*Bon idée,* Ambrose! Move over to my rabbit patch, le Beau. There you can live in perfect harmony like all the world's paternity. So robust you are, Ambrose! Perhaps you will in the end take after Monsieur Rousseau?

Life has many wonders ahead, even for you."

Although Ambrose le Beau had missed the gist, as everyone could see, he shot a condescending look at Jadot. And the hair rose up like spring chives on all Georges Menard's knuckles where they lay on the bar. Quickly he prepared to intervene. "Mind the furniture," he was already stating firmly in an unpleasant voice he reserved only for the grand displays.

"But, of course, I take the wake of Rousseau in even his smallest thought," le Beau went on. "Who could do otherwise and hold up his head?"

"So you *would* trundle your children to the orphanage," the Rabbit Catcher goaded. "I thought you said you would not."

"What has Rousseau to do with the orphanage? You have really gone too far, Monsieur le Lapin, in the drink tonight."

The Rabbit Catcher lay his head on the bar as if to concede.

Ambrose grumbled to himself and turned away, choosing to ignore late night lunacies. He called loudly for his pool partner to return at once from the toilet and finish the game.

"I begin to fetch the meaning of this, le Beau, which is more than you do in your present besotted circumstance," Pierre Jadot jabbed. Ambrose turned toward him again. "Either Rousseau's children were evil indeed, or Rousseau hit upon the intriguingly new philosophy: Let anyone with children more than one or two in number send them off to orphanage. They are the people's war fodder. Here, I salute Rousseau, I say!"

∞

Pereault de Poste, a cleanly shaven man with a small golden-brown head on a small but well-shouldered body, who completely adored five children of his own, was perhaps additionally brooding over quite something else. That unprecedented hysteria in riding helpless in a yellow inflatable from village to village during the flashflood had been so publicly displayed, yes; perhaps it was this that haunted him. For nights and weeks, he had dreamed that still he found himself riding to work on a gigantic banana that everyone could see.

Doctor Benoit, renowned cardiologist of St. Y, who also specialized as a hobby in dream therapy, had consoled the little postman earlier that day. Benoit had offered early on the suggestion that perhaps Pereault actually would have preferred to have had the yellow canoe to having the post office emergency inflatable. It was a great disaster to be cast out in a boat without oars, in all countries that was known. Pereault, their valued postman and sentinel, had survived and even made the essential call to The Beloved, the call that had saved Père Martin's life. Indeed, Doctor Benoit said now, it was highly likely that Pereault de Poste should expect continuing stress and even sudden unpredictable actions for at least six or seven post-traumatic months. "Sleep with a water bottle on your chest whenever your wife moves to her side of the bed," Doctor Benoit advised, but Pereault of the post was not listening to him.

Under the effects of such continuing nervous tension, it was indeed difficult for the normally congenial postman to keep from striking the unsightly Jadot who was decidedly not a small man and who was at that moment at logger heads with the gargantuan le Beau, both of whom now had leapt to their feet and were nose to nose staring each other down. More than once the little postman managed to stomp onto the great toes of The Rabbit Catcher's steel-toed work boots, before the brutish man noticed him. Then several drinkers did have a difficult time holding Pereault the Postman back. Before the hour had passed, in spite of extraordinary efforts by many, including Juliette Menard and Camille Desbordes, Pereault de Poste had taken a bloody blow to the end of his nose, one blackening, side-winding knuckle sandwich to the left orbital, and another to the right.

It was all too obvious to Pereault, long before it occurred to the others, that not one of his blossoming injuries could be adequately concealed upon arriving home that night to his unwittingly defended, lovely wife and brood. Mortified, Pereault de Poste curled up as the Rabbit Catcher stomped over him and out the door. Now his bloodied and swollen appearance would create yet other disturbances in his aplomb. Would it never end? Now he was nothing but two extroverted eggplants staring hopelessly out over a nasal fig. How, he now groaned, was he in the next days to make his way through every neighborhood, being asked again and again to relive all the unfortunate moments that had led to his new face? And, all on account of bad weather! And then, too, on account of a sudden revelation about the life of his heretofore favorite philosopher. To be sure, his villagers would try to console him when they saw his silver nose splint, and he would turn away yet again in shame.

Yes, it had been a disappointing season for nearly everyone, he muttered to himself. And, who would know it more than a postman, he asked himself in that rhetorical fashion that was his wont. Who knew anything more of a village than those who served the post?

The SEPTUM CONSIDERS *his* SENTENCE

 **ALTHOUGH PEPIN WAS VERY SHORT,** smaller even than Pereault de Poste, he was perfectly formed, Pearl admitted to herself. He had beautifully sculpted, delicate ears, almost electric looking. One nearly expected his perfect ears to have tiny antennae protruding from their upper hemispheres. A similarly fine, pink membrane supported the interior of his well-furred nostrils. Although his eyes appeared close together in his head, particularly when they shifted about like that, they did resemble those of a kiwi bird she had once admired in New Zealand. It seemed as though his features were about to fold in upon themselves when anything remotely emotional overtook his course. A serious fault in a man, perhaps, or in a woman, certainly. His chest did not expand like those of other men, or those of birds or other male animals when challenged. Was he leering, one asked, much as a young gorilla might fake strength when threatened? Or, was he the natural descendent of the platypus? Pearl and Camille and Ambrose could not decide. Nor could anyone else.

∞

Père Pepin leaned back at an angle in the chair from whence the much older Père Martin had normally officiated from under his great mass of silver hair, but for the one spot at the crown that had gone to balding. An appropriate natural tonsure, a gift from God himself, he said. What a lovely disposition, people said Père Martin had, full of generosity and good humor, brimming with advice more than humanly sage. And so it was pretty much universally said of him. Anyone would have had a hard time filling the place of such a figure, much less a tiny young platitudinous creature of the cloth.

Pepin put his feet up on the desk and tilted back until the couple and their closest friend had a good view of the soles of his shoes, which they could not help noting were barely scratched and were in any case undeniably elegant.

In the next moment, time had shifted and the bride was staring out that same window through which she had first seen him from the street. She was hearing for the first time the new priest saying the incomprehensible: "I'm afraid I must advise against your marriage."

"Oh, but it's all arranged!" Pearl exclaimed. "We didn't mean to offend you. You told us to go away and come back. We just kept waiting for Père Martin's recovery, don't you see that? Don't worry. This will be our last visit to you."

Pepin considered recanting momentarily. "Postponement is one possibility, of course. Or perhaps you will decide not to marry this man after all. And he, you? How do we know? I have not had the chance to counsel you."

The bride gripped the groom's upper sleeve and twisted the fabric.

"Some do not even bother with marrying," Ambrose began to suggest. "We live in a predominantly secular state now."

Père Pepin winced, seeing the scheming drift of the immense man's implication. In self-defense, Pepin flared the channels of his nose, though his narrow chest displayed no expansion. "I can only say that I do not condone your marriage now," he pronounced, tapping the ashes of his cigarette neatly into his palm. Then he let them drift overboard, into a receptacle. For a moment he considered revealing his own experiences with those in the matrimonial state, but then he thought better of it. "Or ever," he decreed.

"But, why oh why?" Pearl cried out. "I have to have a church wedding, even if it is Catholic, or my mother and sisters won't come!"

"I suspected as much," the little man sneered, lifting his eyes above their heads. "Not a Catholic, not a believer, not French," he said. "And," he whispered to himself, "not fleshed."

"But I have taken the instruction!" she declared. "So that I can be married in the Church!"

Ambrose le Beau, endowed with keen hearing, had already stood and made to exit the room. Following, Pearl nearly managed to beat him to the door and ran into him, as he turned around and made again for the side of the priest's desk.

∞

She had been thinking, at the back of her mind, even hoping a little hysterically, that if that priest were not careful, he might burn an inappropriate hole into his hand. Later that night in her dreams, she would consider further the image of him wandering the earth, bleeding falsely on international talk shows. He would appear in clips of operas on Arte on the television set. That night she sat up in bed astonished at herself, considering her dreamed fate for Pepin, a far worse fate for a priest than that which Père Martin had recently acquired after a bad dream about something the Blue Mother had said to him about automobiles. In the dream, Pepin progressed to etching unmistakable little red, starfishy stigmata with a ball-point pen into his palms.

Fully awake, Pearl wondered now beside his desk with Beau, whether The Septum had taken up piercing his feet. She would have been encouraged if she had known that across town, for the past few hours, Père Martin's worries had been tranquilized by the sight of the little flying machine that Madame and Monsieur Hauberk had sent over with Ambrose. At least he had ceased his shrieking. Henri Béranger and Christian Malaplate—the only ones allowed in to see him, except for Juliette Menard and the Mayor's sister—-had tied the flying pirate ship to the ceiling by way of a cup hook and a string of dental floss.

Towering over Père Pepin, Ambrose tried to contain himself but knew he was failing. Why else would he have returned to face the obstinate, inexperienced substitute? He thought now that perhaps he understood him. Pepin, he thought, was trying to fail in St. X so that he might be called home. Why else would Pepin be behaving in such a manner? The heat went up in his face as he spoke, yet again, "We already fixed our plans with Père Martin," Ambrose stated in a flat and immovable voice. "This is our visit, merely a formality. Our wedding will take place on a new schedule, when Père Martin recovers, or by le Maire alone. Our guests have been reassured. No matter what you say are the ominous effects of Père Martin's flash flood upon you, you can not even imagine it, or our resolve, much less claim to have been at the scene."

The substitute priest smiled thinly up at the groom, and the bride felt her outwardly undetectable blood slow to a trickle. The not elderly, suddenly not young, priest leaned gingerly forward as if onto push pins and heard himself through the tips of his ears wheedling away at them, "As you may have noticed, Père Martin has been imprisoned within his own wrought iron bed-frame for some time. No one has let me speak to him, even though I have filled his post. Don't you think that extraordinary?"

"Doctor Malaplate and The Beloved told us," the bride asserted, "Père Martin will be well in time for our wedding. So, we will have no need of you. We only came as a courtesy to you. And, and, just in case—"

Swiftly Père Pepin interrupted, with only a slightly triumphant note entering along with his surprise report: "Doctor Malaplate conveyed to me this very morning that Père Martin has very little chance of living in a wheel chair, or even—*pardon bien*—living on this earth. For personal reasons, Mademoiselle Queneau, the outcome is decidedly not my own preference that your beloved priest should pass from this world and leave me to carry on for him in this place. That would seem to put us on the same side. *N'est pas?* Well, it makes little difference. Consider the possibilities of something new in your lives: rally, accept, and tolerate! You can put off your marriage until we have had time to meet and determine at a later date the advisability of entertaining yet again the thought of such a grave act as marriage for the two of you. Certainly not now, during a time of compromise in the village."

Then Pearl was shaking her finger at him until she found that Ambrose had gently nudged her back into her chair again. "Don't talk about Père Martin that way!" she raged. "Ambrose and I have full confidence in Père Martin's recovery! Everyone in St. X, everyone who has ever met him, loves Père Martin; they told us he wasn't dying! And, besides," she stammered, "our mayor, The Beloved, he will marry us, even if you won't."

At this, Père Pepin shot out of the leather wing chair like a small fruit bat and thrust his hands into the dark drapery of his sleeves. "It is interesting," the priest insinuated, "that you in this village call your mayor The Beloved, rather than your priest. Such a secular place on earth I have come to occupy, against my human judgment! I am against your marriage in such an atmosphere of strange occurrences and inclement weather. If you persist, you should wait a year to be married in this village in this church. Hopefully by then I will be out of the way. And someone else less ambitious will be ensconced in your nightmares. Meantime, if you wish to be married without me and without your family, be my guest."

Pearl had never heard Ambrose truly shout, except for the once when their tipsy friend Tomás had fallen into Ambrose's favorite guitar case and splintered the bridge of the gorgeous instrument. Now Pearl's eyes opened up like two windows in her head as her intended's pressurized voice extruded into church chambers. *"Je m'en fous!"* Ambrose shouted. Even in his rudeness, Pearl could see that Ambrose was trying to contain himself: "You arrive in our village, as you yourself say, Pepin, against your will, and you will not condone our wedding?" Ambrose held out his immense hands as if to strangle him. "How dare you defame Père Martin? He is the Father to our village! No one knows more that he is loved here than Père Martin himself!"

Pearl stood up beside her fiancé on his weak-eyed side, but he barely felt her grip his arm as his logic began to disintegrate. "You say weather is your reason for denying a sacrament? Perhaps you come from some primeval territory where you worship the sun or the sheen on rain! To call you a priest! What a sacrilège!" Ambrose wrung his hands dramatically. His breath came in colossal huffs and suspirations; even visible quakes seemed to be pounding out of his shirt.

From among the books, the sepia-toned eyes of Père Martin peered out at Ambrose in a reminder of the previous century of teachings in the village; Ambrose's own father was pictured on that wall as a boy taking his first communion from Père Martin.

The new young priest held his ground; and then, as the couple turned their backs on him and on the room itself, he shrank down at the desk. Father Pepin stared into the blotter and realized his very own stubbornness had sealed his fate. He would never be allowed to leave the struggling little village after this.

This village of coincidence and accident, this St. X with an impending marriage with a priest's pronounced curse on it, Père Pepin's own curse, all of this he had been allotted. Pepin could not think why or how or what he had done to deserve being even the smallest part of it. Perhaps the white bride, as he thought of her, had not been told of Père Martin's own concerns about them. Pepin had refused to look them in the eyes directly: the gigantic one—he must have surpassed two and a half meters—the one who occasionally called himself Ambrose the Cyclops because of some childhood accident no one spoke about, and the other, the female, with hardly an ounce of pigment. No, he would no more look at them than he would have looked a rabid dog directly in the eye, and his first marriage ceremony in this village was not going to be theirs, that was certain. He took up his pen and began again to circle on his face, ever smaller toward the corner of his upper lip, where once his mustaches had been teased by the same motion. This time, however absent-mindedly, he held the pen the wrong way out and left behind a blue-black snail to smile at him on either side of his mouth.

SANTÉ!

"ALLONS-Y!" **AMBROSE ANNOUNCED,** grasping his consort by her shoulder blades. She had a sensation then of having been transported on a jet stream out of hell and into Jerusalem. In one swift movement, they rushed out the sapphire door of the Quandary and turned to watch it slam shut like a wall of sky before them. Then they found themselves on the familiar *rue* under a comforting veil of cascading pink and red ivy geraniums.

For the good of those on bar stools or at nearby tables that midday, along with the two distraught lovers, the postman had dropped in for lunch to recount his own eventful story. While delivering an express letter from a religious source, into what he called the 'inlet' of the sanctuary, and having blithely mentioned Ambrose and Pearl's impending ceremony to Père Pepin, while assuming the substitute priest would be presiding, the new priest, in no uncertain terms and most inappropriately, had announced that Ambrose's marriage was not something in which Père Pepin had any intentions of assisting! Since no one had shown him the courtesy of mentioning that plans for it were still, in defiance of him, going forward, no, he would not assist! In that next very moment, The Septum had accosted the postman verbally for flinging his envelopes through the mail slot in the blue door just as he had always done, rather than politely ringing the bell so that The Septum would not have to bend down to retrieve the envelopes. So the postman now raged, thumping his glass about on the polished limestone surface for emphasis.

A crowd of twelve or fourteen clicked their tongues at this, which led others to gasp and shake their heads in remembrance of a related occurrence in the café-bar some blustery weeks ago.

ASSERTIONS & HERBS
by CAMILLE DESBORDES

 THE NEXT RUCKUS IN CAFÉ ROUSSEAU started with a casual comment by Camille Desbordes, who possessed well known, perhaps even formidable healing powers, a garden of healthy herbs, and attendant forest creatures hanging about her land to vouch for it. Camille had been praising Père Martin's decision not to go to hospital and complaining that perhaps she might have been called in to good effect for assistance to the elderly priest. Pearl had been the first to agree with her.

"I can certainly understand that he might refuse to go to hospital," Pearl said unwisely, and then offered up the interesting information that her first boyfriend Boswell, an Irish boy who, like herself, had gone to the international school in Paris, well it was Jimmy himself who had explained to her eight years before, that if, in France, you fell off a high cliff or got hit by a runaway automobile, you would eventually be whisked away all right by *les pompiers* or by ambulance. If you had had the fortunate foresight to have had a more serious and truly scary near-death experience in remote circumstances, a helicopter would come to rescue you even more quickly—all *dramatique*. But, once in that emergency vehicle, you would receive no treatment whatsoever until you arrived at hospital perhaps forty to sixty kilometers away.

The crowd shrugged as one. Well, what was her point? "*C'est normale,*" they said.

There were very few in France to make it to life support, Boswell had sternly said. "So don't step out before yer infernal blocks of anything that be solid and moving quick-like toward your face." Pearl recounted this further rumor to Camille Desbordes, afraid to offend other less-traveled citizens only to find that Camille Desbordes herself ruffled up in a patriotic temper.

Indeed, Pearl recounted to Camille, Jimmy Boswell had mentioned the excellence of French hospitals, something that Pearl noticed her friend, the herbalist and psychic, did not wish to hear, now that the quality of French ambulances had been thoroughly defamed. For that matter, Camille admitted quite loudly, swallowing her pride, that she herself, having never been a patient in a hospital since the day of her birth, did not wish to think of or attend any hospitals anywhere at all, no matter how good Pearl's Boswell claimed they were.

"I would absolutely decline to go to hospital myself," Pearl bragged then for general hearing over the first course of her meal, almost hopelessly trying to redeem herself. "Only in the case of births, God forbid, might I go to hospital, and only then for the protection of *les enfants*, God forbid that there should be many, or any."

A gasp went up in the café.

"Besides, why would I, or Père Martin, take that long and dangerous trip in an ambulance that offers up nothing on the way but transportation?" The café was beset with sideways glances as the little schoolteacher continued. "Especially when Doctor Malaplate will come right to our door with his excellent skills and his magic medicine? Besides," she said, "we always have Camille Desbordes, who in my opinion may be equal or superior to any number of saints, to say nothing of hospitals anywhere in the world." She took a quick sip, blew her bangs off her sweltering, bright forehead, and looked into her glass again. Yes, everyone was staring at her again.

It was not this latter statement that astonished everyone who was eating or imbibing at Café Rousseau, for many in attendance were in complete agreement with her about Camille Desbordes and also Christian Malaplate.

A meditative moment plunged over the bar as all within earshot of the minuscule, quite oblivious bride-to-be stared through the adjacent door at Ambrose who was just then unconsciously flexing a muscle or two, while racking up balls on the pool table.

Hardly anyone in Café Rousseau, except for Pearl herself, had failed to hear how Ambrose had been bragging all the previous evening amongst his male friends of his emotional goal to immediately father children with her. It was time, he had declared, to father many small *montagnes*, even feminine hills if need be! He was absolutely ecstatic. Mademoiselle Queneau would be the perfect mother, he had announced.

Who among them could deny it? Bets escalated, along with intake of liquid sustenance, until he had committed himself and much of the village's financial security, to having his first child on his lap by the next Bastille Day.

Upon hearing of these plans from their individual husbands and beaus on the preceding night, speculation had ensued among the wives and girlfriends as to whether or not Mademoiselle Queneau might already be with child—*Elle a le ballon?* they asked. Did she already have the balloon? And, if so, how many were in there and of which kind to give Ambrose such confidence? Perhaps they had already been for the sonogram at the clinic in St. Z? Ah, but no, that would be cheating! And, Ambrose was known for an honest fellow. Of course, impending marriage could change a man, it was said. Yes, but not that much. A man was the man before and after.

But, just now, to those gathered in the café, it was all too clear that Pearl Queneau had denied and even denounced any possibility of personal yearnings toward motherhood, even though she loved children and had made the nourishment of their intelligence one of her life's works. *O, c'est normale*, some of the café discussants proclaimed, so normal, was it not, that Ambrose would not know of Pearl's terror of childbirth. In the throes and throbs of love, one often forgot to ask even the important questions. One just assumed that the loved one was like oneself. And then, anyway, fate would have its way, wouldn't it, no matter what had been said.

OPEN SEAS,
LITTLE FATHER

 **SOMETIMES A ROD WAS JUST A STICK** and a staff was just a staff. And the crossbar was the intersection that did all the complicated math, that's the way Père Martin figured it. Sometimes two lines were more than three to six dots on a graph. Sometimes the paddle floated more easily than the spear and sometimes it did not, to good effect. The memory washed the illusions back and forth among the drugs the doctor had given him and underpinned Père Martin's concussion.

But, from without, le Maire and Doctor Malaplate had not noticed the priest's inward-turning expression, the tiny crenellations appearing near the bridge of his forehead. After all, the priest had barely spoken since they had taken him down and carried him across town, on the back of a ladder, and up the stairs. He had clenched his eyes shut all the while the body cast was being applied like a second skin to his naked body. It had been as cold as a snake's sting, he'd thought, as another glob of it had come into contact with his ruined hip and thigh.

In between the repetitive shocks, the priest bobbed about, still on the open sea of invigorated memory. The theme was pain at the moment, he had resigned himself to that. An undertow came vividly whenever he recalled an old injury, even in a minor way—a stub of the toenail against the sheet, a bump, bash, cat scratch, rose thorn, or bee bite.

And when he smelled it now, even his own excrement, the dirt of life, that would bring back the worst day of the war, the beginning of the turning, for certain, not just every day but every time. Bales of hay, or newly mown grass, green tea, or a baby's diapers, or even someone's accidental squeaking of gas, anywhere it could happen. That horrid day long past, at the ready in the moment to descend.

They called it blessed now, even heroic, but it hadn't seemed anything like that. So few had been sent from this sector, mostly boys and old men already injured who had never seen one another before. He had been attached to the unit for good measure and support. There was never any thought of a priest fighting until the fighting started and then he thought of it himself. Well, that was not exactly it, was it?

Soon enough, within seconds, first the men were there, joshing with him about his illness, for he had had the misfortune to come down with it. Heaving all night and losing water out both ends, and then they were all dead. No one ever said what you were to do if you got sick during the big wars. His own filth oozed from his body, and seemed to melt into the realm of others. His neck refused to turn, he was aware of someone screaming, perhaps himself, he could not be sure and he wasn't sure it mattered. The fever probably saved him from freezing, or it felt like it. And so he told himself.

There was so much sound that he could no longer hear anything. Mushroom clouds of fabric drifted over him from time to time—people's clothing, parachutes. Le Clare's ankle melted into a net. He wasn't sure how he knew that it was Le Clare's ankle. It must have been the clock on the socks that he had teased him about a few days before. Somehow it had seemed almost cheery.

He supposed the invasion must have been well under way by that point. He couldn't see why it would not have been, and then looking out over the vast array of detritus, he could not see why it would have progressed in the positive at all. Perhaps it was a stalemate, or even a failure. The screaming had not stopped and the nail in his neck seemed to have either gotten longer or penetrated farther. This would have been the time for him to have called on Father Soufflé for assistance, as the young priests liked to call the old badger, to give him the royal neck twist. Soufflé was an expert at the back crack and the neck twist. Nothing could deflate pain the way Soufflé could.

Perhaps the entire world had received the royal neck crack in that one go-around, so Père Martin was thinking as a group of legs appeared nearby on a set of further arms and legs, all of them or some of them, he could not be certain, still functional.

And then some of them had grabbed him up and he had been upended, cast adrift into the lost planes of gravity. His vision seemed to turn three-quarters sideways and then disappear into what was certainly unfamiliar and stinking, surely himself, he considered as the stretcher laid him out to flail like a dislodged insect. It seemed then that his attendant countrymen had all died or departed. He was divided from reality, stunned and stultified, blood left his body and seemed to enter back in on its own, a tiny dog rode by at an angle and disappeared, barking, into a G.I.'s jacket. A voice joked that it wouldn't do any good to shoot him, he would stink as bad dead as alive, now that he had seen fit to get the dysentery. At first, they'd slept ass out for self-preservation, face to face in the snow, when they could find a few minutes to lie down. When they could not even pretend to be dead, they slept on their feet, leaning their backs against one another in groups of six or more like sheaves of corn.

And, when the sickness got so bad, and he could stand no longer because his knees were shaking so badly, the two Americans swept him up—yet in his fowled priestly garb—through the thickly falling snow, cored the edge of a hay stack, and corked it with him. Before he knew it, they had fully shoved him in and under. Straw rained down upon his head.

One of them said something awful, grinning widely, but in another language, slang perhaps or dialect, perhaps not even ordinary. He didn't need to know to understand it. Then those boys, too, were gone all together, into the fray, into the deafening upheaval. Their last words to him should have been his last to them. *Pray, little Father*, one of them had said and kissed him on top of the head, grinning, stunning blue eyes beaming down at him through the fodder. The ones closest had leaned in and burst out in a momentary silent cantata of smiling as they disappeared into a wave of smoke and blizzard.

Voilà! he thought. He had arrived! At least the two Americans had saved him from Father Soufflé's whispered last rites and that lethal neck crack that his departed comrades had begun to consider.

IN *the* VINEYARD

 **UP AND DOWN THE ROWS OF TORTURED VINES** that spread from the mountainous horizons to the Great Crevasse and back across the plain, in among the black vegetal skeletons, nested the multiple yet exceedingly small, the discolored, and incomparably crenellated crop, the hopeless-looking grapes that had turned on the vines to mouldering *raisins sec.*

"It does no good at all to pay workers to take in a crop like this! It's completely dead!"

"But all these unplucked vines will fail year after year if we don't take these grapes!"

"All you hooligans ever think about is now!"

"But they stink and they look like flies!"

"Don't be such a greedy-guts!"

Small children gyrated like changeling caterpillars in the rocky soil.

"Zut alors—"

The Mayor's father's, father's, father's grandfather had started up a strain of grape that had fathered many of the finer vines to be found. Beside him, earlier that morning, the pinched Père Pepin, reluctant substitute for Père Martin, gazed condescendingly over the crowd as *le Maire* spoke:

"We have been worrying this matter since Père Martin asked for peace for us from the arms of The Blessed Mother," The Beloved began again. "I have considered every point of view that has been offered to me, and some I have forced out of a sickly, nearly drowned person who does not wish to be seen right now by you. For the first time in memory many of you wish to abandon the crop. For some reason, some have come to think it impolitic or even bad fortune to bring this one harvest in. To me, this is inconceivable. It is certainly not forward-looking for our village, and it is not French. Our crop is our grand and natural mother, just as we have always said about this our dearly beloved village of St. X. *Zut alors.* In the worst of all possible days, if it were my mother, I would at least prepare the body. I would not leave her here to rot in the fields before the world!"

With which impassioned comparison, *le Maire* waved a protective silence over himself, fearing that he might dissemble even more. He removed the hand of the ingratiating and pockmarked new priest from his arm, and dismounted from the tiny truck onto the back of his aging *motocyclette*. In no time he had zoomed home to bed where his sister placed a sprig of thyme under his pillow and an ice pack on his head.

Meanwhile on the tailgate of the *camion*, Père Pepin pulsed and scowled and pitied himself for having been disemboweled from the inner cavity of his former city life, as the entire populace of his new parish turned their backs on him and receded into town along the Rue du Porche.

ON *the* CHEMIN *de* TÊTE GRIMAÇANTE

 **ON THE CHEMIN DE TÊTE GRIMAÇANTE,** the Street of the Grimacing Head, the pre-marital duet eventually found The Beloved, Monsieur Henri Béranger, in his parlor of elegance, bent over his famed motorcycle where he had propped it on a protective carpet he had made of the *International Herald Tribune,* which he read to keep his English up. He also enjoyed a number of other newspapers in other languages; a simple hobby of his, he said. A linguist at heart.

Oh, so happy and relieved they were to see him! "*Bonjour, bonjour,* Beloved! We've come to ask you to marry us!" they called in at his open door.

The Beloved lifted up his hand in affectionate, if a bit more than slightly distracted, acknowledgment and then he motioned them in. In a moment he came around to putting down his tools, wiping the oil from his face. The robust gentleman offered them each a glass of the miraculous new grape juice that had as of late overtaken so many conversations among his countrymen. For a moment the couple hesitated, twirled and sniffed and marveled. Should they drink it or not? Just last night over pool, Ambrose had heard a rumor that the post-flood grapes might have acquired an instantaneously poisonous streak.

"So delightful! And yet, still merely the juice!" *le Maire* pointed out.

"And, why not?" he said, "Everyone is thinking it! Being soaked, boiled, and baked on the vine, and yet to survive even to the *vendange!* With the slightest fermentation, who knows, but perhaps for the first time, our humble village will live in the maps of the finest French vines. Perhaps our dear Père Martin will yet recover health and wit and the grand flashflood will have been just a little bit of the Godsend!" so *le Maire* said, perhaps a little too hopefully, trying to sip grandly all the same and not mention the possibilities of the wide-spread financial devastation that loomed nearby if not directly overhead. "*Santé!*" Out of respect, and hope, they lifted and drank.

As though from distant shores, Pearl looked on while *le Maire* took up the fuel cap from the motorcycle. With Ambrose, *le Maire* sniffed at it by turns. The two men frowned, and then *le Maire* made a production of pinching at one tire. "*Et alors!*" both men said. At last, The Beloved waved the couple over the newspaper-covered, antique Savonnerie carpet toward his sofa. The two lovers sank into its cushions, immensely relieved to be again in sagacious accord. The future appeared from there to open up.

Ambrose had been a school chum of the Mayor's late son, and in many ways Ambrose had taken on the role of surrogate son, being without a father, due to desertion from late childhood himself. Mademoiselle Queneau also had turned for guidance to *le Maire* during her years in the village for explanations of language differences and local customs, for the sake of her travel articles, often out of curiosity, and then plainly out of affection and friendship with the old gentleman.

Le Maire pressed his cap uncomfortably down on his head and removed it once again to hang it on the handlebar. He rubbed at the bridge above his nostrils as though something grave were troubling him. Very seriously he pulled up a chair, draped a piece of newspaper over its gold brocade, and perched on its edge. Hands planted on his knees, handkerchief wandering, polishing his face and precipitously balding head, The Beloved spoke to them quietly. They thought for a moment that they had misunderstood. "But must you marry now, Ambrose? Pearl?" he asked. "With Père Martin still in bed?"

"*Bien sur,* Beloved," Ambrose responded politely, but with worry in his face. "That is what we planned with Père Martin. It is our wish, out of respect."

Pensively, The Beloved stood up again to wipe the rear view mirror with his face cloth. "You don't want to be blessed by someone, well, so— It puts a taint on things to have such a man as Pepin put his thumb in your ritual. Already you live together. What's the stampede anyway, Ambrose? Mademoiselle Pearl?"

Nearly a foot taller than the elderly mayor, Ambrose now developed an uncharacteristic whine in his voice as though a young *cigale* had put a chirrup onto his tonsils. It tugged at the little schoolteacher's heart to see him like this. "But, Beloved," Ambrose said, "for ten years it's been: *Why so tardy, Ambrose? When will you marry, Ambrose? Why not now, le Beau?* And you know how everyone says it. How about my daughter, Ambrose, why not marry her? Younger and younger the girls and still they say it. *Zut! Zut alors!* Besides, everyone loves Pearl."

"But, of course," *le Maire* replied, rubbing his hand over his head again. "We all love Pearl, especially the big and little children, and their families. Mademoiselle Queneau will make you a beautiful and fascinating wife."

A wave swept le Beau's face. "Is it because Pearl is pale?"

Pearl took in a quick breath and thought she might faint at such a question from her fiancé. "Ambrose!"

"*Mais non*, Ambrose. That is not the reason. In our village, we do not let fear dictate in mere matters of personality! Make no mistake. We are Old Resistance here. *Mais non*, you have been with us three, maybe six years, Mademoiselle Queneau. Already you are nearly one of us. *Non, non*, Ambrose, it is not your Mademoiselle. Think. When have you ever heard of it? It is the weather, he is mad. You know, Ambrose, I tell you, this new man, Pepin, he telephoned while you were on your way to me. He thinks it would be better to wait. And it is very late to inform him of wedding plans. Don't dismiss, don't dismiss so easily. First Père Martin had to be saved by the Blessed Blue Mother herself, after who knows what strange experience. And, Ambrose, you may think more seriously about what Pepin said, now that this drought has begun. This may be a very dark year. I know we thought Père Martin would be healed by now."

"Because of the weather!" Ambrose le Beau cried out in disbelief.

"Because of superstition?" Pearl said.

"What on this earth has the weather got to do with our wedding?" Ambrose asked in all innocence. He had never known *le Maire* to make an ill-advised pronouncement. Even this strange statement, he was willing to consider—for an instant anyway.

"You will want to start a family, Ambrose. Be cautious how you start." He looked carefully into the bride-to-be's eyes as he had many a time. But she said nothing now.

"*O!* So *vivante!*" *Le Maire* fingered the vein at his temple and then he bent to tinker with his motorcycle while reflecting again. In a dejected swoop, Ambrose and Pearl sank down deeper into the sofa before one of the two most admired men in their community. Ambrose actually groaned in despair as he draped his other arm around Pearl's frail shoulders. He tapped his other fingers protectively on her thigh.

Mademoiselle and Ambrose, both, were welling up, as *le Maire* could see. To see the Colossus in tears, well, that brought out the fatherly nature in him. "You must stay to dinner," he said. "Please."

RECOLLECTIONS *of a* BRIGHTLY PAINTED YELLOW CHAIR

 **A BRIGHTLY PAINTED YELLOW CHAIR APPEARED BEFORE THEM** beside the kitchen door, empty all these years. Beside it, arrived Brigitte, the Mayor's aproned sister, who had reached the time known as the joyous middle age some time before, and with her on a large flowered tray came a baguette, *saucisse sec*, a covered soup and other steamy courses cloaked in the celebrated orange and blue pottery of St. Z. Soon the lid was lifted from the tureen. The little bulbs in the mushroom soup presented a steam that was heavenly. Afterward, soon enough would come a moist and tender sliced duck with peppercorns and asparagus, braised courgettes, and then salad, and *tarte aux poires*.

Le Maire poured out a glass for each of them, making clicking sounds at the back of his throat, not unlike that of a tin, wind-up toy. The Mayor's sister herself plumped up a flower-embroidered cushion and rushed to set it behind Pearl's back each time she sat. "So happy! So happy!" the Mayor's sister exclaimed. "And, how are your wedding plans coming along?"

"My sister's coloring is pink as a peony, whenever she inadvertently interferes—" *le Maire* warmly said. And, indeed, his sister was as pink as a Chinese peony; she blushed so at her brother's odd acknowledgment.

"Why then! Are you not marrying this month? All the village has been looking forward to it. And there has been nothing much to look forward to for such a long time. What a boost to our little economy! I myself have bought a special dress. And presents, to be sure!"

"The children are thinking about whether or not to wait for Père Martin, Brigitte—"

"Ah, yes," she murmured. "I can see that, Henri. But the poor doves are anxious to get a common nest, everyone has heard of that. And their invitations have gone out. We have it on top of the bureau where it picks our spirits up."

"Ah," *le Maire* understood. "But already, Brigitte, they have their common nest."

Brigitte, who had never had a common nest with anyone other than a passing soldier who unfortunately had been killed not so far from home but none-the-less in war, sighed, letting her disappointment show. She took the pillow out from behind Mademoiselle Queneau and pressed it onto her own lap where many times imaginary infants sat, thinking that there must have been a miscarriage—of babies and perhaps justice at the same time. "Ah, so then, may as well wait."

Pearl would have been the one to change color now, if coloring had been within her range of possibility. How had she lost control in the last few days? How had she become the subject of this familial judgment? she asked herself more philosophically. What was it that she did not quite grasp?

As the meal progressed, the stricken Pearl Queneau expected her marriage plans to evaporate progressively, or to hear stories once again of The Beloved's war conquests, how he and his comrades had saved one another from the Nazis on their mountainside and plateaus.

Instead, *le Maire* asked as though the young couple had never thought of it, "How old are you?" And when they had offered up their ages, "Only thirty-nine and thirty-one?" he asked, nodding toward his sister. "Doesn't our little schoolteacher look even younger than thirty, Brigitte? Still thirty is not too old. But who can judge? We ourselves approach the true old age." His sister Brigitte painfully affirmed this with a nod and handed around the sliced *courgettes* under their blanketing of cheese.

"Ah, but Ambrose now, everyone knows his age!" The Beloved continued. "We thought this Ambrose, who is like a son to us, would never marry; or perhaps we always thought every time that he would marry. Every young woman and girl has tried to get a hand on him, Mademoiselle Queneau. He is our pride *robuste*, and so accomplished! The women do not call Ambrose day and night for nothing; every mother has wanted him for son-in-law. And if I had had a daughter, we would have had Ambrose living here with us for the last ten years—not that he hasn't been to visit me nearly every day of his life. *C'n'est pas vrais, Brigitte?* We would have kidnapped him!"

Le Maire tested the sauce accompanying the duck with the tip of his fork, placing it slowly onto his tongue. His eyes closed, and the young couple could see through the Mayor's nearly transparent lids, his eyes rolling back with the pleasure of man. "*Oui-da!*" he wheezed. "That is another fine sauce that my sister makes! And, that is a good pair of ages for marriage—especially if you would like the infants. Do not think for a moment that I forget or forsake you, lovely ones."

Pearl Queneau thought that perhaps she was witnessing a ritualistic courtship dance as occurred among many of the brightly colored birds and animals about which she had already written for travel magazines. Perhaps their mayor, as official and former *bon vivant,* must make these declarations before the bride could sweep Ambrose into flight! She hoped so. She had decided, even before they'd left the church, to try, for once, to be still and let Ambrose handle the customs of his own village. Yes, she had had the one little outburst, or two, each time they went in front of The Septum, but now she was determined to hold her peace. Such an approach was usually to her advantage in this country, though it was rarely possible. Her blood might not give her color but it certainly gave an upward rising pressure to her temperament.

"Establishing family is most serious, not only for you the lovers, but also for St. X," Mayor Henri Béranger told them now.

It came out suddenly, in rather a high voice like steam when it first starts to keen out of the kettle's spout. "You mean, I'm not what you want for your village?"

Le Maire finally spoke, in that tone that signaled a lengthy parable of sorts. Ambrose set his chair back on its legs, not altogether unhappily, and sighed.

"You see, Pearl, it was my *trisaieule-grandmere,* who took breath over such an exceedingly long time, as many people do in our village of good health," so The Beloved ever pontificated, holding her hand as if to study the white veins pouring through her skin. The Mayor's sister offered Pearl *tarte aux poires* and also pulled out a plate of *petits fours* on a silver tray to comfort her. "We send our spring water in little green bottles all across the world, as you know. In this way, proudly, we extend our health to anyone who cares enough for it. That is the loveliness of our village. She is a village with a heart for those we have never seen, for others who appreciate us without seeing, too! Faith has a place even in the small things of this world. *Ouais, ouais, mon grand-père* explicated for me the year that began so nearly like this one—fraught with unusual weather. *Mon Dieu.*"

"Inclement weather!" Ambrose scowled under his breath. "What is this weather madness anyway?"

Monsieur Henri Béranger narrowed his brown eyes at him and Ambrose set the front legs of his chair onto the tiles again.

"*Exactement! Mon fils!* The effects of the Revolution, they occurred, even here in St. X, you know, because of bad weather." He drew a finger across his sunburned throat. "Large and small battles depend on weather, Ambrose. Even in the family."

Ambrose tipped his head, trying, if not for understanding, well then for renewed tolerance.

"Ambrose, the world over, weather means something. P.M.S. She means the same thing in all languages to her men," he held a straight face for as long as he could and then he laughed.

Pearl prepared herself to be less than amused, but she rolled her pink eyes and laughed with the kindly mayor—in an act of broadmindedness toward members of what she called the 'hirsute sex—' waiting for the inevitable end to the Mayor's joke.

"I can not understand this burst of English now!" Ambrose complained. "What is this joke?"

"*Préparation militaire supérieure.* P.M.S.!" le Maire roared.

"Later I will explain it to you," Pearl said, relieved that the joke was at an end, "if you insist."

Now *le Maire* reverted to an ancient and, to Pearl, incomprehensible dialect near to Catalan. The two men sparred briefly and then they were smiling, having seen eye-to-eye and returned to common ground with, among other things, the joke explained enough to suit anyone. Both men raised their eyebrows up and carefully set them down, acknowledging the company of women as they did.

"This year also will be a hot year, like the others, even like The Year of the Frequent Throat Impediment. Har, har." *Le Maire* again indicated a strangulation of his *gorge*, and a slicing—almost comical. "For your marriage, children—try to wait."

The unusual heat of the street roared up behind them, along with the village traffic on rickety wheel and foot beyond the stony grounds; then it receded. "But we can not help ourselves!" they pined openly, and without apology, before him like any number of the school children they worked with.

"But my mother is coming from the Isle in two weeks—" Pearl whimpered, lip trembling as she edged her fork tines under a pale pink frosting floret, very much like the ones she still envisioned for her wedding cakes.

Henri Béranger stood up and seriously hesitated beside his motorcycle after this buffeting with the young couple's woes and familial news. The couple could not keep from silent thrilled commentary between themselves with their eyes at the sight of the mayor rummaging in the motorcycle's worn leather saddlebags, first one, and then in the other famous pouch in which The Beloved had carried an ultimatum to the few, but dominating, French collaborators in St. Z in the form of the grimacing head of the regional German commandant.

"Your mother will arrive in just two weeks?" Henri Béranger repeated. "From the Isle of Man?"

"No, from Michigan; she is stopping off with one of my sisters on the way!"

"Everyone we know is coming, Beloved!"

"Yes, just everyone!"

"Pearl's mother is a sweet woman in her pictures," Ambrose encouraged. "I'm afraid to let her down."

"I'm sorry, Ambrose," *le Maire* said. "What if the entire crop failed and some other catastrophe commenced, an epidemic for instance, or another flood. I, as someone who would grieve for you, if you wanted grief, must say I think you make a bad mistake in going to your wedding now. Beau, we do not want to frighten Pearl. But you might know what I mean."

"Might it be possible," the new priest had asked with *le Maire* on the phone, "might it be possible that the town could blame all of these on Pearl?" When the priest had said it, the mayor had wondered whether Pepin was likely to set it into the villagers' minds himself.

Ambrose rolled his massive head in his hands, despairing. His black hair stuck out from under them like a pile of sticks. "It will be no surprise to me if Pearl will leave me, now that she sees what weird superstitions we must go through in order to do *quelque chose correct*. Already I must disappoint the mother-in-law I have never met. My own mother arrives in two weeks!"

Pearl nudged him in the ribs. In return, Ambrose breathed out his resigned reply.

Le Maire laughed out-loud infectiously, and Pearl did the same, if a little nervously. "She is true, or you would not marry her. We will get you married in time for all your plans, even if time seems too quickly to flash by." Mademoiselle Queneau began to protest, but in a moment she thought better of it. On second thought she realized she did not know about what she would be protesting anyway.

Ambrose sulked, carried away as usual by his sensitivity. "If I could only get rid of that Pepin—"

Béranger revved the motor a bit with a little switch on the motorized bicycle, and a cloud of gas overtook the living room. Suddenly it seemed cavernous as the walls lost definition and their counterparts in the conversation disappeared. They coughed, politely, under their fists, and Ambrose laughed a little then, disingenuously, as life itself seemed to come back. "*D'accord*, Ambrose. I see that you are heartbroken. Forget that crank Père Pepin's weird refusal. Ask Père Alban in St. G for his blessing. I'll give you the civil ceremony here in St. X. A wedding must have an official blessing from the church, for all of the family. I know you appreciate that."

"But I don't understand. Père Pepin has already agreed to marry us!" Pearl Queneau interjected. "Whether we want him or not. He shouted it to us on the street as we left the church in a rage."

Ambrose turned and looked at her.

"A lie?" she said. "Surely not! And from a priest."

"The change of heart comes before the change of mind," The Beloved equated. "I truly think you should wait," he said again. "But, you choose."

NEWS *from the* CAV

AT SUNRISE, A GLUM CONVOY OF VEHICLES BEGAN. The sky was clear, and the heat itself was seen to shimmer over the spectacle. In open-backed carts and on tiny tractors, villagers and immigrant workers descended upon the fields. To and fro they went, carrying the aberrant grapes to the *cav*.

Eventually everyone laughed. *Tout le monde!* And cried. These grapes had been completely submerged for no less than three and one-half days during Père Martin's Flood. They had been steamed, boiled, and baked on the vine. And now they were to offer up exquisite nectar? There was erratic singing in the vineyards as is sometimes heard on Parisian psychiatric wards.

"*Ouais, ouais,*" Monsieur Henri Béranger said looking concerned when next Pearl and Ambrose met him quite by accident at the *cav* after a visit to the vats that he would not discuss. "It is as if we in our village are now under the gigantic magnifying glass. *Pour moi, il est tros chaud!* I don't remember ever being so affected by the heat like this."

It was true, the heat was most intense, extraordinary even for that month, which could be cruel of itself. The Baker's brand new, blue-feathered coq, which spent his time yodeling and fixed by his vulcanized living feet to the sign outside the tobacconist's shop, had fallen off, stricken dead by the boiling of his own blood, the butcher said. Hauberk's wife declared that not only was it a bad portent, she had not even had to fry the meat. It was all but smoked. Certainly no one in the village would have challenged the butcher or the butcher's wife's word about the nature of meat.

Most days Pearl Queneau went about dreaming of her upcoming wedding, wearing long, brightly-colored sundresses for their airiness, accompanied by the requisite long-sleeves. Ambrose was clad boyishly in shorts and sleeveless t-shirts decorated with one or another depictions of rock bands or of skulls or eyes that looked about after you wherever you tried to hide. Ambrose was too hot to make his usual self-deprecating jokes about the double-tinted glasses he wore. The weather had turned Ambrose's mood toward an even broodier attitude. As everyone native to the village phrased it, Still today *he* did not rain. *O, c'est normale,* they said with a collective shrug. The foreign inhabitants put it slightly differently, in slightly different forms: Today we have Hell itself for chef outside in this God-forsaken place.

Le Maire cleaned his own blue-green spectacles on a sterile part of his handkerchief and fastened the springy curvature of the bows about his jutting ears. He leaned pointedly toward Ambrose. "But one thing more," *le Maire* said, smiling rather pacifically, Ambrose thought. "Your music store, Ambrose, it will remain open until the last moment, if you do get married at Christmas time? So the parents can buy the children's Christmas presents? I have heard from my esteemed sister that we have received your latest, exquisitely engraved invitation. You are having your wedding after Christmas and not before. Brigitte and I are *très content.*"

"As always, we will open for regular hours until seven in the evening," Ambrose said with great dignity, considering that *le Maire* had managed to put off their wedding for more than a quarter of the year.

"*Bon!* And you might be persuaded to conduct the village concert on New Year's Day, as is your usual?"

"And why not?" The Bandmaster said. "As usual, it will be Mademoiselle Queneau's and my greatest pleasure to see our students there. We agree to take our marriage and honeymoon after that. *C'est vrai,* Pearl?"

She gave her resigned but positive response. "All my students will be looking forward to it, Beloved."

"*Bien,* Ambrose! *Bien!*" *le Maire* said, with a tear the size of a small grape just now squeezing out from one of his brown-centered eyeballs. "I have listened to you play *What Child Is This* every year since you were seven years old at our Christmas Festival, along with the Grieg you love, and also all our favorite carols. Such exuberance! Such exactitude! I will sit in my usual spot in the front row where I can hear your notes—I will sit up close, but only if you agree also to play your lovely guitar—not only this new bass viola that has captivated you—though I adore that, too."

Without waiting for Ambrose's response, *le Maire* moved toward the counter of the *cav cooperative* and purchased a glass for each of them to taste from a year long previous, when The Beloved's, and also Ambrose's, family had still been intact. It was light, dry, a slightly nutty wine, warming to the taste and also the sentiments. "We keep our pockets sewn closed then, Ambrose, until Christmas—but for a few necessary musical instruments—until we see the fine result, we hope, of this year's tragi-comic yield."

For a time they stood and stared out at the passing of the third truck moving household furnishings from the village that week. They turned the other way then to peer into the great void that the future had become within the stainless metal vats and oaken barrels, all the sparkling bottles and all the sanitized reaches that lay beyond. Over and over they turned the wine from a previous season on their palates, contemplating the time when Ambrose and the Mayor's curly-headed son had run wild in the vineyards and had taken their first tries with the sharp curved scissors, bearing up the gigantic sensual clusters in their baskets toward the little trucks. Now the three of them spun the intoxication around and around on their tongues while the unspoken heady scent of joyous reminiscence and conjecture rose into all their sinuses.

"*Ouais,*" *le Maire* sighed tearfully. "*Mais ouais.* But why concentrate on what may not turn out to be disaster. We have a wedding on our charts. Finally my little boy's friend Ambrose will marry, their childhoods are truly gone now, and already Ambrose will marry one I like very much. What a grand surprise, Ambrose, already you have grown up!"

"Do you have any substantial advice for myself and Mademoiselle Queneau, Beloved?" Ambrose asked.

They could not help but think of him, the week before, in his living room, balanced on his famous war-time motorcycle, alongside a rack of large and extraordinarily historic weapons, next to his late-wife's blue satin Louis XIV settee. Monsieur Henri Béranger mopped his lower lip.

Yes, the portrait of his wife's ancestress had smiled down on them from over her exquisitely beaded throat. It was the famous 'cut on the dotted line portrait' that The Bandmaster had described to Pearl on one of their earliest dates.

"*Ouais, ouais.* You want my advice? Take your time about everything. That is my advice. Never for one moment submit to *l'ennui*... Together or independently. It is not the battle against the bad guy that is important. Your battle against boredom must be incendiary! That is the battle worth winning. Together or alone, every single day you must wage dedicated warfare against this most invisible enemy. If you win, *voilà!* Then, long or short, your life is many blessings. *C'est tout.* If not, well then, it is not exactly *catastrophe*, but then, well--you are like all the rest of them. *C'est tout.*"

The fatherly friend took their empty glasses back again and handed them to the attendant. He offered them his hands. They had his little kisses, and they were on their way toward a wedding after Christmas, at the beginning of the new year.

"Felicitations!" The Beloved called after Pearl and Ambrose as happily they went up the lane toward the Rue de Porche, where Père Martin had first seen the immense Green Flashflood Unforeseeable cascading down on him.

To the LOWER PASTURES

 **WITH SO MUCH UNUSUAL FLUCTUATION IN TEMPERATURE,** the trees had already begun to drop their leaves, the upper pastures had also dried, and the weather was turning suddenly bitter. In response, the shepherds were bringing their flocks down early from the mountains to the lower pastures, three hundred, possibly more, bells clanking. "One sheep, one bell, that is the rule," Ambrose laughed, pinching Pearl. "And, try not to lose yours!" Live wool tumbled down the narrow streets up to their waists, clogging every passage as the young couple leapt into the safety of Madame Meulemeester's doorway.

"*Salut! Salut, tos animaux!*"

"Beau," she said, whimsically. "We might invite them to ring in your evening concert—at the beginning of our so-called honeymoon."

"Smell that," Ambrose replied, unimpressed by her suggestion.

"*Très naturelle.*"

"No," he said, smacking his lips. "Sniff with *ta bouche.*"

He was thinking stew, she could see. Ambrose was a magnificent cook, so she had heard more than once before she had even laid eyes on him nearly eight years before. For some time now, she had had the privilege of cooking with him. Mademoiselle Queneau rolled her eyes. "Mmm, I prefer the live animal, and the sweater," she said, nibbling at his shoulder. Pearl Queneau mutton, and she refused to eat lamb or veal. She had a bad reaction, she told herself, to the idea of eating infants, in whatever form. It was a difficult thought to hold to in this land. As her sisters had said to her, Oh! It's good you're not a vegetarian! You're going to that place where they know how to eat anything that moves, aren't you?"

"Oh yes," she had said. "They know how to make everything about life absolutely perfect!"

"Mo*n Dieu!*" Ambrose exclaimed when finally they emerged from the doorway, and the wooly din could be heard jangling down the road, trampling across the wooden bridge, angling along the green river again. Past the Abbey, through St. G and toward the lower pastures they would go.

By the looks of his brow drawn together without forewarning, she saw yet again that Ambrose had emotions that went up and down without notice. She wondered that, after so much time with him, he could keep surprising her.

"*Zut!*" he said again. "Did you notice, Pearl, the last time we saw The Beloved, just last month, The Beloved had hair *extraordinaire*, full, grey and black. How did it happen? A man so virile? Over night? *Horrible!*"

"But The Beloved must be eighty now, Beau."

"*Impossible!*" Ambrose swept his hand through his own thick, dark hair. "Now I think of it, it's too true. In two years only, I will be older than my father, that I barely knew, ever was, or so they tell."

Ambrose, at a little over six feet seven inches, was made even brawnier through the shoulders from slinging guitars and speakers and boxes of equipment and books around for his students. His latest conquest, the stand-up bass, was the first instrument he'd ever had that made him feel precisely equaled in mass, and also in tone, he bragged to her. His expertise was known throughout the area on any number of stringed instruments. He had also a twelve-string, an electric-acoustic, a solid body—all guitars--and a very mellow hand-made lute, all played to excellent effect. He wanted desperately someday, he said, to go to India and to learn to play the sitar there.

"No wonder The Beloved is afraid of what will happen next!" Pearl agreed, avoiding carefully that fruitless topic of Ambrose's aging when he was feeling sensitive and already annoyed. "The drought has certainly had a personal effect on the Mayor."

"That drought again? The drought did it? Such superstition! You have been here for years, and still you do not recognize that here in September it is always oppressive!" Ambrose chortled nervously. He made a boyish and terrifying face then, pulling his good eyelid down to show to his lover the inner rim, to show her exactly what he thought of weather superstition. He could not have said why it was that he had not told her the whole story of Père Martin's odd dream on the night of the engagement celebration. Perhaps it was fate, he told himself, that she had gone home just before the priest's frantic arrival.

As for their mayor, he had some large store of zest remaining, so they found out at the annual autumn picnic which was held along the pride of their village: their beautiful, willow-lined, emerald river. Luckily, the cold snap that arrived over night fell away and the weather improved extraordinarily and continued doing so through that weekend. It might have been June! It was that *parfait!* At the picnic, *Monsieur le Maire* Béranger distinguished himself by ripping off his shirt and pants. Like an over-fed ray, he flung himself into his element. Decidedly, so they decided, he did not for a minute look like he'd been bitten by the olive tree bug, although, for a time, he seemed to float pensively on his back, scratching and considering. Perhaps he could not help but think how close he now found himself to reuniting with what and whom he had long ago lost to these very same surroundings.

If only Père Martin had not been in bed now with pneumonia, after his rescue by the Ultimate Mother; surely then Pearl and Ambrose would have been granted the marriage they had been planning for the weekend. Yes, that was something, The Beloved thought, while floating down river, humming to himself, that was something upon which heartily to reflect.

From his bed Père Martin also saluted the couple on this the very early autumn day when their wedding was to have taken place. He saluted them for waiting for his recovery while he lay increasingly elongated in the traction set. The recovering priest could imagine himself clearly at the annual riverside gathering, so he'd said that morning as Pearl and Ambrose came by to pay their respects. This would be the first autumn picnic Père Martin had missed in nearly forty years. All that week, he lay cheered on by reports of the goings on from Doctor Christian Malaplate, who daily came and went, came and went, tending the effects of the flood.

"*Pas de problème!*"

WEATHER *from the* MOUNTAIN TOP

 **TOO SOON, THE AIR TEMPERATURE PLUNGED DRAMATICALLY;** and then it plunged again. There was little relief indoors. All the linked stone domiciles, set so determinedly on both sides of their narrow *rues*, seemed like crypts within their meter-thick walls of concrete and stone. As in nearly all of the homes in the southern regions of France, central heat was practically unknown.

Ambrose merely rolled his nut-brown eye whenever Mademoiselle Queneau mentioned it; after all, he'd been listening to such complaints from her for years. Yet, this year, Pearl overheard Ambrose bewailing the extraordinarily wicked frost to his male friends. It was too hard to work with the hands, they said. These musicians were also masons, automobile mechanics, a veterinarian, writers, and doctors. Their intelligence was especially conveyed through the deftness of their hands. The laying on of hands, Père Martin had often said, is not necessarily so far from some of our own powers.

Although in that region of France there was hardly ever any snow, that year it was as though someone had burst a duvet over St. X. They had swirling white descents of it. And, there were the great winds of madness they had also, *les mistrals* barreling down out of the Alps, both with and without snow, not unlike the serious build-up to a true tornado.

"*O, c'est normale,*" Ambrose le Beau said, as was his habit. "*L'hiver,* he is just commencing. Enjoy."

The winds moved at record speed over the ruined 10th century chateau on their little bit of mountain, over its crumbled ramparts. The villagers reported that around midnight one night, they had all bolted up in bed after peculiar nightmares. The first time Pearl heard *le mistral,* she thought giant cannons were being fired down the single-lane streets and conduits. "I hear cannon fire!" Pearl said.

"Perhaps they were cannon once, in another world," Ambrose merely answered, rolling over. Shutters banged; the wind burst forth in repeated volleys. "Now that is weather madness! I concede!"

That was the one desperation that Pearl, ever the stranger in those parts, seemed alone in experiencing. Pearl could not overcome her reaction to the cold. She had come there to avoid cold and yet here it was. It was the lack of pigment in her skin that made her even more sensitive, she thought, to both heat and cold. Yet in the discomfort of that winter, she felt the luxury of it too, immobilized as she was by her own incessant chattering and trembling. Winter guests gathered around, near the blazing fires in both their kitchen and living room. How she loved to share in the camaraderie. As a party, they shared in Ambrose's extravagant cooking, and then always in a festival of synchronicity. Laughing long into the night, they draped their coats over her, the lump by the *cheminée.*

Occasionally they humored her by letting her play her harpsichord along with them. "Have a glass of dark red wine," they said, "it will cause you to circulate more efficiently. If you're too cold to play your harpsi, shake this tambourine. Sing very loudly! Have no fear! Good song, it makes you happy, it will not cause you to fall over without a franc on one of the benches near the fountain and despair." It was said that the group could play almost anything by then.

Among those of his band, Ambrose's ivory face was borne up on the top of his frame on a long masculine neck. He seemed otherworldly to his bride-to-be beside his new instrument, the double bass. Broad at the forehead and cheekbones, his mouth a very pale pink with a mauvish cast to the thin lower lip, his was a stunningly masculine face that always seemed to be in a meditative trance, when he was not angered by something he considered a slight to logic or good sense.

In his music shop, he had many village children to cajole into exuberance and regular practicing. But, because of his height, so he confided in Pearl, he worried that he might appear to them "*tros intellectuel*," he said; or, even worse, especially frightening. An ogre *extraordinaire!* Each morning, therefore, he worked in a ferocious lather at the bathroom sink, foam flying, to keep back his heavy beard. He kept his hair slightly long and soft, yet very neatly trimmed.

On Sunday, very early, Pearl curled up in her usual place next to the kitchen fireplace. Ambrose bent over pen and graph paper at their long table. Already he had written the requisite letter to her mother and had had a satisfying response. Pearl's mother would come after New Year's for the great ceremony of her most unusual child.

Like a monk copying scriptures, he drew the blanket now around his massive shoulders; again he erased, charting. He tapped his pencil against his temple, flipping bits of his hair into makeshift curls with the tip. His slippers beat an intriguing syncopation against one of the blue and black starburst tiles, while his pencil took up counterpoint against a glass. Pearl got up and poked the fire into a steady burn.

He wore the red flannel shirt as he also did when outdoors practicing in spring and fall; she'd purchased it from the American shop in Cannes for him, to encourage his musical dreams, she said. In all nice weather, even usually in winter, it was his pleasure to walk on the mountainside before he went to work. There she had seen him from their back terrace, before it had started snowing: he was a small red cube with appendages dwarfed by the backdrop of vineyards, mountains, and castle ruins, playing his bass and thrumming the warped branches of nearby grapevines into orchestral sympathy. It was good for the wine, the local vintners said. On his way to work, Pearl would see the two of them like traveling companions: Ambrose driving, the bass sitting in the front passenger seat angled out through the sunroof like a gigantic ostrich neck.

Now it grew even colder in their southerly climate. *C'est impossible!* Woolen sweaters filled the shops, dark wool coats seemed to float down every *rue*. Children ran past with brightly colored neck scarves on display. Since Père Martin still was not receiving the younger visitors, Père Pepin taught a grim version of the children's Wednesday morning catechism, focusing on his more irritable days on the tortures of the saints. Incredibly, Pereault de Poste reported, some of the middle-aged ladies had begun to send Pepin crossword puzzles to keep him from being bored. Camille Desbordes went out of her way to claim that she, too, was now supplying the church's incense and trying to think of The Transplant, as she called him, with affirmation and good will.

At home, Ambrose put up wooden rods for Pearl, and strung heavy tapestries on rings between their plastered stone chambers. An electric heater was moved at considerable expense, from quarter to quarter. In this way they might begin to hold onto whatever regional warmth they might be able to generate. And then, too, they huddled together. She was nearly elastic in the way she wound about him, shivering beside the fire and then under the sheets and duvets. There Mademoiselle Pearl lifted her nightclothes for him and Ambrose stretched out in her flannel cave as if newly breech born to her. One late autumn Sunday evening, carried away again by his enthusiasms, Ambrose took a tiny bite out of one of her lips and swallowed it. To which, she let out a defiant shriek. "What have you done?" she cried.

"Now I've done it!" he cried, startling her. "And so! What do you think?"

"Think?" she squeaked. "Think? When you've taken a bite out of me?"

"It means we can never now be separated. I will have to have another bite."

"No more bites," she exclaimed. "I am not about to marry the Cannibal of St. Xavier!"

"*Exactement,*" he cried, as though this newest of pet names had finally suited him.

Market Day

 **It was his temperament as a musician,** the bandmaster said of himself, that made him so completely flexible, all the plucking and friction, he said. His hands, he bragged, were so malleable that he could have had many other hand-oriented professions.

"Such as?" Pearl asked

"*Plombier,*" he answered.

"Yes, plumber," she could see that.

"Watchmaker."

"*Oui.*"

"Mid-wife."

"*O, Beau.*"

"I would love it so!"

"Indeed you would adore it. Whatever are you scribbling, Bandmaster?" Ambrose's good eye swirled over her, and in response she could feel goose pimples dotting her flesh; but he continued without answering. She thought of him as having a very playful and balmy nature. Nothing seemed to bother him but for the tortures of others.

❦

Camille Desbordes, recovering from her second marriage to the same man, one day told Pearl on the way through the bitter cold to Saturday market in Pearl's little Renault that she knew the reason Ambrose had grown to be a man so strange and wonderful. Ambrose as a child had had to conquer long and grave illness, she said.

"*C' n'est pas vrais!*" Pearl cried, nearly driving off the road. It seemed impossible to her that Ambrose would not have told her such an important element from his past. "Even now? Is he not well?"

"*Mais si!*" Camille Desbordes assured her, "that history is of the past."

But, it was certainly true about his childhood illness. She knew it, Camille said, because they had been closest playmates as children. Ambrose's mother and sisters had nearly gone mad, doting upon him, restoring him to health in his father's continuing and unexplained absences. Camille Desbordes' own parents had thought she'd marry him. "A silly thought," Camille said. "Such parents."

Pearl thought for a moment then, probably mistakenly, that perhaps her friend looked a little wistful at that thought. "But what happened to Ambrose?" Pearl asked. "What was this illness he's hidden from me?"

As a boy, Ambrose had been confined to bed for nearly a year and a half. *La maladie* had left him tall and determined, Camille said, not weaker, but even stronger than before. "Yet he has the chest of a wine barrel, and he is a thin-legged boy." Camille Desbordes frowned as though these were earth-shattering faults. In fact, they were the traits Pearl herself had found extremely provocative. Her own father and grandfathers had been built that way, though somewhat smaller, and without prerequisite suffering.

"He is not well-formed like most French men. Ambrose is not compact. And, as you know, he is a little crazed," Camille Desbordes clucked. "Perhaps you see now," she prodded, "that his handsome features are not so perfect as you thought?" Ambrose had been roughened, she said, by that early ordeal of sickness in his childhood.

Pearl Queneau replied coolly, taken aback, "Surely, Camille, you must have noticed—that I notice no deficiency in Ambrose whatsoever."

"That's right," Camille Desbordes encouraged her, "think with affirmation. Never complain."

"No, it's true!" Pearl cried out, but there was no way to make Camille, who was not to marry him, believe. Perhaps it was just as well.

"It is his heart. And surely you must know about his cocaine. He must not take this, yet always he persists! Why do you think his emotions are so volatile."

Ambrose's Magical Mystery Tour

 **THERE WERE ALWAYS CHILDREN IN THE MUSIC STORE,** and Ambrose could be found there laughing and jesting, playing harmless tricks on them to keep them interested in their lessons, and the children responded by hiding behind the French horns and even in the tuba once. There, with him, transformations were astounding. They loved coming to the store and devoted themselves to practicing and calling for advice. Daily the children mixed up all the sheet music; and, Ambrose set them straight.

Now it was time to ready themselves for the Christmas concert. One by one they were earnestly squeaking or pounding out lessons in preparation for the concert. When at lunchtime Pearl joined him, as she so often did. Ambrose cocked his head and she waited for that fierce encouraging word, the stiff upper-lipped adjective about going forth into the responsibility that she had often heard him proffer to his musicians and students and even to elderly women in their neighborhood. But instead, Ambrose rushed out of the store and saw nothing of what he passed.

It had begun to rain; whole metallic sheets of it drove against the windows of the shops. Down the street the front window of Madame Meulemeester's dress shop blew out and was left leaning against Gond the Florist's back door so that when Monsieur Gond came out carrying Christmas roses, he cut his arm. The miracle in it, so Gond said, was that along with the plate glass had arrived the dress, all in one piece from off the mannequin in Madame Meulemeester's store. Gond, of necessity, had used the sleeveless pink silk shift to make a speedy tourniquet until the postman heard his cries for help and sped him away in his yellow truck to Doctor Malaplate.

Alas the sudden downpour was not enough to ease the winter drought. No one had come into the shop for hours. There is weather, but there is very little wood. Pearl looked out into the flooded street and said to herself, *Everything is made of gravel here, and stone.*

Ambrose put out the closed sign again the next day, locked the doors, and lowered the window shades for lunch. When Pearl looked up later, it was to see a towel flung onto a music stand, and the face of the deaf Beethoven staring out from under it.

Mistral Madness

 **OUTSIDE, THE WIND HOWLED.** When Ambrose had finished persuading her out of her clothes, she clamored toward him in the hot water that fell from the showerhead into the vast bath taking up much of the room. When he had surpassed her navel, pressing on her from the back and front, slapping ever so lightly against her skin in a very gentle and provocative way, electrifying the juncture between the interior and exterior, adjusting her limbs as he wanted them, holding down her sudden movements on the floor of the bath with his heft, he indicated again and again the vast amount of space inside her. He massaged so deeply that she could feel each of her inner organs.

Her arms and legs jerked of their own accord. Writhing with desire, she called for his presence while he continued emptying and filling her with his hands. She moved in increasing wonderment; yet, above her, his face streaming with water was strangely apathetic and hard. On opening her eyes again to see, if he had been a stranger, even in some public place, his face alone might have been enough to have made her run.

He set her down out of the shower's spray. He had begun dipping the wash mitten into the paste. He smeared a soapy glaze across the bridge of her nose and onto her cheeks, then down and onto her breasts, lingering at their tips. At the contact, her nipples turned up, significant as two small immature grapes. Ambrose massaged a semi-circle between her legs. Even in the bath, Pearl could hear the wind howling through the village outside as he lapped along her neck.

"You are afraid to have a baby, Pearl?" he asked. "Because you are too tiny? Yet we get no younger."

He went to the sink then, and she watched him through the steamed mirror. He stood, brushing his teeth with false intensity. The room seemed too fiercely cold. Her clothes were flung about the room. She began to shake. She held her arms out to him, saying, "Please come back. It's cold." Then he put the protective barrier on; and in a nexus somewhere between pleasure, pain, and grief, silently Pearl howled while his hands hoisted her body and released her onto him with sudden dispassionate jolts.

That night he slept in the living room, while Pearl Queneau, acutely aware of his absence, tossed and turned in their bed under the semi-circular canopy.

The next evening Ambrose came home covered with dirt and seemingly subdued. It was the anniversary of the tragic river incident in which he had lost his eye, his childhood friend, and his friend's mother—The Beloved's son and wife. This history Camille Desbordes had recounted to Pearl that morning over the telephone. Oh, it was so natural that he would feel *bizarre*, Camille said, considering all the bad reveries that must come back on such a day.

After he'd showered, the Colossus began to spoon up the soup Pearl had made for him. He went to the counter and retrieved a pinch of rosemary where it grew in a little blue pot. For a moment, they almost seemed meant for one another: the plant in its beautiful pot and the shaft of light penetrating the room.

"So much cold wind, so loud!" Pearl said. "It's nearly a hurricane."

Pearl went to the cupboard for the rosemary. It was exactly right to add just a pinch of summer to their winter soup. Pearl sat down next to him. He put her rosemary in the mortar with his and ground the pestle about. Then he rolled the powdered spice between his hands over both their bowls. "Wait for it to heat," he said. She watched it settling to the bottom. He poured out a taste of wine and sipped it up. He doled out spoonfuls of crème fraiche and gave a deft stir to both.

Ambrose was inordinately silent, bent over his bowl. Then he told her what had happened that day. During the worst of the wind, during the early morning hours just as he was going to work, approximately half of the heavy terra cotta roofing tiles from the baker's house had blown down.

"Was anyone hurt?"

"The tiles flew across the street and onto the rectory, onto Père Martin's—"

"Oh, no!"

"Père's roof—his roof collapsed on top of him. I drove out the east road or maybe I wouldn't have seen. All this morning we have moved debris. Finally they could take him, he was gasping for air; Père is in hospital. The Beloved is with him. Doctor Malaplate—in and out, and the old woman, too. Georges Menard plays at salvaging the house—in case Père comes home, he will have his place. Camille is on the frame with Georges." He pressed Pearl's fingertips and then he shrugged.

"The Rabbit Catcher's arm was badly cut on a piece of glass while he was trying to carry Père Martin out to the ambulance before the last collapse. He lost too much blood."

"The Rabbit Catcher died?"

"*Mais si.* But, of course! What did you think?"

In the next days, the pounding noise of the mistral grew worse, and with it, Ambrose, madly animated, leapt about, yelping. "*Fun!* Pearl! It might be *fun!*"

"What might be fun?"

"It's like this," Ambrose instructed, suddenly far too serious, drumming his nails impatiently on the oak tabletop. He directed the point of his pencil through the air at her, executing a little thrust. At the end of this trajectory, she fidgeted. "When the musician inserts himself into time, Pearl, he must work *with method.*"

Normally his hair had an impish nature. The *Monsieur Beethoven*, Pearl called it. It was thick hair, and glossy, almost black, long though neatly trimmed. It shimmered under moonlight, given the chance.

A chill went up her neck; she got up to stir the pot on the stove and cleared her throat. "Don't instruct me. Please."

"For a *purpose*, Pearl," he said behind her, eerily.

"For a purpose? What do you mean?"

"But didn't you always crave one? Really crave one?"

"What?" Pearl turned around; he gazed at her until he, too, grew aware that in irritation she had ceased to stir the chocolate. Beside the kitchen fireplace with its blue and white hand-painted tiles of real villagers and animals from hundreds of years before, she sat and stared, as if into their individual lives. The ladle dripped into the air.

"What are you saying?"

"*Enfants,* Pearl. What did you think I was talking?"

"Oh, that," she said. "We have plenty of time to think of that. Years and years."

That night Ambrose, embarrassed, even humiliated, fully dressed in a suit, appeared just before dawn beside their bed.

"What's the matter?" she cried out in alarm, thinking that Père Martin must have died. Or that his death was imminent. Why else would this be happening? But he would not tell her. He insisted that the two of them had to rush off to see Henri Béranger. He had chosen a dress for her, her favorite. He was holding it out for her.

"What is it, Ambrose? Where are we going? It's so early. Is Père worse?" She slipped the dress on and started looking for her shoes.

"I wish to do the right thing," he said. He kissed her brow. "I know now why I didn't see it. Hurry, Pearl."

The headlights of their little Renault tunneled around the bend before the sun had risen along the stonewall toward the north gate.

"Do you think we will get there in time?"

"In time for what?"

"Isn't Père dying?" she asked.

"*Mais non!*" he said. "Where did you get that? At least, I have not heard. Such absurdities sometimes, Pearl."

"But where are we going then, at this time?"

"Why, we are going to get married. *Bien sur*, and why not?"

"But, our wedding! What are you trying to do?"

"I see it now. This is what you wanted. I didn't see that you wanted it so much. I have bruised your sentiment. I apologize. So many times my apology to you, Pearl!"

"You want to go to *le Maire* tonight? This is *not* what I want! The Beloved is asleep or going back and forth to Père Martin. Take me home right this moment, Ambrose."

"But you wish to be married before I give you a child. If it weren't for all this weather madness," he barked most angrily, "we would have been married by now! Everyone does and does not want my wedding. I do and don't want my wedding. I am too old suddenly with all this weather eating us up!"

"Old? Don't be silly."

"All the Fathers of our village will be gone soon. Look at Père Martin." He leaned across the front seat and took her by the wrist. The car veered and she was forced to grab the wheel with her other hand. "I am trying not to do the crazy things, Pearl," he said. "I can be funny or I can be crazy. That is for you to decide. Today I will marry someone. You are bride of choice. You will be my bride?"

Pearl Queneau leaned forward and pulled her coat around her further, wondering in what life she had awakened. "Are you threatening me, Beau, with marrying someone else? Take me home immediately!"

He drove around for another hour or so, aimlessly, while she stared at him in dismay; and then finally she was home again, looking at his glazed eyes wandering about the kitchen in the firelight.

"You are always free. Every day of your life, Pearl, you are free to come or to go. Have you not noticed the noise that masks everything? Look in the living room."

She followed him down the hall, wrapping a blanket around her shoulders. And it was true. It was not supernatural, it was merely very cold and oddly surreal. In the living room, even though the outside shutters were closed, and also the inner windows, the wind was so strong that the long curtains were cast in to the room at right angles to the wall.

The curtains filled the living room chamber as with veils blowing parallel to the floor. She could feel it in her entire body: everything seemed to shake with the expansive, percussive wind. It sounded as though the town were being fired upon by cannon from many directions at once. She thought soon they would be sure to hear ice cracking on the roof.

She had never given any credence at all to the thought, so common here, that a simple change in barometric pressure and a raging wind could drive someone mad. Why had she not seen the other side to him? What ancient land had come to hold her now in modern times like this? Why could she never force herself to go home, in spite of everything?

"*Ouais, Ouais,*" Ambrose scowled. He tapped the center of his forehead. "For the first time, I have *le mistral* very large in here. My father went away on just such a night as this to die. And now, last night I almost went too far with you. I have heard stories of murders and the sudden reversals in men's character since I was a child. I have never once hurt you, Pearl. Even last night in my madness, I did not hurt you. I only stopped myself by sleeping away from you."

"You were going to hurt me?"

His jaw hardened and he did not reply.

"*O, c'est normale,*" she lied, seeing his dejected melancholia. But, even in her wildest imagination, she could not sustain this notion. "Poor Beau, so worried about Père Martin that you are not yourself. You have drunk far too much and you worry now. You should not get too excited. You need sleep."

"Do I hurt your sentiments? With my rampage? I did not know anything about Père Martin last night. You are right, the rampage it is so very normal with *le mistral. C'est normale. Exactement.*"

She grew increasingly alarmed. "No, no! I am not one who will be beaten or hurt, Ambrose! No matter your excuses. I never will stand for that. Or, be coerced. I would rather put a gun to my head, than live with someone who hurts me, or anyone!"

Grotesquely, he laughed at that, as though she were telling jokes, doubling over, his voice going high, "Hurts you!" and then rocking with the depth of it. She was shocked to the core at this response and could not even pretend to smile, even enough to walk away. She could not bring up the other things Camille had told her, about his heart and the drugs. She could not force herself to make them real.

WATER MUSIC

 **THAT MUCH WAS CERTAINLY TRUE:** Mademoiselle Queneau was not one to be coerced into being damaged, or so she said. Ambrose bundled her into his massive chest and made the little dismissive sound with his lips that the French people made so frequently. He began to hum and then he sighed. "My little Pearl. You can't help yourself. Yours is a country cut down from your history. A mere few hundred years. It affects everything. I see it in you, your haste," he said. "You want to be married now. You cannot take the disappointment of that priest, so ridiculous. All this waiting I have put you through. And now you must have this mistral. You are going mad; I see you must marry now. I know Père Martin will not be himself by Christmas. Now we despair."

"I am not going mad, Ambrose. If anyone is, it is you."

"*Non*! No waiting! Now I hear your thoughts for once. Don't deny. We will marry now. I have taken the decision. You cannot change me. Not again! I, you, go mad with memories in this wind! Yes," he muttered, unconvinced. "It is like the wine. You have to bring it home from the *cav*; in the end it is no good in the bottle." Her slippers came off in his hands; absent-mindedly he rubbed her feet.

"But, Beau," she said. "We're together anyway. Not the wedding. Not the baby now. Please. I want to wait. I'm not as old as you are. There isn't any hurry. I think I will go home for a week or two, if we aren't going to marry right away."

"That is your *Isle de Man*, and perhaps your Grand Lakes. That is their way. Rushing. Waiting. Rushing. But you live here, Pearl. Truth before ritual." He took up his espresso and she took hers, while thinking perhaps she should quickly slip away. He stood in front of the bedroom mantle. And then his shoulders shook and his head was on his arms.

She went up on tiptoe behind him. She put her arms around. She felt her heart breaking. "Ambrose?" After all, had he asked anything so terrible of her, but that she ease his pain and be the mother to his child? "Ambrose? Is it your heart again? Don't worry. Camille told me about your illness. Père Alban can marry us in St. G, if you wish. We can be married there. You know my mother is coming just before Christmas. And, all my sisters. It's not long now. I only thought it was important to you, and your village for some reason, that we wait until the New Year."

"*Non*. It is all superstition! I want none of it. Now I see it, you do not want to marry me."

"I have never before felt this way," he confessed. "Perhaps I should move to another room for tonight, and a few days." He cradled her face in his large hands. "Open your eyes," he demanded. "Look at me. What more can I offer? I offer you everything. And you refuse. You are afraid to have a baby inside of you?" He squeezed her cheeks. "Say."

"I am afraid."

"You only repeat, Pearl, to make me happy. Say it's true."

"I'm afraid to have a baby."

"Inside of you?"

"Inside of me! And also, on the way out!"

"Close your eyes. Close them." Ambrose ran his finger down the side of her face, and she could hear him fumbling at the bedside table. "Close them. Open your mouth."

Still, he was not listening. He did not know how hard it had been for her even to make love to him at first. He had not been paying attention. He leaned down then and kissed her lips. A small, acrid sliver of flesh slipped between them and lay on her tongue. Dark thoughts, hatred entered her mind. He put his palm over her lips and held her tight. Was he not her best friend just days ago? The raw fish reeked of garlic and wine inside her mouth. He would not let go so she had no choice. She tried to move her face out from under his, but he would not release the back of her head. But then, with horror, she knew. It had begun to squirm. A tiny creature flipped insanely about in her mouth. In and over their tongues as he tried to kiss her, the creature clambered, trying to save itself.

"It would be better to swallow it now. Swallow it," he whispered.

She tried to shake her head. Tears engulfed her face.

"Swallow it," he said. "It will be okay."

Her head went back and forth, as she tried to cast him off of her. She could not look at him. Again he manipulated her with his fingertips. A jet of heat raged out from under her waist. She could not breathe. "No, no," she cried, nearly choking. The little fish flipped against the back of her throat, and she began to gag. She could no longer breathe. Its life encompassed her throat. With a deep shudder, finally, she swallowed and gasped in all the air she could.

Pearl was then intensely aware of him, of Ambrose's body crushing her own. An involuntary wave of despair moved over her as her head fell to the side and the air went into her lungs. Her hatred rose. She felt as though they were finished for the moment. It was over, and she could only hope he would now move aside. But he was grinning at her, grinning with triumph, after such a cruel feat. She closed her eyes in revulsion and tried not to move. Her eyes iced over with tears as he smiled on and on at her, failing to realize that anything at all was amiss; and then, she could feel it: It could only be the fish reviving in her gut.

Pearl was all motion then. She began to pant, and contract, and churn out from under him. Sweat poured down her belly. Insanely coughing, churning, and gagging under his weight, her upper body went into a paroxysm that threatened to make her faint.

But she could not do it slowly, or quickly. She gulped and then a cascade swept into her belly where still the creature thrashed. Up and up, she tried to shake herself, crazed with trying to shake the fish out, beating on his chest to get him off, but Ambrose threw himself sideways across her belly now. He banged his chest down on her belly again; he lay hard on her, crushing her down now while inside, twitching and burning, the little minnow whipped itself against her interior, making its way toward her intestinal canals, trying in a last series of instants to save itself. Her breath wheezed out from under him. His chest bashed down with weird intent. For a second she could feel it so clearly: the fish writhing in the dead space beneath her lower ribs.

Endlessly she called for him to stop without result, until finally she began to hope that he would indeed have the early heart attack that her friend had mentioned. Perhaps he had taken the drug tonight and that was what was driving him mad, perhaps it was not the cacophonous, bone-deep wind, as he'd claimed.

"It is your best time! I can see it," he exclaimed. "I can see it is good for you. *Parfait?*" But he was not listening. "*Parfait.* It was my best time. It was my best time in my life."

Could he comprehend nothing? she asked herself.

He smiled tenderly at her as he smoothed the cream over her, onto her forehead and feet. A milky salve he rubbed over her whole skin. Then with his shirt, he cleaned her as though she had been his newly born calf. From between her legs, he looked up at her where she lay completely lethargic, scheming for escape.

Yet uncomprehending, he blocked her with his forearm. His mouth arrived at the underside of her chin, then entered his tongue into the delicacy of her ear. When she had completely collapsed, he, in his further bizarre momentum, laid slices of kiwi in her mouth; when even her eyelids had been cleaned and slices of cucumber placed on them and her flossy hair combed up over her, he uttered, "Well, now are you still afraid to have my child?"

Yes, she wanted to say. *Now I am more afraid than ever, because now I know you have the madness—both real and synthetic. And, I will never ever be able to forget it.* But, "No," she lied, so very afraid. "No, I'm not afraid anymore. Not now I'm not. Now you can stop. Please, please you can stop your madness now, Ambrose. I understand!" But, she added, only to herself, I will never forgive you as long as we live.

She heard him puttering about in the kitchen. She lathered herself briefly with the honey soap he had handed her. The soft warm spray moved over her stretched and aching parts. And then with embarrassment and wretchedness, she began to laugh like a maniac, like one of the brightly colored birds she had watched mate and then attack.

When she stood to pat herself dry, she grew aware of her face in the mirror: her skin looked like ice, smoothly radiating light like an alabaster lamp. She wrapped a long white towel around herself and bent over to brush her hair down nearly to the floor, trying to cover her quaking. For a few moments, she jerked then stretched her limbs. And then she hunkered down and began to cry again. Inside of her a creature had died without a chance. Never again would she be able to trust him.

She would need a chair to reach the overhead cabinet where he'd put her bags. Still, she was not sure she would be able to reach them herself, when she left.

In the kitchen, Ambrose was inventing distant arias again. She pulled aside the shower curtain. But Ambrose had already been there; the water in the tub had been drawn. Steam rose from the large pool. She might run away now, if she were very quick, she considered. She took off the towel again and stepped in. The well water was so hot she thought to draw her foot out, but soon she could also lower her other foot and the rest of her.

When he arrived, "Close your eyes," he said. She heard him getting into the water. Horrified, she felt him lay something between her breasts. "Open," he said.

But it was merely a part of himself.

WEDDING DAMAGES

 **VAGUELY SHE HURT EVERYWHERE,** and was relieved that it was over. She could not forget the imagery of his solitary banquet. But what he had done further—and there had been much, much more later—Ambrose had no knowledge of because he had done these things to her afterward in the depths of her dreams. What he had done in reality had been bad enough. For this, she could have left him. How could she explain the absurdity, the cruelty of what he'd caused her to encompass?

She heard him hustling about in the coat closet, and then she heard him on the telephone. She flipped about in the water, reveling as if in newfound fins. She lifted her head to listen. "But, I have the madness!" he was shouting to himself in the next room. Then she heard him on the telephone: "Père is dying, Beloved! My heart beats out of my chest! *Le mistral* is in my head. Marry us, Beloved. Or I do not know what I will do. Today I am not responsible. To anyone! You must help her now. No, of course I do not still think of going away. That is all *I know*, I see it now! I'm going to have *la crise cardiaque!*"

As she removed herself from the bath water, for the first time she began to think of him as worse than mad. She thought of him as not particularly intelligent, which was a great surprise, seeing that he was so incredibly talented.

So powerful was the village concept of *le mistral* that within the hour she found that he had hurried her into her own clothing, even while she protested, and then she had been taken, again protesting, to see both The Beloved and the repugnant Père Pepin. To her surprise, both of them asked after Ambrose's health, and then she and Ambrose received both blessings and a marriage certificate as well. No one seemed to notice that she was not interested in the truncated ceremony, or that she was in fact objecting and had never said the consenting, binding words of the ritual!

What was this? she asked herself. Bewilderment upon bewilderment. By lunchtime on the day following, because she had not wanted him to come into her on one day to make a child before their marriage, they were married in haste on the next!

Until it happened, theirs had been a union that she was certain deserved celebrating—that was the way she forlornly would always look at it. And they had had many friends who wished to solemnize her vows. Her mother was heartbroken; there was no other word for it. Now she refused to board a plane and come to her. Her sisters berated her for her impetuousness.

The villagers looked at her with sympathy and some returned to church, tolerating the presence of The Septum now in the outer moments of their faith. Although The Beloved and his sister continued to attend services in St. Alban, the elderly Monsieur de Graff at last allowed himself to die and be buried in his family crypt at the hands of Père Pepin. The upturn of the economy crept on, the spring water production was regained, and jobs were restored at the bottling plant. Hope persisted for the prospects of the new wine.

For Pearl, personally though, this time was riddled with disappointment and uncertainty. She found now that the color seemed to have left all the elements in the surrounding atmosphere; she felt a lack of color for the first time in her future, too. Just when she had come to question her own wish to marry Ambrose, she had done just that in the most perfunctory way.

Early Days

"IF YOU THINK SO," HE TRIED TO SAY LIGHTLY; but there was dismay in his voice, as if for one of the first times he had encountered his own fallibility. There was menstrual blood for her again, and he had been having his own pains. He would disappear into the bathroom and then he would emerge with a pain. She began to suspect that it was in his chest. He said nothing, would answer nothing, but his jaws would clench until it passed. Now he placed his hand between her thighs, protectively, as if to ward off any further thought of loss, and then to both their astonishment he began to cry. Just as suddenly, she laughed. And then she too cried.

"I know how you love children, and I could see you were too afraid. I didn't mean to force you, Pearl, to have a baby. You know that. Don't you like being married to me now? Are you disappointed there isn't a baby, too?" But she wouldn't say, even when he asked her again and again, even when he pretended to pout at her. She felt she had been unfairly and brutally used, if only, as he would tell her, in a mood that had been brought on by strange weather. In the end, after her mother had been notified of the couple's rash decision, none of her family would ever come to see her in this strange land which she had so hoped to share with them in all its splendor and perfect simplicity.

The frantic energy of pretense flooded into Ambrose and Pearl when they were in public, laughing outwardly, fingers entwined. He called her his lattice; she named him the vine. She said she loved him, without truly meaning it. They cooked incessantly for large groups of their friends, smiling quietly at one another as they orchestrated the dishes for their gatherings, laying out each article of food onto each finely graced plate. Secretly, she longed for the quiet hopeful days when they had taken dinners to Père Martin's bedside while waiting for their wedding to take place.

At night, Ambrose held her with new tenderness. Often he would carry her from room to room draped in a blanket, her arms about his neck. She had never known there to be so many places to visit, so much space in their one habitat.

HOLIDAY TIDINGS
from ST. Z

ON THE BENCH IN FRONT OF THE THEATRE IN ST. Z, the Pearl sat waiting for Christmas beneath the row of radically stripped and pruned plane trees. Children rushed back and forth, screaming savagely, fully cloaked, leaping from one rocking, metal giraffe to the next. She could not stop crowing hysterically. Was she crying? She didn't think so, yet a complete stranger stepped up behind her to place one quieting hand on her shoulder, and then disappeared without comment.

"I will take your place '*hatching*' on the egg, when you get the *ballon*. That is my promise," Ambrose declared that night. "*Et alors*, Pearl, you must make it a very sturdy egg. A very, very *grand oeuf*."

"Oh, Beau, don't be so silly," she protested, giving way to his physical coaxing, his digits meandering up and down her arm and around her waist, into her sleeves at the innermost elbows.

"But Beau, it took each of my sisters at least three years to conceive!"

"*Trois? Trois année?* You say, *trois?* Three years! For each *bébé? Ce n'est pas vrais? C'est ridicule.* Each of your sisters and their men may have taken so many years, Pearl, to make for each one *bébé*. But that does not apply to us. None of your family before me was French—even with that Queneau name. That is obvious."

A momentary urge to defend the virility of her countrymen rose up, but she fought it down. It was pointless to embark on that kind of argument, offering up questionable and definitely inflammatory proof. "And also, Beau," she sighed, "for four weeks you'll be on tour. At the end of June and the start of July! You won't be home until almost Bastille Day!"

"I will be here for Bastille! Count on it!"

She wilted momentarily at the thought of his being away from her, she felt so protected next to his mammoth form. No one would dare to jeer at her when he was along, as they had when she was a small girl. No one would chase her down the streets and fling small heavy objects and rotting substances at her. In their dissimilarities from all the others they had ever known, the two of them were united in their secret feelings about their physical presences in the world.

Miraculously, so quickly then they resolved almost all of their own differences and were once again set upon their daily course. They had become nearly interlocked these past weeks. All this passionate melding and withdrawing had come as a complete and tantalizing surprise to her. She wanted a while to be 'newly wed,' she'd tried to explain. "We're not planning to die tomorrow, are we? What's your rush toward fatherhood?"

"I had the lemming dream," he laughed.

"And you ate them, *sans doubt*! What a horrifying thought! Oh never, never mind. Sometimes I think I should run away as fast as I can, far, far away from you."

"Ha," he laughed. "Try for it. I have you now under the spell. And, compared to me, you are just the tiny girl."

Normally, she was inclined toward the luxurious savoring of every carefully and slowly approached moment, while Ambrose was all for instantly devouring every opportunity, and then prolonging it—something that she heartily admired but could not do. If there was a difference between them, this was it, they both knew.

"You think it can not be done? Even by Bastille Day? Ha! *Pas de problème*, my little cotton ball," Ambrose shrugged confidently. To her surprise, he set her aside as though she had been only a piece of sturdy porcelain statuary. He picked up his guitar. "It will be enough, I'm sure."

He could be so abrupt, and always, always, it seemed he got his way. Perhaps always she got her way also, he had pointed out earlier in one of their spiraling conversations. "Say one time, Pearl, when you did not have it your way!" And she could not name one, other than the wedding, and the sorrow over the tiny fish, which she refused to ever in her life recall again or admit—it had hurt her so extraordinarily. Best to let it pass by, her mother had consoled her by telephone. Better to have a good marriage and a foolish wedding than the other way around, most certainly! Still, she wondered aloud, why would a family visit for a ceremony but not visit otherwise? Just to see her? Still, their lives had been so much quieter since Pearl had left home. No evil children slashing their tires and throwing stones because of her.

She could see it in his face, a moment of graying, the shadow of a thought. "Yes, I see," she muttered, although she did not see. Right before her, she could envision him as an old man, a childless man, conducting the orchestra of other people's babies as they endlessly grew and left.

MOTHER *and* DAUGHTERS CONFER

"IMAGINE GIVING BIRTH TO AN OX!" her eldest sister, Cornelia, confided by telephone. "Then you'll have a small idea of how it is."

"Or, a whale!" her younger sister Sylvia remarked.

"Or, a tractor trailer with a horse cart on the back coming out of you!" her littlest sister, Marvel, already grown with two children, said.

"Or, a tractor trailer with a Mack truck on the top!" Cornelia stressed. "Ripping right out between your legs."

"Or, a military tank with a gun turret slashing you up and down on the way out."

"Stop, you wicked girls, at once! You are frightening your sister," her mother had shouted into her extension of the call. "And Pearl is always frightened enough, girls. And, why not? She hasn't got a thick skin like any of you. Why, my poor little darling has practically no skin at all."

"Oh, Mother!" all the girls had said at once into separate phones. Only mothers knew these things. Others could be taken in. One could make oneself to appear brave, except with mothers and lovers. Especially mothers, that was true.

Their mother had planned to name her sisters and Pearl for the four seasons. Pearl was to have been called Autumn, until they had seen her pale self; it was an idea to which Pearl had warmed and was still attached. And, considering the circumstance, her parents had decided that Winter was too obvious a reference, and even perhaps pejorative. It was said to have been her parents' only major dispute, and their recourse to other names had led to one of the girls' biggest squabbles.

Cornelia, Sylvia, Marvel, and she, Pearl, quarreled relentlessly, long into their adolescence and well beyond, in fact. They all wanted to have had Marvel's name. Marvel thought it impish that they should want what was hers since birth. When Ambrose heard this story of his mysterious otherworldly sisters-in-law, he began to call her Marvel himself. About which satisfaction, she did—marvel, that is. How silly, to take your sister's name. She did not report to her new husband the silence that had fallen between continents when on the phone she had inadvertently called him by one of his nicknames.

"You are marrying someone called Colossus? I thought his first name was Beau, Pearly? Now I don't know what it is. Is that his surname, *la*, or *le Beau*? I looked it up, or tried to," her mother said timidly, as though the breath had been suctioned out of her. "I hope this means he is good-looking, at least."

"Well, Mother, what can you expect?" Cornelia, ever chipper, chirped thoughtlessly from the other line. "Pearly is an albino. What choice did she have?"

"Cornie!" absolutely everyone on the line had shouted.

"Well, if he's a colossus, how are Pearlie's babies going to get out without killing her?"

"Cornie!"

"I'm sure he's very nice, dear," her mother said much too quietly.

On her end of the conversation, Pearl had merely managed to blink repeatedly. Saying that he was gigantic with only one good eye would have done nothing for her credibility. And now, there would be no wedding ceremony, not even a visit. The silence of it crashed about as though off cliffs.

BUILDING *the* DAYTIME NEST

NOT LONG INTO SPRING, Ambrose began the process of expanding his music shop. Although he claimed that he could not sing at all, he sang extremely well with a broad range from a sweet upper register into a deep resonating lower baritone. One day, she found him keening both high and sweetly from his head and then deeply from the bottom of his chest again, putting forth bits of songs and phrases he had written that day as he set up a new desk in the corner of the store.

There, between the sheet music and the saxophones, he said she should come to write her articles about flowers and birds whenever she wished to be close to him. It would always be her place; he would never tamper with her papers, not even to move her pencils around, or to borrow them. In the back room, which he had painted and made pleasant for her, he had already set a cradle, on to which he had fixed small oiled wheels for easily ferrying the crib about the stone floors, and newly padded carpeting in the entrance area. There, too, he had placed a sofa—for any number of their impending little family who might need to *evaporate*, one of his English vocabulary words, administered with an ill-chosen twist.

She added to their nest by painting the table that he'd found, in her favorite color: a soft, Mediterranean blue, a color she'd always thought an imagined one before she'd come to this part of the world. On one corner, the table had been a little tall, so Ambrose sawed off the leg and leveled it. "It is just this high," Ambrose pointed out a point waist-high for her and knee-high for himself, "in case you need to change a whole choir of little babies on it, Pearl! Twenty or thirty *bébés* will be good for me and certainly for you."

He laughed, ever readjusting the numbers upward or downward according to his mood, until he had created a rocking coffee table upon which babies might be diapered while their parents were sitting on the sofa in front of it, or kneeling on the floor. "We might make little twins at first," he coaxed. "Or quintuplets. Perhaps Camille Desbordes knows a good herb for making rocket-propelled deliveries."

Early on, Ambrose added a rocking chair he'd found at the Saturday market as a surprise. Soon it was to this room they retreated during the two-hour lunch the villagers took each day. This elongated lunch hour, she said half-seriously to Ambrose, would be the greatest contribution the French could make to international peace, if only they could get the rest of the world to adopt it.

"But yes," Ambrose frowned, considering, "you say you have school in your country Monday through Friday? Even the littlest children do?"

"Yes," she said. "I have always been impressed that here there is no school on Wednesdays. When we are parents, we will appreciate that."

"*Ouais*," he said, "early the Americans give up their children to be the little machines. Who can learn so many days in a row, when fatigued? We do not give over our babies so easily. Mondays and Tuesdays to get up early and work for the teacher, we do. And then Tuesday night--stay up late, playing with friends in the vines, reading the Asterix comics until asleep. Then Wednesday morning the little Catechism with Père Martin, or, well, now The Septum, then all day play to rest, catch up and cuddle in the family, and do homework Wednesday night. Then another two days to morning Saturday class.

Et voilà! Le weekend arrives! We like to see our babies before they grow away from us.

"There is something to be said also, Pearl, for superiority in French contribution to peace, literature, medicine, arts. As you may not know, all the world begins here, even also in St. X!"

She knew better than to bring up the Greeks, the Romans, the Aztecs or the Egyptians, and better than to say anything of the British at all. They didn't need to talk about French literature. French literature, as they had discussed many times, was the reason she had come to live in his country in the first place.

"Medicine, too?" She knew how he loved to go on about this.

"*Mais si!*" Ambrose declared, puffing up. "We are very advanced in medicine, except in emergency. For emergencies you need the Americans in the flashing van like in the television show. We do not have a need for emergencies in France, Pearl. *Mais non!*"

"No?" She would not bring up the rapid transportation of Père Martin only recently.

Ambrose shrugged. "It is not for nothing your great favorite character Molloy had trouble with his transportation, Pearl. It is the getting there—" Ambrose shook his hand in the air, as though he had burned himself and were shaking off his skin. "*Très dangereux!*" Occasionally she found herself 'transported' to her own past by these peculiar conversations that she occasionally only half understood.

Her beau at college, and then, too, at university in Paris, Jimmy Boswell, like herself, had been a great admirer of Beckett and his great fictional character Molloy. The Beastly Boswell had once or even twice, after spraining his ankle, tried Molloy's flights on a rickety bicycle while simultaneously employing crutches, only to end up in an ambulance himself on the way to hospital, with one side of himself badly concussed and scraped—with a bloody exudation to show for it. Boswell, or 'the Beastly Boswell,' as she called him ever afterward, explained endlessly to her the cultural innuendos that he, like Beckett, had encountered, coming from an Irish upbringing and having moved to France.

How had she wandered off from that relationship during their twenties? she infrequently wondered. Her Beastly Boswell had gone off to report on wars in South Africa, while she'd had assignments based in Paris for the *Herald Tribune*. At first, daily letters and clippings had arrived, and then she had begun forgetting to write back to him. Writing letters was hard, she found, something of a busman's holiday, even for writers in love.

In response to any somber Boswellian moods when they were together, Pearl had played her electronic harpsichord for him. He could listen to her playing, or even practicing scales, for hours. How strange that now she herself felt the same way about Ambrose's repetitive exercises on guitar and now also on the bass-cello. Before he went to work, once again after he returned home, and often just before he went to bed, he could be found rapt in his latest musical passages.

And, even after so much time together, Ambrose, who noticed little around himself, never did have knowledge of how great her accomplishment at the keyboard had once been.

∞

"So much can be done at home," Ambrose said now, studying the effects of his new lair on his bride. "The baby perhaps she or he would like to be born at home? It is up to you, of course, Pearl, where you have our baby. Naturally. I think to be at home is best, naturally, if that is what you think. We will see."

"Naturally, Beau, I'd like to be at home," she said, brightening.

"The birth it *is* natural," he suggested, as though he had been an understudy in midwifery. "Consider the pores in your skin, Pearl. Think of all the liquid flowing out. Natural things are the most frightening, if you think about them too, too much."

At times, he was so self-centered that he eclipsed his own intelligence, she was thinking to herself.

A Giant Sings

Telegrams and gifts from their friends in other compartments of the world, right along with a flurry of Christmas cards, had been arriving for weeks after the word got around about their cancelled wedding ceremony. Ambrose strung throughout their house all the white bows and streamers of silvery cotton lace that were to have decorated the church and their reception. He could hardly keep from laughing at himself: "I, brave young groom, run this gauntlet of the metaphorical white underpants." Pearl discovered later, on her morning walk through the thickly falling snow, that Ambrose had also placed a white bow on the fig leaf of the male statue in the frosty village garden.

As the snow increased daily, they swerved from blizzard to blizzard, burrowing. Here it was, not yet Christmas, and in a land that usually had no snow! Boys on small bicycles with bells and boys with scoop shovels veered along their narrow stone-walled lanes in an attempt to free their unaccustomed town and pick up petty cash. Each day the whole village was out, shoveling, and at dawn a minuscule tractor came forth, pushing the white beast before it, breaking down at the main intersection so that traffic through their village was backed up for two and one half days ending at the final sundown. Café Rousseau was crowded with stranded visitors.

Ambrose's musical friends hiked in to stay with them, just before they closed the mountain pass. Beside her fireplace, Pearl recalled for them her tales of Michigan and how they had tied red flags to their radio antennas when she was a child so cars could be anticipated coming around the towering banks of snow. Oh, but cars in her part of the country were big! she realized. Or were, then! And the antennae went up maybe six or eight feet! Oh well, she said when it became clear that they thought the story had been told in service of big American automobiles from Michigan. "No, no really," she said. "It's about snow," she said. "I, too, prefer the little car." In her frustration, she had broken into her schoolgirl German.

"We thought you were *Americaine!*"

"But no!"

"*Mon Dieu*, be quiet," Camille Desbordes picked up her flute. "Stay in tune before we have an international incident."

Pearl and Ambrose stoked the three fireplaces in their house while the eighteen travelers huddled that night, some within the cases for their larger musical instruments, and others curled under the carpets. Two weeks later, all the snow was gone.

∽

Daily her moods switched back and forth. With tenderness, the newly weds watched one another, knowingly, whenever one of them left a room or wandered over in the café to talk with someone else. She could feel his heat rolling toward her long before they even touched. She knew exactly what he was thinking; however, one day she saw him look away toward the lower half of their kitchen door and for a moment Pearl was confused. No, no, she thought. The doctor said I shouldn't have children. It's too dangerous!

But already she could see as well as hear his intentions in the light motion of his fingertips. A desperate loneliness overcame her; had they lost their beautiful moments together? Would their baby ruin it, or never come? Would she die in child birth? He, too, was imagining it. It was not the edge of the door he was seeing. There it was, she could almost see it, too: another smaller being, a combination of the two of them, in one gender or another, a combination of light and dark, here, then there, lithely moving about, already another mortal presence in the village of St. X.

REHEARSALS

AT NIGHT **A**MBROSE HELD REHEARSALS IN THE CHURCH, and she nestled at the back and watched the children, many of whom she had taught and who still stopped to visit her classroom. They were developing their parts from what had seemed like chaos minutes before. All of the little flautists that year had been in her class only the spring before—it seemed so long ago now. They particularly intrigued her with their straight-backed stances, their flutes so tightly held, and their seriously shrill din, their thin straight legs like the legs of a line of seaside plovers—so unlike the little individual high-spoken voices they had offered up from behind their wooden desks.

The goatherd's red-haired boy was developing into a prodigy at the piano now, she could tell. Often she saw Ambrose striding down the street with the boy practically running like a little flame at his side to keep up. Ambrose spent a long while each night writing a solo the little boy could play.

The child labored in their house, filling it with chords and scales at the electric piano Ambrose had brought home for him. Ambrose waved her out until finally she set to fuming and cooking in the kitchen. She laid out snacks and dinners in the dining room and was forced to retreat to the bedroom to try to read. "You have to let him eat!" she finally shouted from under the covers. "He's a little boy, he's not a machine! Start with a little tune. Scales can't hold him! Now let him eat!"

Guiltily, the two of them appeared and devoured everything in one sitting that she had laid out for them throughout the afternoon and evening. The little, large-eared child seemed not to mind the fact that hours passed in their evening musical preparations, while his mother was bringing in the goats. Together, Ambrose and the little prodigy sat by the open fire, on mismatched chairs, repeating and even rewriting phrases as they went along, altering and extending familiar carols. One evening the boy came to sit on Pearl's lap and confessed that of all the composers ever in the world, his favorite was Beethoven. She'd come in once, touched to find the child sitting on a pile of books to lift him before the beautiful little cherry harpsichord that had arrived from her three sisters for a "late marriage present," even if they couldn't see her "day of happiness."

SMALL DOSES

"YOU ARE TAKING PILLS!" Ambrose declared one morning, sulking even before breakfast.

"No!" she said, slapping down her napkin. "Now that you mention it, Camille says you are taking drugs!"

"Do not change the subject. Non! Secretly you take the hormone birth control! Now I see it."

"Beau," she objected, rising from her chair. "Please tell me seriously you think I would lie to you. If you do, then I will be completely free to leave."

"Non," he said finally, after a long brooding silence. "I do not think that."

"Okay then," she said. "I'm sorry I haven't got a baby for you today." She looked away from him for a long while then, and back again. "What about what Camille said?"

"I take the medicine for my heart, that is all," he said. "Camille is the fool herbal. You should not listen to her when you have such a one as me." He stalked out of the room. After quite a long time and the sound of crashing behind the door, he came out of his retreat. "I admit. I can not lie. I do think you don't want it, that's what the matter is," he mumbled in her direction. "Do not answer me, Pearl! Only you can know whether or not this is true. You do not need to say! Already I know." His heels crashed down the stairs. The front door slammed.

A HOLIDAY *with* LA GRIPPE

 JUST DAYS BEFORE THE CHRISTMAS SCHOOL VACATION, an outbreak of influenza closed all classes. Three-quarters of Pearl's schoolchildren had already gone home with *la grippe*. Even the little piano prodigy lay at home in bed, Enid had called to say. She and Ambrose, too, lay in a fever of aches and pains. Still, on Christmas Eve, Ambrose arose from under his icepack to go to the store so that the children of St. X would not be disappointed, as he'd agreed upon with The Beloved. He waited six hours for the usual influx of parents, and in they came looking truly miserable. Then he lay in the back room on the sofa bed, waiting for the bell to ring on the snow-smitten blue front door, waiting for Pearl to come to get him. He was far too ill, he'd said, to drive himself to the concert.

By nearly eight o'clock, Pearl arrived to say that *le Maire* had called with apologies. For the first time, they had cancelled the Christmas concert. Ambrose was instructed by *le Maire* to have a small happy evening, if possible, at home beneath the tree Pearl had prepared for them. But, they spent the evening much as the rest of the village, shivering under the covers and cursing the bell ringer for carrying on with his usual midnight carillon.

By the time the town recovered, New Year's Eve had passed without notice.

During the last few days of the year, the influenza did take a life:

Madame Meulemeester passed into her next world during the only night when the wind had stopped howling. It was said around the village that the sudden silence that had made the whole village sit up and take notice, had been the exact moment of her passing. Her funeral was badly attended because of extensive winter sickness. Père Pepin gracefully prayed over her in a nearly empty church, and then she was slid into her final rest, right next to Père Martin's awaiting drawer, one of the most coveted places in the mausoleum wall of the cemetery.

Looking a little green herself, Madame Menard came by her friend's shop and draped the blue cerulean door with Madame Meulemeester's own black satin opera stole and a wreath of black satin roses, to which someone in the middle of the night added her red ballet slippers.

During these small remembrances for Madame Meulemeester, during the dark months of the influenza, one surprising fact slowly came to light. Père Pepin had made preparations for his predecessor's death almost immediately upon his arrival, long before Père Martin's death had seemed imminent to the rest of the village. And in these preparations he had assigned the impending ghost of Père Martin to the shortest lease possible, renting for him the economy drawer vault, occupiable only for the minimum number of years allowed at the ossuary in the cemetery.

After several particularly vociferous protests at town meetings, by spring, the villagers had chipped in and assured the bones of both Madame Meulemeester and Père Martin additional time. "An astounding extra eight years—which takes us up to twenty-five, or for eternity," Père Martin's contract had said, "whichever has the grace of arriving first in our most incomparable village of St. X."

BENEATH *the* CHESTNUT TREE

 **MOISTURE RAINED FROM AMBROSE'S PORES** before their springtime feast, as Madame le Beau slipped along his enormous hide hidden deep within the woods. When finally she grew too tired in the heat to move, he would lift her again and again until she regained her verve. An acceptance of fate had begun to enter into them. He no longer thought so much of designing children, or so it now seemed to her. The birds nesting in the trees above seemed to sing shriller and shriller notes of joy as he impaled her.

The berries had ripened two months early in this year of extraordinarily hot and unpredictable weather. Oh how joyfully she began to pelt him with *les mûres*. Wherever they struck, a bright, blue stain like a pockmark appeared on his handsome, naked hide.

"Plague! Plague!" she cried, running from the hideous blue face she had created. Round and round he chased her with his cinnamon eye leering at her. Into the lowly branches of a good-sized holm oak she sprang and from there onto a boulder nearly her own height. She squatted down behind a ledge in the glossy leaves, and lay in wait for him.

Twice he passed by her hiding place, calling out her name, until finally she, with a flying leap, catapulted from her camouflage of branches onto his broad back to bury her chin in his shoulder. "That will teach you—" she started to shout, playfully hammering on his head.

For a moment Ambrose staggered and she thought that perhaps she had made a vast if giddy mistake and injured him. He swung around, and their voices were corked at the sight of what lay before them.

In the bushes, practically at their feet, lay two of the most beautifully formed human beings, man and woman. There seemed to be cast a coral hue about them, as if the meaning of sunlight itself were pouring through and from their skins. Every hair upon them seemed a sun-struck thread. Afraid to stir, Ambrose squeezed his hands around Pearl's ankles as the other couple moved gently apart and together. The tiniest white hairs glowed on the sides of the woman's face as her elegant head tilted back until the crown of it nearly touched her back. Her ribs shone out. For a moment, the youth—for could he be old enough to be a man really? Ambrose asked himself—took the whole flower of the young woman's ear into his mouth and sucked at it.

Quietly, Ambrose began to step backward, holding tightly to Pearl, trying not to look at the beautiful couple, and trying not to fall into the foliage. When safely out of sight, Ambrose set her down on the path. Later they would speak of the way they could not stop remembering the splendor of the young couple's embrace. After that, they avoided that particular part of the woods, granting to the strangers all privacy. As though by agreement, neither of them mentioned the occurrence to anyone. It was as though they had rejoiced before the painting of a great masterpiece.

RIVER *of* EMERALDS

 **CAMILLE DESBORDES HAD HAD MANY LIVES—** or so she was indicating on the beach, under a gigantic sun hat and bikini briefs, during another lunchtime retreat. Camille Desbordes had an exquisite speaking voice, as well as an operatic talent for singing, packed into her forceful body. When Camille Desbordes spoke, it was impossible not to listen. Her intelligence was noticeable because she did not try to hide it. Her chestnut hair swept around an almost rectangular forehead and a straight nose that, if it had been any narrower, would have appeared to have been mechanically sharpened. There were many reasons Pearl liked her, least of which was her experience.

Camille had in her earlier days written a book about cooking which had been published with many sun-glazed pictures in it of herself beside her cook stove. When she had tired of the kitchen, she had upon occasion designed perfumes for friends from substances she grew in her own garden. Camille had also run a small café; and she had been a carpenter for a time, specializing in scampering lightly like a goat in her hiking sandals along steeply pitched orange roofs, replacing roofing tiles. She had married twice the same brusque man, with no children either of those first times. But now, to her delight, she said, she found herself divorced and temporarily unemployed at the same time. If she were engaging the affections of a man, she volunteered almost matter-of-factly, it was usually a tourist or even an itinerant, delaying his departure for a week, maybe two at most. It was a Thursday when Camille Desbordes stepped into the water again for a quick swim across river and back when something caught her attention. *"Au secours!"* Camille Desbordes cried out.

The picnicking crowd stopped all movement at her so unusual, serious tone.

How could they not have noticed it? Could it have happened all at once? Down river, where the falls had the day before been a torrent, a child was sitting on the dam itself, slapping his hands on the surface, immersed to his hips only. There were no slender yellow boats today, they realized. They stared at the ripples about themselves, at the lower banks. In the inordinate heat, the clear green of the water had, without their notice, ever so slightly been shrinking and thickening.

When they scampered up beside Camille onto the bank to look at it, it appeared as though individual emeralds of moss were spraying past the child and over the crude stone obstacle onto the other bathers who, from below, now stared up at them.

Madame le Beau would remember sometime later that another seemingly minor, yet unusual, moment had occurred on that day. Just before Camille's outcry, Pearl had brought her head up from under the surface of the river and gasped at the sight of her new husband on the bank, appearing from among the branches as if from out of nowhere. *Un homme très beau!* she'd thought. How beautiful the man is!

But no, she'd thought directly on the heels of it, I can't have already married him! Her old thoughts were upon her, her mood swinging wildly. Can I? I'm far too young for marriage! And, where was her beautiful wedding ceremony? She had a momentary flashback then to her Irishman Boswell. She had almost been able to touch him, he'd seemed so real, nestled in, all shaggy beside her on the bed, singing badly, and drumming his fingers lightly on her naked chest.

It was upon this absurdity that Pearl was pondering and marveling just as she dipped under again and broke through the surface of their river into the dazzling vision of Ambrose so confidently grinning back at her. In that moment of astonishment, she found herself gasping and railing and choking upon the slightest sip of the ailing waters that had fallen into her lungs. She'd swallowed only a driblet, she would later remember, but then her body had managed to cough nearly the bottom of her lungs out of her in trying to expel it.

HOUSE CALLS

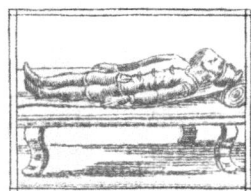 **HOW SLOWLY TIME MOVED FOR THEM,** sweeping them along, while everything around them in the intensifying heat seemed to stand and reverberate. It was not long at all until rumors commenced in their area. One case only had been reported, and that diagnosis had been declared uncertain and then false. In a few days, Madame le Beau lay in Ambrose's arms in quite another way than they were used. She had begun to be more ill than she could ever recall. "*C'est normale* for the *grippe*," her friends tried to reassure her.

She had had it twice before, since coming to this country, this influenza called *la grippe*, and recently, just this past Christmas Day, had been the worst. How fiercely this French ailment could take you, particularly in one so slight as she, and with a foreign system of immunity. And yet *la grippe* was nothing much in the relative world of deadly disease, especially compared to this, whatever it was that had started in the green mottled waters of an early summer swim.

They went on for a few days before she would agree to the doctor. Ambrose had had to shake her like a little doll to get her to wake, and then her fever was so fierce that in touching her he had recoiled. He sat on the edge of the bed and stared, as though damaged, at his immense, nearly-burned fingertips.

Within half an hour of the call and through a barrage of her own feverish moans, Madame le Beau could hear Doctor Malaplate wedging his white Renault up the barely navigable slot of Rue de Versailles toward their limestone house.

How many people must have died in this house before even the commencement of their century, Madame le Beau began to ponder, almost pleasantly, most dreamily floating in and out of an extraordinary febrile disease. She began counting backward through its previous occupants, known and unknown, increasingly imaginary, increasingly like a little blue and white tile hand-painted at the breast of her chimney. This stone house had stood at the corner for at least seven centuries. Now she hummed a little nursery song to herself, as often her little mother had done when Pearl had had to overcome some passing, yet threatening, childhood illness.

"*Calme-toi, Pearl, calme-toi*!" Ambrose called out far too loudly, bounding down the stairs to street level and flinging their heavy door open. "*Le médecin* arrives now!"

This call for a doctor to come to the house had not been easy for her. She was used to waiting while others, perhaps or perhaps not sicklier, even well or dying persons, some barely able to sit up, were stretched out around her, crying in the halls. She had often been there, to the hospital. She was afraid that they would take her to hospital now, if Doctor Malaplate were to come now. To her on that day, she felt sure it meant that she would leave her beloved house and be taken in the tiny ambulance to a place called hospital and die there. So firmly she believed.

∞

When it had become for her as though she were falling down a well, she began to change her mind. She dreamed of the arrival of Doctor Malaplate who had so kindly soothed her arms with the olive tree bug medicament. Although she recalled that it might have continued to swell a bit, the bite itself had no longer hurt and had even the

171

added pleasure of causing a stir around her among her students.

It had been the beautiful Doctor Malaplate who had finally, at *le maire's* insistence, against his will almost, stood up with her and her new husband on the spur of the moment for their hasty wedding vows in The Beloved's office.

Now increasingly, the room swung around and around. To the edge of the bed she clung now, her little nose barely over the mattress edge, as though inching over the rim of a cliff outwardly collapsing. The mattress under her was in process, day and night, of tilting and shifting with revenge. Continuously, she now called out for help in a weakened voice. No amusement park could have proved so perpetual. On this ride, it grew apparent to her reluctant self that there might be no getting off, no acceptable end to it. Finally she discovered that if she could tilt her head a mere fraction to the right, for just one hint of a moment, the armoire, the pale green chairs, the mahogany tables, the fireplace mantel, the delicate silk shades on the lamps, and even the flowers in the maroon tiles, might for just one moment stop their kaleidoscopic circumnavigation. Her skin grew unearthly clammy. Pearl was at the center, while it all swung around her, until it could less frequently be stopped by any movement, or by any drink, or by any pill anyone could offer, or she might think to swallow.

By the time Christian Malaplate pulled the sheer veil of mosquito netting from around their bed, Pearl was already twelve pounds less staunch than she'd been on that Thursday before, when they had had their swim and had seen the beautiful couple. Her head tossed on the pillow as though she were cast out on an ocean.

Quite suddenly, out of the swirl of unfamiliar objects, Doctor Malaplate's long mustache appeared before her. There the mustache was now like two, dark slur marks in a line of musical notes. Whenever it wiggled, she lost her place and the music ran off without her in a field of snakes. Within minutes, his eyeglasses had come to have a peculiar gleam in them, too, twirling about her as though he had become one of the multiplying identical ornaments.

Christian Malaplate absolutely insisted she turn onto her back; and when she could not, he slipped his palms beneath her side and actually turned her, swiftly and in one motion, like a pancake. Then, the many mustachioed Malaplates began to hang up their intravenous plastic packs; and then she felt all of them put the many needles in the tender corner of her many elbows. She closed her eyes and felt them all sit down and hold her arms firmly at her sides within the comfort of their cool hands. She heard him sighing and clucking.

During that hour or so, somewhere in the vast and whirling chasm where she now trembled and tried to steady herself, she became aware of the image of the head of a bull, not unlike the one made of bread dough that hung over the counter in the bakery. At the center of the bull's horns roared the likeness of her new husband. Then both of them were gone and only their voices trailed behind them.

"*Pas bon*? What do you mean, *Not good*?" Ambrose bellowed from the kitchen. "*Pas bon*?" he demanded, as if the doctor were the cause of her affliction and not potentially the maker of good news.

A GIANT PROTEST

 **"PUT ME DOWN AT ONCE!"** the doctor hissed. A silence followed and a little squeak. In her mind, Pearl sat up straight in her bed; yet, in reality, she had not moved. Perhaps, Pearl told herself, I have dreamed myself finally into a cartoon, just as my students might have wished. Or, I have entered into the realm of hallucination.

"O, pardon, pardon, Christian!" Ambrose apologized in a deeply frightened voice, getting ahold of himself, lowering the doctor by his lapels to his stance on the floor once again, in front of the adjoining doorways.

Pearl listened on with remote interest in her case, as the meaty Christian Malaplate whispered further. The words came! What a delight it was to hear him say it! The doctor was afraid, even refused, to even attempt to move her to hospital until she was better!

How odd, the little patient was thinking, that it occurred to neither man that in her high fever everything in range of her hearing might dramatically be amplified. Even her mental French seemed intensely accurate, if only she had had the strength to speak it. If they had spoken in German, her understanding of that, too, might have been renewed. Perhaps languages she had never studied would have been given to her automatically, she mused. She had always wanted to speak Hungarian.

The doctor poured out a glass of something for them both; she could hear it splashing twice like twin waterfalls down the cool sides of two glasses. All the while, the newly-arrived Camille Desbordes silently stroked at Pearl's feverish temples, leaning toward the doorway, trying to listen to what was being said in the kitchen.

"*Mon Dieu! Mon Dieu! Ceci la typhöide!*"

"Certainly not!" the doctor declared. "There are no cases of *la typhöide* here. *Mais*, something similar perhaps. But, not the same thing, Ambrose! Get ahold of yourself!"

"But the river—"

Perhaps it was true that their beautiful river now barely moved and was not beautiful, that in the last few days it had grown to look as though it had an illness itself, and not a very nice one. "No one can deny your observations regarding our river," Christian Malaplate was saying. "I have my own suspicions."

Above her, the slow drip of the medication bubbled and tumbled forth, down the long transparent threadlike passage. Camille's gentle breathing filled the room, as Pearl floated in the slight up and down movement of her motherly arms, while she placed Pearl's hairpins to keep the million lengthy white hairs from falling across her face in her vertigo.

It was in this circular dream that perhaps even days or weeks collapsed into history before Pearl heard the doctor pouring out yet another small chalice for Ambrose. The sun was trying to edge its way around the shutters and through the lace curtains. The liquid in the kitchen came to crash this time down into the husband's glass as if over a chute inside her ear. A pen there scratched out instructions on a pad. She could hear the fabric of Beau's shirt crumpling across the shoulders, the recipient of the doctor's fatherly pats. Then the footsteps of the doctor padded down the cut stone stairway as though he were wearing only stockings. A car door creaked open and closed, and then the tiny vehicle was attempting to reverse and turn up their street.

The street was no larger than the sidewalk in front of the house where she had been raised, where the image of her family still lived so very far away. Always it seemed to her a miracle that any car might get through their street, no matter how small, much less that it might be able to turn around in it.

For a moment all was still, and then off and on over the week, she heard Christian Malaplate reappear and retreat, rev and reverse, rev and reverse, until he could get onto *la route* that would take him to that nameless larger village six distant kilometers away.

∞

All the repositioning of people and objects in the outside world made Pearl dizzy. Paradoxically, the memory of the intense jockeying of the doctor's *voiture*, reversing and reversing again and again, making every centimeter count in its slow but steady circular repositioning, almost calmed her until against Camille's good advice she opened her eyes.

The bedside lamp began to swing at once, and she prayed that no one would come in to further disturb her peace. And if they did, mercifully she would not be aware of them. She could not now speak to anyone without the vertigo beginning again. The present met the past in a continuous winding thread. She dreamed a thick, deep trance, and in it she watched in horror a Hitchcock movie of the most vicious and vertiginous nature. *Vertigo*. Never again would she watch that film, she thought. If she lived, never! And, if she did not live, *voilà*!

It was Camille Desbordes who came to sit with Pearl then. And, it was Camille Desbordes who gave her the news: Ambrose had been offered a recording session and a tour. Ambrose had been planning to cancel it so that he could stay and take care of her. His band, and in it many of their friends from the shop, had not only agreed, but also encouraged his cancellation.

"*Oualou*," Pearl began to cry on hearing this news. "*Oualou, oualou*." She could barely speak for weeping. She felt so sad for Beau, and so terrified of him.

"Terrified?" Camille demanded of her, startled at the strange word. "What do you mean you are *terrified* of Ambrose?"

That morning, Doctor Malaplate had told Ambrose that his bride was starving to death. This, Pearl had overheard and now managed to explain to Camille Desbordes between sips as Camille Desbordes held her head and fed her a tepid broth. That week, five or six times a day, while Camille was gone, Ambrose had insisted on preparing dishes to restore her health.

The normally tantalizing smell of Ambrose's cooking now nearly killed her, she confessed to her friend. Again and again, he had knelt by her on the bed, insisting that she eat increasingly spiced foods meant to stimulate her appetite. She had asked, and pleaded, then begged, that he take the trays away. Twice he had force-fed her, and she had nearly choked to death.

In a torrent of hiccoughing, she began to cry as she related how Ambrose, in his compassion and anguish, was inadvertently torturing her. "When finally I am fallen asleep," she trembled on, "he pokes my head! He is trying so hard, but he sits by me, touching, touching, touching. The avalanche comes when he sits down on the bed! I can't stop the vertigo then, and he can not remember not to do it."

There was no concealing her exasperation, and also her love and pity for Ambrose. "It is so hard to get to sleep! He wakes me when finally I am asleep, Camille. He wakes me to eat those horrible things he makes. He wakes me just to see if I'm alive! Only when I'm asleep does the pain go away. I can't stop the whirling if I can't sleep. And he is obsessed with me!"

Camille Desbordes was not above singing lullabies to a grown friend when silence made the pain intense. When Pearl slipped under to a peaceful rest, Camille knew to let the silence carry them both away. Camille assured her friend that she would very gently speak with Ambrose. And, she promised, she would try not to offend.

A Good Chef's
Cuisine

AFTER CLOSING UP THE STORE, Ambrose came quietly up the stairs, only to be led into the kitchen by the headstrong Camille Desbordes. Pearl herself saw him through her closed eyelids, looking through the doorway at her, as though afraid that she had passed away during the hours while he had been away at work.

"No, no, she is asleep." Their chairs creaked to the side and then against the floor tiles again. The packets of biscuits and cheese crackled as Camille opened them. She heard him settle into the hand-painted chair he always sat in.

"Pearl is too sick to be able to mend your worries," Pearl overheard her friend too firmly say. "Having such rich passions aroused, Ambrose," Camille Desbordes went on, "when she needs her strength, could cost us all her life. She cares too much for you."

Ambrose coughed then, and she heard the sound of a small biscuit in his colossal hands, cracking in half, and then again. She heard him clear his throat as he did when he was fighting back tears. "You must go away for now, just as you planned. You must make your recording just as though Pearl were well. She wants you to have your tour. You must know that."

"I will not leave my wife when she has the malady," Ambrose hoarsely said.

In whispers, Camille shushed him. "Ambrose, Ambrose," she said. "It is dangerous to continue this way. Everyone knows you love and worship Pearl. Anyone would be moved to see your compassion. You've been trying to save her for weeks."

"I will not be the one who runs away when my family is in need! *J'm'en fous! Camille Desbordes!* You may run with louts and pigs, and even marry one after another of them again and again, but I am not such a pig as to leave my wife! As you know, I am not one who married you! You can not make me go!"

Already the armoire commenced to swirl; the ceiling plaster undulated. Soon, she hoped, the neighbors would come to the door in protest. She feared even worse, the worst thought in her life. She burned with agony, and the fear came again, as Ambrose countered Camille's suggestions in a hurt and defensive voice. The argument entered into absurdity. Then he declared himself the best chef in the *département*. Camille Desbordes did not have to counter with her own claim for excellence in the kitchen.

Were those the dishes cracking? Or, was that the sound of a pencil being tapped emphatically on a plate? She heard only bits and chards of their conversation now. In her imagination, she, too, began to bawl.

"It would be better, Ambrose," Camille Desbordes whispered, "if you would leave so that all of Pearl's forces could concentrate on her recovery. You would not be letting her down. Just for now, just for now, is all I say."

Desertion was not one of the husband's duties, her husband declared. Who would cook for her? he worried aloud once again.

Now Camille Desbordes absurdly asserted that the patients in the hospital in Cannes were not asked to dine at the resplendent *Moulin à Mougins*.

"And that is why the American Hospital no longer exists in Cannes, Camille Desbordes. The cuisine it was too bland to sustain life!" Yes, it was all a very loud cartoon now, and a roller coaster ride.

Face down, Pearl scratched back the edges of her sheets and blankets and held to the ridged edge of the mattress, pressing her head then beneath a pillow where she could feel all the feathers caving in upon themselves, and she, completely captured in their midst, became merely a whirling white particle. The room rocked like a doomed boat in a storm of fog.

Mercifully, she no longer understood what they said. Merely a passerby to the commotion, Pearl managed to stand. Her head pounded with every syllable, understood or not, as she groped her way into the bathroom and closed the door. She only wanted silence. Oh, to be deaf! she thought. Pearl thought herself lucid now, barely able to stand, but oh so lucid, and miserable.

Perhaps they heard the silver sound the toilet made when she gathered enough strength to get up and manipulate the cold round knob at the top of the tank and then to sink down again. The water ran and ran until she tried to stand and shake the knob up and down, tried to stop it, this sound that also made her ill. All sounds and motions did the same. Whatever had caused the utter stillness in the adjoining rooms, Pearl was too weak to do anything about it. She lay back, relishing the peace. It was as though she had been swept up on a cooling cloud of cumulous.

Against the flaking plaster wall were stacked the remaining old tiles.

"Nesting, nesting, we are always nesting, Beau," she had teased. It had been one of their dreams to make their little house beautiful. They had enough of the blue market pattern of village scenes to completely line the Roman bath.

Now these hand-painted objects seemed like portents of some great catastrophe that was even at that moment taking place in their own lives. Pearl drifted out on the cold, crisp currents the floor gave to her. For a moment she felt she would be well, even resplendent, and then from the kitchen came the slinky odor of a liver broth Ambrose had begun frantically stewing up to save her life.

"Get out of my house! *Immédiatement!*" he said to Pearl's helpful friend.

"Are you deaf?" Camille Desbordes demanded. "If the little girl can not eat your *épice de Catelán*, so be it. If the little girl needs to sleep and not have her handsome French *gigot* here, in order not to die, let it be so! Have you no respect? Pearl is not the experiment *gastronomique!* You talk about her life! You are not the only one who loves her. She means something to many others here as well. Nearly every child in the St. X school adores her."

It would have been impossible for her husband to strike a woman, no matter how she threatened his integrity, or so Pearl thought. Yet in the bathroom, Pearl lay on the concrete and trembled for fear that Ambrose, in his rage, would do just that. And, she feared, then in his horror and humiliation at what he had done and at what he could not do for her, he would leave her forever. She lifted up her head and tried to shout something of reassurance at them both.

"How dare you ask me why," he was hissing at Camille. "The doctor says she must eat or die!"

"Ask her yourself, does she wish to eat your food, Ambrose? It is you who make her unable to eat or sleep! This is not the Grand Hotel. *Espèce d'imbécile*! Ask her yourself. You are killing her!"

"*Merde! Merde! Merde! You ugly, heartless woman!*"

"Ask her, I say!"

"*Et alors*, my wife does not want her food, but that is because my wife is ill. I will tempt her into being well. I can save my own wife. I know what it is to be sick and to have your friends abandon you."

"Sick persons do not wish to eat exotic food. Any idiot knows this. Boiled liver! Turn that stove off! If you do not leave, the doctor tells her, he will take her to the hospital today. Even the doctor agrees that she cannot make that journey. You brute! You will kill her to have your own way!"

"And you, Camille Desbordes!" his immense, grating voice countered, "you who throw away all your husbands! You drive a wedge between us, even at this time? You think I do not know. It is me you have wanted to marry since you were six years old. There are afternoons between us you cannot forget. Now you take your revenge on us."

"*Tu es stupide à la fin!* So be it. For the sake of you alone, pig pride, you lose your *musique*, your first recording, and we bury her. Everything! Is that what you want?"

The towel beneath her soaked into the crumbling floor. Her skin seemed, too, to melt into the animation of objects. From the level where she lay, her left eye peered at the mirrored panel slanted there against the wall. Ambrose had purchased it for its gilt frame at the *marché aux puces*. The room lurched to a halt then; and, in the corner of the mirror, an emaciated face drooled into a sodden towel. She looked at it with curiosity. It was hard to tell where the portions of skin left off and the towel and hair began. White hair was plastered to all surfaces of the troll's head and neck, even onto the small breasts. Why, the features had no human distinction, she thought, if they had ever had them. Who had let this creature in?

Up the hallway fell the heavy hullabaloo of their sandals. They passed by the bathroom and then she heard them stop at the bedroom. She heard a horrified gasp when they saw the empty bed. She heard their squeaky shoes turning. Ambrose tapped on the bathroom door; and softly the two of them said her name. The corner of the door slipped by the back of her head. She knew for a second they thought her dead, because at the sight of her lying on the torn up floor amongst the loose tiles, a cry escaped from Camille. Ambrose began at once to sob in loud heaving rhythms.

A FOUR POSTER BED

MY THOUGHTS DRIFT AWAY FROM THEM, Pearl thought, even now. Someday, somewhere, she realized, all that happened here would be the case again. Someone, somewhere, would come upon her, as someone must come upon everyone, and gasp in just that way. No one moved. In the mirror, their feet shone just beyond her head. They could not from this angle see her eyes. She could not signal anything to them of reassurance. She managed barely to move her palm ever so slightly. It was as though a conductor had signaled the overture. Camille Desbordes began to babble and cry at her side in relief.

Cooing to her, sighing and soothing her with pet words, together they picked her up and carried her back to bed. Camille Desbordes sponged her with cold towels and dried her skin and Ambrose sat beside her bed in the big armchair, head bowed as if in a trance, without touching her again, not even to hold her hand. Soon enough she had slipped off into an hypnotic sleep even while the doctor came and went, changing medications and reports, droning out his restorative songs and drugs.

∞

Later that night, Pearl had to ask herself, What was that beautiful eerie sound welling up in the house and spilling out the windows and down the stairs, echoing off the continuous stone cavern of their street, around the corner to the South, and down the other alleyways? She would never forget it. After a while, Ambrose's wailing song seemed to weave itself into the bed sheet. It ran in and out, a blue thread. She threw her cheek upon it and would not let go of him.

Later, on their last night, she tried to get out of bed to go to the sound of him sequestered somewhere in the very room in which she lay. She knew he was there, but she could not so much as raise her head or open her mouth. A terrible entity lodged itself between her lungs and began to ache with every sob she heard from him over her waning life. It was her belief that all their village sat silent in that night, listening with a deepening sadness as his voice cried out the window, from between the open shutters on the hot night. Ambrose, they were saying. They shook their heads. That is our Ambrose; our bandmaster is crying such a very sad song. Soon we will all weep.

For the first time, on that last day, Ambrose did not disturb her fitful sleep or cook beyond the broth the doctor asked him to make or pace wildly back and forth in the room, stopping to touch her every time he turned. He did not shake her every time it seemed to him that she had fallen into a sound sleep. Camille Desbordes sat vigilantly on a chair just inside her door, supervising him. Occasionally Pearl would open her eyes and see him hovering, his hands extended like wings, as if to land on her brow or place his lips on her arms and chest. But there his limbs halted, mid-air, as he thought better of it.

At the sight of him, about to touch her, she could not help herself; she winced. She had meant to compare him with something simple he could readily understand even in his frenzied state, an anchor perhaps, to tell him that he was steady and serene. This she had thought to spill out so tactfully and powerfully, but she could not speak the words herself. She had hoped for his understanding and enlightenment. His benevolent face fell into gloom as he sat back down in the chair Camille Desbordes resolutely pointed out to him.

Three days later Pearl awoke to the force of a slamming door. She heard Camille pick up the telephone and call not only the doctor, but also Père Pepin.

That night she felt her husband's presence once again in her fitful sleep. She opened her eyes and found his one, tormented iris staring back at her and beside him the dreaded Père Pepin, crying out her last rites in a rather strangulated voice. She tried to protest but could not elevate her eyelids. Perhaps she was paralyzed at the nearness of the mealy-mouthed priest who had not long before refused to marry her because he thought her to be a freak. Or, perhaps she was paralyzed not only by her illness but also by the daunting thought that these breaths might actually be her last. When she woke again, both men were gone. Camille Desbordes snored lightly in the hall, her head up against the top-most wrung of a straight-backed chair.

The doctor had given Ambrose the typhoid vaccine, and Camille Desbordes as well. "Just as a precaution *plus*," the doctor said, denying any reason for worry at all. "Gastro-entérite," he was calling it. Then Christian Malaplate smiled, pecking both Pearl's skeletal hands, beneath the ardor of his black mustache. "Not a problem, little Pearl. Sleep now, Pearl. Soon it will all be nothing more than an unpleasant memory." He kissed her hands and tucked her blankets up over her arms. He helped her to roll onto her side. She pressed her brow into the tiny, soft, warm hairs at the backs of the doctor's quiet hands. "Do you want to go to the hospital tonight after your rest?" he asked. "I think it might be good for us to go tonight."

In the hallway, Camille's chair scraped the tiles. "But I will be with her," began Camille's protest. "And, Ambrose will be away on business. I promised him I would stay. She's afraid to go to hospital."

Ambrose entered again, an apparition of himself by the bed. "There is just as much danger in moving her as in her staying here, you said so yourself."

"If you will be with her then—" the Doctor said to Camille. "And you, Ambrose, will you leave her to her peace?"

Pearl closed her eyes. What difference could it make? She was too tired now to think.

"*Voilà!*" the doctor's voice said, close to her, suddenly in her ear. "You will see it for yourself, Pearl. He will be renewed also when he returns. You must believe in that. But, Pearl, this is for you to decide: do you wish to travel to the hospital? Or stay here with your friend, Camille. Ambrose has promised to leave for his tour, just as you request." But, the patient could not nod or in any way affirm, as she was once again whirling in an endless sea of darkness, streaked with the palest of acrid yellow lights.

"Squeeze once if you wish to stay at home now, twice if you wish to go to hospital. The hospitals are very good here, Pearl. You are not to be afraid of them." She squeezed once and clung onto him. "Good," the doctor said. "I don't think she could stand the trip. I will give her another *pique* and soon the carousel will slow down a little, if it does not entirely stop. I will be back before mid-day, of course. We can take her tomorrow if she does not improve."

She felt the cold crisp pain of his needle in her muscle; and then the hope of it entered her consciousness even before the drug could take its first effects.

∞

The next day, with great emotion, Beau knelt beside the bed to say good-bye, kissing her lightly on the forehead as if it were the end. "I promise," she tried to say, but she could not go on with it. He held her hands then lightly, but no one else could have looked into her eyes like that. She felt his strength move into her and hold her there. If only he could have been so calm for the past weeks. Then, she would not, for the life of her, want Beau to go away from her.

"I asked Pearl," the doctor said again to him, to be sure he understood. "This is what she wants. She knows you are not deserting her, Ambrose."

She opened her mouth and the most peculiar shaking sound came out. She saw Camille Desbordes reach out in horror and grip Ambrose's arm at what they thought to be the death rattle. But the false moment they had feared soon passed.

All, as planned, was under way. Camille Desbordes bathed Pearl's face while she promised her husband that by the time he returned, if it was at all in God's will, his wife would be well. A fond stubble appeared before Pearl's face, and then the quarter note of the eye patch, and then his bloodshot, golden eye. She tried to speak and swallowed instead. He reached out for her and left his hand lingering above her in the air. Then ever so calmly he stroked her cheek. In her mind she moved into the reservoir of his palm. Could she not live there all her life?

She could not go to the window to see him, but she heard his reluctant feet on the stone street dragging along, less and less audibly, heading north. And then she hoped perhaps the footsteps were a little sprightlier as he moved toward the recordings, and perhaps even the acclaim he had awaited for so long. Perhaps now he did share his hopes with Camille Desbordes, that his absence would indeed be exactly what his wife needed. She could imagine him then: she could almost smell his sweet breath, and feel the splendor of him, could sense his strength moving into his arms and shoulders and into his legs then, as he left death behind. Surely it was better for him, she told herself. The giant was moving along a bit more lightly on his feet, her Beau, slipping up the street, packing the immense bass and his electric guitar.

FRIENDLY SOUP

IT HAD BEEN LIKE BREATHING TO HER, to have his music in the house; she knew that, in an even deeper way now. Always she had enjoyed her solitude, yet it was even the slightest sound laid upon another musical sound that had always given her existence bearing. Without it, Pearl was unendurably alone. For a day or two, she rebounded, and then faltered under Camille's care, and prepared to die. She slept in a fever of nausea, panting for air. She fell continually through the hours. The doctor came and went, no longer knocking, just appearing in multiple whirling forms beside her bed.

Pearl was helped back and forth to the bathroom, again and again, until she was too weak to stand. People from the village came to help. They bathed her and took her fluids away; yet she was not sure which of them they were. They seemed a blurred chorus of existence around her, though she could not make out their song. And through it all, encouragement came from their blend of incomprehensible patter, and from the simplest sounds rising toward her, from the smallest babble on the street.

Some days she knew of time again, when the tolling of the church bells reeled in from out of nowhere, or when the dawn chorus of insects and birds gently reminded her of an external life to her misery. Somewhere, winged things called to one another in intricate joy as well as in despair.

Increasingly then, she could not understand even Camille's speech, or even her healing sign language.

On the fifteenth day after Ambrose's departure, Camille Desbordes would tell her later, there began a change in her. About that time, Camille Desbordes had a notion to turn on the radio or CD player the moment Camille awoke on the cot she had set up beside Pearl's bed. Partly, Camille did this to relieve her own discouragement, for now she believed that she would lose Pearl and that she would have to tell Ambrose that she had failed and Pearl had, in his absence, died. But soon she found that Pearl ate a little when the music was on. From time to time she opened her eyes and was less distraught. In the middle of the night, when Pearl grew miserable with pain, Camille turned it softly on again. She played lovely pieces, only those songs that were not of her native tongue, so as not to be too taxing, she said. She did not play rock music or jazz, she said later, because she was sure it would bring Ambrose to mind. She played Debussy, then Mozart, Brahms' *Intermezzi*, and Grieg.

In the third week Pearl regained some of her strength, yet she mourned for Ambrose as though he had been the one dying, not herself. She called repeatedly for him, even in her sleep. Incessantly she inquired whether Camille Desbordes thought Ambrose would return. At the first asking, she reassured her, but by the third or fourth time, Pearl could not be sure whether Camille Desbordes truly believed he was coming home, or whether she was humoring a sick friend, and after that, Pearl, for whom time was so elusive, lost count. She merely called for him, to make time pass or to call their lost days back.

One day she began to pick at some eggs Camille Desbordes had poached for her. She had mashed them with a fork, just as Pearl had described to her, just as her mother had done when she was a tiny girl suffering from serious kidney ailments. For her tongue to toy with those shredded bits of eggs in their brothlike yolks was to regain the memory of her own mother crooking her arm around her back, and of holding out the bowl before her mother's trembling spoon. Camille Desbordes held the glass of ice water to Pearl's blistered lips. As the wave of cold fell into her, she thought perhaps now she had a hole in her belly. She felt as though the ice water would flow through into her legs and out her feet.

Camille Desbordes pushed her hair back, and clicked her tongue. "What happened? Too much all at once?"

Pearl pressed down with her arms into the mattress. The bureau ceased to move. She could see once again: Camille's short white skirt and her petite gold blouse. Her brown hair was tied back and she seemed more than tired without her makeup on. Camille Desbordes herself seemed almost ill.

Pearl held her own spoon now, if clumsily. "*La typhöide?*" Camille Desbordes put her arm behind her shoulders and held the bowl out for Pearl to take the last of it.

"You are not to worry about that, Pearl. There is no epidemic in the village down below us." She massaged her arms and ankles and then covered her; Pearl had begun to shake again. "*Ouais,*" Camille Desbordes confirmed. "*C'est fini.* It is the end of that bad story!"

"*Oui?*" she rasped.

"*Ouais.*" Camille Desbordes placed a hot towel on her friend's forehead. "There was only one."

"*Un?*"

193

"Ouais. The patient died."

The syllable bolted out of Pearl's mouth. "Died!"

"C'est fini. The patient died."

Camille Desbordes looked at Pearl's flooded, drawn face. Pearl laughed nervously then, a small squeaky kind of amusement for the sake of them both, and then she laughed until she cried, in fact. Well, Pearl thought, with an odd disinterest, that *would* be the finish of a flood and an epidemic, wouldn't it? When all the epidemic patients were dead. And then she sputtered and coughed a little, as best she could. Of course! She felt a burst of red corpuscles entering her system. She sputtered again. Either way, whether she lived or died, it would be the end of the pseudo-epidemic. She was the only patient now.

Camille Desbordes cooed, touching her lightly on the nose as though she had been the tiniest girl. "You are very lucky to have survived, Queneau," For a moment Pearl hunched her shoulders, afraid the vertigo would begin again, but it did not. She opened her pink eyes. She squeezed them shut, and then again gazed upon the world of her small room. "Only two were chosen, you and Robert Castille. And you will be the one to live. I am here to insure the good outcome of that!"

"Robert?"

Camille shrugged. She did not know who he was.

The next day Camille Desbordes had news. "Even more interesting than *la epidemie minuscule,*" she announced. "Pearl, think of this— you have new neighbors," she said proudly, as though she herself were responsible. Pearl could feel her own face at last perking up.

It had been a preoccupation of their friends to imagine the neighbors who would someday live where the old people next door had resided. The house, which had been empty for two years, its owners off on permanent holiday in Switzerland, had been finally offered for lease in the past few months.

"How lovely," Pearl thought. "New neighbors." But Pearl was now in a faint again and could not explain it to her.

Every day Doctor Christian Malaplate whistled first as he opened and shut his creaky car door. Pearl was glad not to be in *les États-Unis* where she would have had to go to him, sitting in the waiting room for hours infecting everyone in sight and losing what remaining strength she had. And, she would have had to have gone to some impersonal hospital where they might have lost all her charts and treated her for something else by mistake; that had been her experience anyway as a child. But then, the ambulance ride in France with only the comforting hand, the tender word. Perhaps that was why Doctor Malaplate had agreed to leave her at home.

Now resounded the doctor's familiar brisk knock on the street level. Her blue wooden door groaned open on its iron hinges at the bottom of the steps. Then came Malaplate's brusque *"Allô!"* He bounded directly up without her having to expend the energy to call down to him. Such kindness, she thought.

She slept continuously then for three or four days and nights, or was it a week, then two, then three, more? And, who knew who came and went? Ambrose had not written to her, she found out when she woke; her worst fears had been realized. Père Martin had also died, while she was asleep, and had his services. Now—as it was said repeatedly in Café Rousseau, or so Camille Desbordes said—Père Martin could hold Madame Meulemeester's hand for twenty five years, or for eternity, whichever came first. Somehow it was comforting.

Again Pearl dozed, her head propped up, swathed in the blue duvet, her mind reeling.

"Each day, so much *antibiotique!*" Camille Desbordes huffed, smearing bits of *terrine* on the soft inner parts of the baguette. Camille instructed Pearl to hold each bite as long as she could, beneath her tongue, until the urge to swallow was inevitable. Camille shook her head at all the bottles lined up beside the bed.

One day Camille Desbordes held out a long rope of garlic heads. "You require a touch *du l'ail.* Place it--*up.*" She jerked her fingers skyward, and pursed her lips.

"*Non? Mon derrière?*"

"*Mais non!* Up the *front!*" Camille tersely warned. "*Après l'antibiotique,* the fantastic itch could soon begin."

In dismay, Pearl studied the large garlic chain of twenty or more heads, within which lay all the multiple clustered cloves like toes in all their too-tight shoes. "All of them?" she gulped, showing her big, questioning eyes.

Camille Desbordes howled with delight at her sickly friend's mistake. She bent over and laughed until she coughed.

"*Ça va pas, non?*" She poured out a glass of water and spilled it all over herself, she laughed so hard. "Not all, Pearl! Just one clove! *C'est tout.* You are not a waterfowl for Christmas holiday!"

On the way out of the house, Camille started sputtering again, as she patted the bulbous chain on the table. "Remember, Pearl, only one!" she laughed. She started out the door, but came back to Pearl's bedside again. "*Ma copine,* now you can stay alone sometimes. But promise me, use your tiny brain! One small clove only. *C'est magique.* And soon, soon, Ambrose will come again."

And so Pearl did just as Camille said, and that was the last she thought of it for some time. She lay in bed for several days more. She could not say how many.

Camille Desbordes came and went now, always leaving the radio on for her. Each day Pearl cared for herself more and more. She began to sit up longer. She wrote the beginning to a small article on the idiosyncrasies of nesting birds. She sat in their large bath a long while with Bach's cello suites turned up very high, hoping that her next door neighbors with whom she shared the wall to the East would not be disturbed by the deeply sonorous tones. But slowly it occurred to her again: no mail had come.

Camille Desbordes studied the candlesticks on the mantle of Pearl's kitchen fireplace. She rattled the silverware in the sink. A few yellow plates she put in the rack upon the wall. No, she admitted finally, no mail had come from anyone.

∞

Blessings on the healing powers of food!

Camille Desbordes, according to some mystical system, had decided along with Christian Malaplate what to feed their Pearl. Many times the patient had heard the doctor conferring with Camille; they were correcting one another, changing plans. Bananas one day, clear soup and bananas on another, finally touches of pâté on bits of bread until the food would stay in her system and build her up. Then came the healing powers of *roquefort*. A cold soup that Camille had made for her from mushrooms took all Pearl's nausea away.

TO *the* FÊTE

 **WHEN FINALLY SHE STUCK HER HEAD OUT,** a new mosquito net had materialized to replace the one she'd ripped during her fever. From a perfect, metal ring it fell down over her bed. Out she looked through the haze of it, toward the light. The window had been thrown open, the blue shutter thrown back to the outer walls and latched open. "Pearl! Pearl!" voices called from the street. Quickly she moved to the window and popped her head out over the paved way. For a moment she was afraid she might tumble out between the shutters to land like a bundle on the street. In a dream, she had done exactly that: she lay like a shadow melting into the grey black rue below, next to the yowling cats.

But now, what a joyous sight! Her friends from Perpignan were hailing her. "Can you have forgotten?" the wispy, dominating Tomás called out.

"Look at you!" Mimi cried in shock. "Whatever is the matter? Are you sick?"

"I've forgotten something?" she asked, in a daze at the sight of them dressed up, as though they were on their way to a grand festivity. "I didn't know you were coming, please come up."

"But today is *la fête*. It's Bastille Day! My God, you're thin. Get dressed, we'll save you a seat."

"*La fête*? It's today?"

"That must have been some time you two had last night!"

Time had slipped her by and here it was Bastille Day. Here were Tomás and Mimi come to join them for the feast. She watched them striding away, easily, limber and fit. Mimi practically danced with happiness in her short, sleeveless dress. It would be hot today, they had said that. She could not know what temperature it really was. Perhaps it was a fever. But no, her fever was gone, Camille had said. She sat in the bathroom and stared at the mirror on the floor where still it leaned against the crumbling stonewall that they had not had time to plaster. In that mirror, she had seen what Ambrose had seen: her ravaged face. And, in the mirror, she had seen another thing: Ambrose's feet turning away from her, hesitantly, and then turning back toward her again.

∞

"I've packed our basket," he'd whispered in her ear, "I've placed it on the window sill. All our plates and glasses and silver are there. And our tickets are inside. You don't have to do anything, just show up. And get well. Remember—make it to Bastille!"

Ambrose had said that he would meet her at home before the banquet, and if not there, then at the fête. His band was to play afterward for the dancing on the *Place*. Parting words? She wondered now. Why had she not realized, she asked herself yet again, that she had had no mail for these months.

Tomás waved. Mimi's face smiled back at her, concerned. How many of their friends might not have known of her illness? She held the basket in her arms and watched her two friends like stringed puppets skipping down the street in the direction of the *Place*. She gazed skyward into a shaft of orange light falling down over the ice-pink geraniums and lily-shaped lace at the windows across the rue on the little seamstress Marie-Odile's green shuttered house.

Now she bathed herself, washed her long white hair, pampered her still-frail skin. It felt as though it had been forcibly shrunken, or stretched, all of it. She lathered her entire body in the partially tiled vault, waving the moveable showerhead from body part to body part. The works would not seem to fit together, be of a piece. On the bidet, she ran a warm, gentle spray up inside of her in pursuit of a perfect cleanliness in anticipation of her husband's return. A sense of healthiness and well-being seemed to hover in their rooms again.

It had become her room in these last months, her house, without anyone planning it. All around her were stacked the rectangular tiles with their hand-painted village scenes. Each seemed so real she might have fallen into any one of them and become the tiny representation in blue of a real St. Xavier citizen from several centuries past. She dried herself with a thick towel and rubbed milky creams all over herself. She could not get enough of the cream's peppery under-scent.

If Pearl was not at the café-bar in an hour, Mimi and Tomás had said, they would come back for her; and yet, here she was, nearly ready and so quickly.

Today Ambrose would come! It was not in him to do otherwise, they had reassured her, but they had not known of anything that had passed between the two of them. Her dress now fit her like a loose camisole after all her travails of the months before. For the second time it was as if she were donning the atmosphere of a bride. What dress could be too small for her now? Only a child's clothing possibly.

∽

Perhaps she would put the thought of childbearing off for a bit, until she was feeling considerably stronger, she told herself. And if they had already managed to conceive a child? Surely her illness had put it down. She had bled with certain proof of that several weeks before, and she had cried then, too. Perhaps it had been the hormones shifting, Camille Desbordes had said to her, that had made her cry so.

Yes, she had turned into a complete suckling, she told herself, at the thought of deciding anything. Pearl, such a sniveler and weeper, she now said of herself. Imagine any other woman getting so upset over an illness that was not even really the typhoid, much less about delivering a baby. It would be the first thing he asked, if he came. Do you have our baby yet? She had nearly come around to his plan, of being ready to announce the coming baby when his band played at the village celebration on Bastille Day. But still, the silky fabric slid over her lean belly, swaying at the hem as she walked. Hadn't all her doctors warned her mother multiple times that Pearl was too frail for childbirth? Out of pride, however, she had not mentioned it to Ambrose. Surely he could figure that much out himself.

Energy bounded through her thighs in answer to the hot summer sun filtering dangerously through her eyebrows and lashes, along the curves of her face. The skirt kicked out around her knees. Her shoes made a clatter on the street. She tied on her apricot hat.

"*Bonjour! Bonjour*, Madame! *Salut*! We are happy to see you so well recovered!"

Her neighbors, one by one, added how well she seemed, how they had noticed the doctor many times coming to the house. Perhaps she had noticed the pot of flowers they had planted by her own, the young bride's, door? Congratulations, they said. And congratulations again! What else were they saying? They were looking forward to hearing Ambrose tonight! Particularly if there was a success at the cav, where the official tasting of the questionable year's wine was just then being held. Swept toward the dank, buttressed cav by the villagers as they approached, she braced for the worst.

"Madame le Beau!" The eldest of the triplet grocers stepped out from under the stone arch of his store to press a little packet of chocolates into her hand. "We thought you would be living up the road before today." He pointed up the chemin toward the cemetery and kissed both her cheeks, then squeezed her arms.

"Too soon gone, too soon gone, it might have been," his sister joined in. The youngest triplet, who had barely made it into this life, shook her head.

At the FEET
of the BLUE MOTHER

THE LARGE SANDY STRETCH next to the boules court had been draped in an array of long tables and, seated there, over eight hundred citizens beneath the St. X plane trees. The grills and stewing vats had been fired up. Old suspendered men pitched and crowed at boules and roosted on the village benches with canes propped against the fountain lion-heads, waiting for their feast. Pearl's little school pupils, long consigned to another teacher in her absence, rushed out to greet her in their brightly colored holiday clothes. Her older students were sturdy enough now to be playing soccer with the adults in the field.

She had seen her protégés everywhere like flowers erupting ever taller in her village garden, daily standing on line retrieving baguettes for their mothers in the patisserie and then in the other line in the épicerie collecting all their animal and bee-shaped candies, counting out Dracula stamps in *la Poste*, or flying by, *à velo*, through the vineyards. Too soon they would be under one's voiture fixing and fiddling and then out again, pumping petrol, or in *la pharmacie* counting out pills to counter one's maladie and advising certain remedies. They grew too fast! That's what all the faded mothers had declared since the beginning of their village. Time was already going fast enough.

Out behind the school just last fall the children held their own small festival, painting the booths and each other as well, building teepees and frog ponds, engaging in one-legged foot races, playing piñata games with candy-filled balloons.

Often Camille Desbordes volunteered to transform the smallest students into magical animals at these festivals in the sandy schoolyard beneath the green draperies of the plane trees. The renowned oil painter Aimée Vernay had a particular expertise at incorporating the ears and necks of the children into the painted masks, outlining essential parts that other less artistic volunteers seemed to miss. In a few flicks of her brushes, she created new species, horns and manes where there had been none before.

$$\infty$$

"Count your blessings! Even she got to play the skeleton once," Tomás shouted, pointing up at the Madonna surrounded with smoke and radiant in fresh paint, but for the white body print where their priest had sprawled. Monsieur Crusteau the painter, too, looked up at the marks where Père Martin's soaked belly had pressed into the underside of her breasts and forearms, removing last year's touch-up attempt. *Zut!* That week Monsieur Crusteau made yet another try at painting a small patch over the edge of the imprint, but the white silhouette of Père Martin bled right through the new acrylic. In his studied opinion, the expert house painter Paulo Crusteau reported to The Beloved, he would find it a sacrilege to deny what he'd seen with his own keen eyes. He would not proceed with any further attempts to efface the tangible record of Père Martin's miracle.

Crusteau, now at the Blue Mother's feet, bounced a second baby on his knees and played the horsy game, braying handsomely—perhaps more like a hyena than a donkey or a horse, Pearl thought—while Madame C., in her new, blue, designer frock with flounces around her shoulders, prepared a bottle and set out two pairs of baby's silver and a knife adequate for mincing meat.

Already Tomás had proclaimed himself to be presiding over their elongated table. Together he and Mimi helped Pearl to unload her basket, and soon all the plates and cutlery had spilled out onto the white-linened table, and each had taken an appropriate place. Tomás perked up Mimi's roses in their vase.

At TABLE *under*
PLANE TREES

THE DISHARMONY OF FEET AND CHAIRS crunching about through sand and gravel, hundreds of voices singing out in mellifluous greeting, the scent of mountain spices, braising roasts and seafood, the heady aroma of uncorked wines . . . Pearl sat across from Ambrose's plate and fiddled with her scarves while Mimi filled her wineglass, but soon the sun was warm and sensual, filtering through the leaves and through the fabric of her dress.

Tomás, what a charming, furry-headed little man, Pearl was thinking—so like a hedgehog in appearance, so like a range of other creatures, practically a zoo in the range of his spoken voice. She herself felt a little dwarfed sitting between the diminutive Tomás and Mimi who was sleeker, taller than any other woman she had ever known.

"Soon the mussels arrive!" Monsieur Crusteau barked, scurrying past in his white apron. Twenty tables, twenty diners on each side, the dappled shade of the laden chestnuts, the birds nearly colliding with excitement over head, the magpies stalking with Hitchcock strides along the apex of the church roof.

The grocers waved, ringed fingers splayed in the air, as Pearl turned. "Congratulations!" the eldest conveyed again.

"Oh," she sparkled from under the broad brim of her hat, "why, thank you." Camille Desbordes swept by, waving back at Pearl with a face as radiant as a sun-struck chalice.

The church bell pealed and there was a rush to sit down. Babies, crawling and mewling on the other side of the Blue Mother, found themselves nestled on their mother's laps; children, darting up and down the old stone garden staircase, were whisked into their places and told to take their napkins up.

A troupe of volunteers popped down the stone tiers and across the boules court, between the rows of tables, through the kaleidoscopic air laden with shades of light and shadow falling upon pollen and seedling fluff while fragile floating insects like dirigibles suspired over the volunteers' long, white aprons. Immense copper bowls, steaming with mussels steeped in wines and thyme and bay appeared.

On the upper boules court, under the intermittent supervision of The Beloved, a core of chefs joked and poked and stirred at vats and grates for all the remaining soups, and vegetables, meats, and sauces still on the open fire.

∽

Finally, all were seated, the bell was quiet, and Monsieur le Maire Henri Béranger raised his glass and saluted the future of his village's economic and spiritual life. Solemnly he twirled his glass and with a grimace seemed to prepare himself. Certainly he had been tempted on the night before to cautiously preview the mystery wine. Certainly he had tried it when it was merely juice and found it exceptional, but beyond that he had not allowed himself. All across the Place, they raised their palms to their brows and peered out painfully through the sunlight drifting over their fingertips.

But, as the first scent rose from his glass's bowl, the Mayor's nostrils flared like the elegant tufts of the tiny scops owl now neatly perched in the bell tower of their church. A quixotic appearance overcame his face. Was it resignation, or was it triumph? His thick, grey brows ascended into the overhang of his forehead. He raised his glass once more, twirling, inhaling, then very cautiously sipping, imbibing. And then: "Santé! Santé! Tout le monde! Salut!"

Goblets filled and raised, then cautiously tilted. A tide of sighs and then a cheer went up. "And so," le Maire said repeatedly, heaving out a little sob, "and so, this is the result of one little prayer from our own Père Martin—who so recently, just fourteen days ago, so quietly ascended." He raised himself from the grip of his sorrow. "Now on to celebrate the miracle of this year's wine, our life's blood, and also, we do not forget the Bastille Rebellion!"

"From our year, this is our year! Our famous wine! Mine! Mine! Mine!" Philippe the Joiner chanted until Pearl thought he might drive her mad. The world was much too real today! Tomás leaned over Mimi to kiss Pearl on the cheek from time to time, and then back to his wife to kiss her at the tiny place where blouse met bodice over her collarbone.

"Save yourself, Mesdames! From too little pleasure! Moules à la marinière! Indulge!" Jean-Luc Redon summoned over six or seven feasting people.

In every mouthful, it seemed the sparse and stony ground erupted into spiny bushes of rosemary and thyme, swept down and met the mussels of the sea. Jean-Luc clustered his fingertips at his fleshy lips for one moment and set them free. "Congratulations, Pearl!" Jean-Luc Redon howled at her.

Mimi's brows arched in two mysterious pickets. Now Pearl regretted most painfully that she had rejected the beautiful soup, as it had been described to her. Her friends could not help pursing their lips like clams and waving their fingers daintily in the air at the memory of the taste and scent of it, just these few minutes past. "Oh, for a good soup on such a fine day," she moaned, but Camille Desbordes appeared as if waved out of a wand to land beside her with a yellow bowl. "Voilà!"

Madame Gautier played the piston of her mongrel-headed cane on the limestone courtyard parapet and then drove it into the sand until everyone agreed: It would not be the same to eat this dinner in any other order. What a pity, too too sad, but even so, so nice to have the soupe all the same; no one would deny anyone the soupe! "Cheers to Camille Desbordes!" the older lady toasted, and their table mewed at the compliment because it was Madame Gautier after all who offered it, the one who had straddled a motorcycle to the rescue of a hundred, some said a thousand, cornered Frenchmen. One by one. And, then they said, she, fearing to do too little in the cause, had chopped off the German commander's head. That part was true.

"But it is just as nice not too eat too much too soon," Camille Desbordes whispered.

To which Pearl did accede; she could not be more pleased.

An UNINVITED GUEST

MADAME SIMONE, THE ARCHAEOLOGIST, raised her glass to Madame Gautier even though her elder neighbor's dovecote was like to drive her deranged each day, and then turned, surprised, to stare. Here was the hand of a young lost friend perhaps, or some young stranger, arriving to the left of Madame le Beau's gaunt arm. Madame Simone, it was said, was never afraid to pry into the secrets of anyone, living or dead. "Who is this who has come to sit with you, Madame le Beau?" she said.

"Imagine, Pearly!" the Beastly Boswell cried. "And, congratulations! After all this time! I hoped, I even designed, my way to find you here!"

Jimmy Boswell—Pearl's old schoolmate and lover at university, philanthropist and talented even gifted humanitarian journalist from Ireland—exclaimed again, "Imagine my finding you! I followed the trail from your wedding invitations. And, why not? On Bastille Day with nothing else to do. I was afraid you'd be in the top of France, tracking down political coups, in and among yer fascinating insect world."

Now that he had squeezed in beside her, she held out her frail hands to appropriate his slender, warm ones. A smile moved across her face. How pleasant his little goatee in that moment, bouncing familiarly about, as if it might dip into an old inkwell and begin writing for him. His narrow face and elongated form seemed out of a fantasy.

Don Quixote! She had heard it touted about that fate always dealt one on Bastille Day an unexpected friend—whether in the prison or out.

∞

When her Beastly Boswell had stopped kissing her all over her face, and brushing up against her with his neatly trimmed whiskers, and patting both her shoulders, she moved farther down the bench until he sat before Ambrose's plate. "Yer man has really done it now," he said, chucking her lightly in the arm. "So, turns out you've run off on me for a better man after all."

"Not so much better," she said quietly, looking at him there in front of Ambrose's dishes, where Ambrose surely would come to sit, as he had promised so many months before when he'd set out for America on his dreamed expedition into the world and onto musical celluloid.

"Come on now, don't be coy," he exclaimed. "It won't hurt my feelings after all this time. And then you didn't even have the wedding shindig, after inviting me. Twice! Sure, it was just me you kept uninviting. You thought I'd show up and fall into the cake or break my knee going down on it trying to win ya back! Married on the private, so I heard. Just the same, you did it. When does it hit the charts?"

Into his happy blustering, Pearl merely gaped. And then she set to fumbling with the edge of the tablecloth. A bottle of wine seemed to stop mid-air on the far side of the table. Most everyone within hearing was staring at her then, everyone she could see.

"You don't know?" he asked, incredulous. "She doesn't know?"

Then, at the sight of her blank expression, he could not help saying it out loud, "Why do you think everyone is hailing you? Six people have congratulated you since I sat down in front of you just now. Did y' not know?"

"Because I am well again?" she meekly said. "Everyone stared at me because I've been sick. That's all. And, everyone is staring still."

"Were you ill?" Mimi asked. "I thought you looked quite down. Didn't I say so, Tomás, when we first arrived? She didn't even know what day it was! I thought it was a joke."

"Camille Desbordes saved me," she said toward her lap. "I almost died."

Camille Desbordes stroked her hair back from her face, and then a quiet moment overcame them all. Who could think of anything to say?

"Why are they congratulating me?" Pearl asked finally. "Isn't Beau coming?" she asked. "Where is the band?"

"Girl, they've taken a recording contract. A good label, too. How could y' not know anything about it, or even if yer man is coming to you?"

Just now it became apparent to everyone at her table and soon to the others, too, that she, Ambrose's wife, had not known even the most vague of details of her husband's success or even his whereabouts for the last months. These fine points they dredged out of her against her will. Boswell gazed at her aghast, until Mimi, who didn't even know him, kicked him square on the kneecap and the table jumped as if it had been shot with a dart.

"It was in all the music papers! It's even plastered on the wall down at your own shop. Haven't y' been to your own plot then in recent history?" Jimmy Boswell took in a deep breath in confusion and let it out again in regret. "I guess I've stuck my foot in it. Ah, so, it's like that then. Too soon, too. Gee, has yer guy already flown the coop, and you not married even a year then?"

A terrible heaviness filled up Pearl's innards, and it had nothing at all to do with the massiveness of the feast.

Odette, one of the bartenders from the café, ladled out the haricots. "I thought Ambrose was going to play tonight. Isn't he going to come?" Odette asked as she stooped over to deliver the vegetables at each plate on the long tablecloths under the trees. The sun sifted down through the broad plane tree leaves, dappling everything.

Jimmy Boswell moved a little closer to her then and put his arm around her shawl. "You see," he said to everyone, changing the subject abruptly, "Pearl's the living proof. Writers, God love 'em, not one has ever been able to resist my bedazzlin'. And I, I can resist ever one of 'em, 'cept you, Pearl. I'll go home now with you sure, if'n you're feelin' blue. Just say the word. But let's finish off the meal first, my little darlin', if you don't mind. All the courses promise to be quite good. You'll feel a little better after food, by the looks of you."

Trying for a smile with lips quivering inside and out, sitting beside her old friend, himself a gift dropped out of the blue sky—so she found herself on Bastille Day. As for Ambrose, she didn't know which questions to ask. She was struck dumb. And she was certainly not sure she could make it home on her own if she had tried to leave. And here was Boswell now, chatting publicly that though he had made a series of amateur sculptures of her when he'd thought himself an artist, using her for his model, he, Boswell, who noticed such things as an artist automatically observes, had never seen Pearl so small as he was seeing her at this table out-of-doors beneath the sun-streaked statue of the generous and very blue Madonna!

"Where have your magnificent boom-bas gone?" he said out loud, but everyone else had moved on with their conversations.

"Ambrose promised to play here for Bastille Day," Mimi nagged and whined. "He better be coming today. That idiot promised us last May."

"Well, at least he's not dead," Madame Simone said to an ensuing flurry of ferocity. "Well, when my husband wasn't coming home one day, it was because he couldn't. He was dead."

"I haven't seen ya for three years, three months, and seven days, Pearly," Boswell interjected, stumbling all over himself in an attempt to shut up the archaeologist who had never been much good at people. "When was the last time I saw you, girl? Just before you met yer huge lad that was to marry you and then wasn't?" It surely wasn't like himself to muddle up so badly, Boswell was thinking, and when it happened like it was happening now, it was disastrous. "Well, oh Jesus, I'd better shut up and just kiss ya. That'd be safer surely. Unless the gigantic bastard shows up and fires between m' eyes."

"*À bas les pattes!*" Mimi reprimanded, progressing into a drunken state, as she was wont suddenly to do at such festivities. "Why are you talking as if he isn't coming? He said he'd come. Two hours is plenty enough time for The Magic Beau to return. He promised me, in person! When he came by Sète, didn't he, Tomás? He promised all of us. Pearl has only got jitters waiting around for him tonight. *C'est normale*. Ambrose keeps his promises, we all know that."

"We do?" she heard someone pipe up. She couldn't see who.

"He came by Sète?" Pearl inquired in a broken tone at this new information.

"*Mais oui*!" Tomás said, "with the band, on his way out to California."

"And you still didn't know Pearl was deathly ill?" Camille Desbordes asked for her.

"Hours?" Boswell asked cheerfully. "Two hours will do just fine. I do love getting completely tossed in the light of day next to a beautiful woman, particularly one I used to tuck in with every night. I'm here to celebrate the tardiness of gigantic people all over the world. And to put things straight. *C'est parfait*!"

"You," Boswell said to Pearl, whispering the bangs off her forehead, so no one else could hear, and leaning toward her ear, "you look *superbe*, Pearly." He poured out from the carafe a little more wine into her glass and reached around her and under her opposite arm. "Why, Queneau! You always were skinny as a little kid! But in places you had—flesh!"

"*Tais-toi*!" Camille Desbordes snapped at him. "You already said that, you gourde!"

Jimmy Boswell looked discombobulated, even shocked. He took a drunken chance then and quickly smoothed down her breasts, at the table. Automatically Pearl shoved him back. Although he nuzzled her, he saw quite quickly that his affections made no difference at all to her. In fact, his Pearl was about to cry. "Aw, kid," he said. "I'll always love ya. No matter what that crook that married ya might do."

Mimi bounced back then, swinging her legs over her side of the bench, showing off how she'd put autobronzante on her calves, right up to her panty line. Not only were her legs tan, but they sparkled as well. "Oh, don't listen to them," Mimi smiled. "*Parfait, non?*"

"Monsieur Boswell," Madame Simone said then. "If you knew Ambrose like I do, you'd know that Ambrose couldn't write a letter to a lover, or a wife, if you held a machete at his forehead. And he absolutely never telephones. I was his *femme* once, you know—"

Pearl stared at her in horror.

Jean-Luc Redon cleared his rasping throat and flexed his muscles beneath his pale green shirt. "That's truth," Jean-Luc Redon said in English, as a kindness to Madame Simone, Pearl supposed.

∞

Pearl worked quietly on her frittons. Since her illness, it was hard to swallow sometimes now. She had gotten so out of practice. She fiddled with her food as though afraid of it. So there it was, the sickening thought. The whole region knew of Ambrose's success and he hadn't even called to let her know. Or even to see whether or not she had lived. This thought took her breath away. She rose up unsteadily, ready to sob, leaving her basket beneath the table, and stumbled out of the Place and down the winding narrow streets toward home, an image of Boswell's mouth agape left behind. She thought now that she must make it there, to be alone. Just thirty meters to the seventh road, then past the jeering mouths to several tiny streets, around the curve of the meanly linked stone homes with their lower windows bricked to avoid additional property tax. That night it was a far longer way.

Their village seemed like a stage set: the cardboard stand-up kind with the false night sky so imperfectly painted midnight blue. There was no one at all on the narrow lane, of course. It was more a stony maze than a town. Half of the homes had not had any plaster or tint since before the war. It might have been a bombing site, there was so much still fallen down. In fact, stumbling along, she knew it had been exactly that in *le Maire's* time.

PASTEL HOUSES INTERTWINED

 **PEARL HAD NOT DRUNK MUCH** at the festival, but she felt herself to be on a rocking horse in the extreme heat as she moved along the cracked road under the moon. She felt she might lose control and careen off the outer walls of first one of the interlinked houses, then the next, knocking into window boxes and flowers and the occasional iron fence. Or, by pressing her face up against the long vertical windowpanes, if only for the coolness of glass against her face, the vision of hand-tatted lace rose right up against her eyes.

Even for Bastille Day, it was hotter than Old Berthe, who sat with her failing dog at her card table in the street, could remember. Berthe had called out this fact in her penetrating voice when, earlier, Pearl soberly, yet unsteadily and yet happily, had made her way in the opposite direction—going to the fête in thrilling anticipation of Ambrose's promised return.

She no longer knew what would happen, even if he did return.

Her door unlatched in her fumbling hands and soon she was inside and lying down again. They were to have started their baby by this day, that's what he'd required. Probably she could have been heard on the street if anyone had passed by just then, but what did she care? These villagers must have known her to be crying, even before she knew the reasons for melancholy had arrived.

Oh my yes, she did dream of him then, and of the trysts they had had perhaps ten years before they'd settled in together, quite a long time before that Bastille Day, and a longer time, years yet, before the day when he, the love of her life, The Woodcutter, would slide from a small plane on an inclement bolt of lightning, along with his guitar and a number of his music fellows into a scorched vortex of sea. Yes, the man's face and other parts of times long past loomed now large in her daydreaming. And not all of the memories were of the pleasantest sort. Why had she not noticed them?

Doctor Malaplate had a vivid way of encouraging one, of making up nonsense syllables to amuse one when in a fever, so that any nonsense one heard come out of oneself because of the affliction seemed to melt into the surroundings almost rationally. Camille called it tuning. The doctor tuned himself to his patients needs. "He is an excellent *médecin*," Camille said, "even if he is a bit primitive when it comes to accepting the age-old remedies."

She had just gotten to remembering Beau's nimble fingers among the pearly buttons of a particularly fitted cardigan she had always liked, when something like his face popped up unexpectedly in the *fleur de laurier*. Her pulse began to perk up in her neck, when she realized that the face had begun to move in reality and had grown a stranger's disconcerted mouth on it.

It was the reverse of the out-of-body experience that Camille Desbordes had been endlessly talking about lately. Camille Desbordes had described it at the festival dinner that night also: "Who would want to leave her own body?" Camille Desbordes had demanded of no one in particular and then had burst out laughing. "It's all I can do to get someone to come into mine." To which she had been roundly booed as being a liar of the first rank! Why, they asserted, there was the lawyer in St. G, the butcher in St. Y, and the handsome lanky ceramist who had spun her on his potting wheel.

Now Pearl went into the inner garden of her home. For a time she fidgeted, counting out the tubules Beau had carefully strung from plant to plant so that she would not have to carry the water herself when he was gone. When she had finished slopping water on the plants, she started around the other way, counting and sniffling as she went as if she'd been forced into a trance.

"Remember—lifting heavy objects does not prove that you are strong, or intelligent, or even that you exist, Pearl," Beau had said, peering over his new reading glasses and across the kitchen at her.

She put her face down near the roots of his favorite plant, *digitale pourpre,* and inhaled, trying to smell his hair. Her heart began to pound up out of her chest almost with joy. The plant was in a kind of frenzied state without his care, yet it still held a few luscious, rose-colored flowers.

Suddenly behind her then, footsteps clattered up the stone stairs, and Pearl leapt, along with her heart, to her feet with unsurpassed delight, carrying inadvertently one of the blossoms away with her. The craggy face of the Beastly Boswell appeared, rising bit by bit above the stairs for the first time, into the home she had shared with Ambrose.

He found her fallen back down, slumped dizzily onto the garden floor as he came in through the divided door. She sat directly next to the gigantic jester's face Camille Desbordes' ceramicist had tiled in Pompeian mosaic into the floor. In sitting down, she had perched right on one white and crimson-pupiled eye. All this beautiful piecework and soon, she dreaded, the room was sure to become again phantasmagoric.

Boswell sat down beside her, smelling of good hair tonic and luxurious food, and took her face into his hands. "I ran into that friend of yours--Madame Desbordes. She says that you've been desperately ill, my little Pearl. Deathly ill, too. I want to offer, always," he said, "to help you, you should know, if there's anything you need or like from me still—"

She leaned against him, but she didn't say anything. He put one hand like a little cap over the crown of her head. "Yer whole curiosity shop here seems to know how many times the doc stopped by to look in on you. But, none of us, your old friends, even knew you were sick or blue! That cad Ambrose! What a bastard to leave you like that! And to take your wedding away from you. We would have come, Pearl. I would have come down here to take care of you. I could have at least got you to hospital. I could have flown with you home to your little island!"

"He needs a new muffler," she said.

He tilted her chin toward his face and pulled her onto his lap. "A muffler? What are you talkin' about?"

"The exhaust," she said. "It makes a lot of noise. Everyone knows where and when the doctor comes. There can't be any secrets here— with cars like that. That's how they know, or should know."

She couldn't help running through the comparisons in her mind, the very ones the Beastly Boswell had given her, even though she'd heard them somewhere else before: Yes, in France, doctors came to you if you were ill; and they struggled just like everyone else. They didn't make a lot of money in France. But they were the best in the world. When she'd told that to a doctor from America, he'd scoffed, "Why do they do it—if they can't make a good living out of it?"

She'd felt like striking the vainglorious doc, but she'd just looked at him in disbelief, not being the kind to hit, or often even to respond.

"We're all screwed into the same gray matter here in this village, Beastly."

"Bergs," Boswell said with dismay. "Yeh, all the freaky, itty bergs of the world." He patted her head as though it might break, and then he fiddled with a decaying leaf until it came off its stem and floated down beside her knee. He began to make a little stack of them, toying with getting them to land on one another in his cap. "So he just disappeared, eh? Just up and whisked himself away? The man of yer life? Just like that while you were sick and all? Pretty astonishing for one so devoted. You're not someone very easy to forget. I, for one, haven't forgotten you."

"It wasn't like that," she said.

"Well, what was it like then? I'd like to break his feet over his head."

"I couldn't accept it."

"Accept what?"

"I'm used to taking care of people, not the other way around. Beau hovered," she said as lightly as though she had been speaking of bread and cheese, or angel food cake.

She got to her feet abruptly and Boswell followed her to the kitchen milking his goatee. "I'll be off, and on to the next course then," Boswell said as if in self-defense. "I can take your little hints after all this time, I'd think. Might as well return to the scene of the gastronomic. Aw," he said, putting his arm around her forlorn shoulder blades. "The old man might turn up yet. And if he doesn't--" Boswell put his hand under her chin. "I'll move in for the hovering. Come back with me to Paris, or just now—to the party. If you get too worn of the chatter, I'll carry you home again." He held his palms before her in the air, as if to say he didn't need to touch her if she didn't want. But when he went out the door, she found to her surprise that she had tagged along, only a few steps behind.

RETURN *to the* FEAST

 **WHEN THEY ARRIVED AT THE FÊTE AGAIN,** the agneau had already come and gone. "It's all right," she said quietly so as to offend no one. "I'm allergic to it." The fact of the matter was, Pearl was allergic to the idea of eating babies—veal or lamb. She was glad she had missed it. It was her own aversion; others could do as they pleased, though she wished they wouldn't. She tried to perk up a little then, for the sake of society. "Oh all right," she said, when the dessert came round.

No one mentioned this time that she was missing courses and wandering in and out without concern for the order of the meal.

"Only happens once a year, they tell me," Boswell said blithely. "Who knows what might happen anyway if you et something sweeter than you'd ever known. Who's to judge?"

∞

Marie-Odile, the seamstress who lived across the street from her, slid over when she returned. Boswell had plunked himself down beside Marie, too, beneath the zebra-skinned plane trees. A golden light filtered down through the leaves over the Blue Mother who seemed to sway with the breeze in the renewed garden of Père Martin's roses. To Pearl's surprise, Boswell turned his attention in another direction, before she had even been seated. She stood on the sandy earth looking toward the empty stage and then back at her old friend who had enticed her to return with him. There the Beastly Boswell sat, with his arm around the piquant Marie-Odile, his fingers tickling under her chin as she giggled.

The whole table of revelers, when they saw it, took silent umbrage, making a big fuss of moving down for Pearl and hailing her with averted eyes and brows of worry. "What a pretty dress, Pearl!" Camille Desbordes cried for the second time since morning. Pearl sat down among them and Camille Desbordes made a point of tying her apricot-colored sunhat in a bow off to one side under her alabaster chin.

Yes, she could see that Marie-Odile wore the yellow-flowered fabric that Pearl had seen her purchasing in St. X. How exquisitely Marie-Odile had sewn the long chemise herself. It came down in a yellow field with small pink flowers cascading to where her sun-tanned ankles crossed. Pearl made a point of saying to Marie-Odile how pretty she was on this day. Marie-Odile took off her pink neck scarf and draped it around Pearl's throat. "See there, how pretty!"

A puff of perfume seemed to float like a little cumulous cloud, Pearl was thinking now, right out from Marie-Odile's breasts as she leaned down beside her to tie the scarf on. The postmistress' little girl, who had been in Pearl's class two years before, came over to put a pink rose in Pearl's white hair. Beside Jean-Luc Redon on the other side, Patrice the Chemist crowded in, and for a moment Pearl imagined that her old boyfriend would perch the lovely Marie-Odile on his knee. Where, she wondered, had Marie-Odile's boyfriend the photographer gone off to that he'd had to miss Bastille Day for the first time in memory?

"Too good," someone said behind them at another table, but at the sight of Pearl the conversation found its cork. Talk of further inclement weather and the compromised grape harvest surged forth.

"Well, that's the end of the music shop," young Rafael the saxophonist was muttering. In the background, the French rock and roll king Johnny Hallyday blared out of a recorded tape.

"Where have you been for the last hour or so?" Camille Desbordes asked. "I've been all over these tables looking for you. I even barged through the queue to see if you'd fainted in the toilet."

"I found her in the men's loo," the Beastly Boswell said.

"You did not," Pearl said, indignantly.

"She wouldn't let the likes of me in the loo with her," Boswell said, and Marie-Odile laughed, looking up into his light brown eyes. "My misfortune," he said, "following her like that. I nearly embarrassed myself."

The narrow-bodied Patrice pretended to puff his pigeon chest out. "The presence of Pearl is essential to the whole meal. We have always for the past seven years had Pearl with us at the banquet. Without Pearl, it is the middle wrenched out of the cinema reel, isn't that so? Aren't I right, Marie-Odile?"

"Oh, Patrice, don't be such a papa," Marie-Odile scolded him. "Pearl has been to more than a few Bastille Day fests. She just doesn't feel like eating—she's been ill."

"*O pardon*," Patrice apologized. "Forgive me that you have missed the point again, Marie. Next we have here, Pearl, *les fromages*. Pearl, you will have to eat twice as much next year, and maybe three baskets of sweets as well. Here, we will help you. *Et voilà!*"

Camille Desbordes took out her bottle of St. X's famous spring water and poured it into her glass. Across the tables, the weary face of The Beloved rose among the crowd, sadly staring, dreaming of his old companion. He lifted a glass halfway and their eyes flared in recognition.

"Let us speak regarding *cuisine extraordinaire*!" Jean-Luc Redon growled.

"Yes, let's," Madame Simone piped up.

"I'm too full," Pearl lightly moaned. "No more food. Even in conversation!"

"The stomach of Pearl is now the size of one dried legume," Jean-Luc grumbled, leaning over her protectively.

Madame Bezier, the third form teacher, shuffled off from the end of the bench and came around to sit next to Monsieur *la Poste* who suddenly was looking particularly pink-cheeked for a married man.

"Consider the foods we love the most," Madame Simone directed. Madame Simone lived in rented rooms, and not very nice ones, everyone knew, adjacent to Madame Gautier's dovecote. Her apartment was overrun with mice on their way to the granary Madame Gautier provided for her pigeons. But archaeologists were not afraid of mice or bats! Only an archaeologist or someone starving would be able to live in such a place. Camille Desbordes slid in next to Pearl again, and the shifting started up again around the table. Camille Desbordes poured more red wine and passed the carafe.

"You don't really mind talking about food," Camille asked, "do you, Pearl?"

"Not at all," Pearl said lightly from the back of her throat. She had been prepared to eat a little, but she had not foreseen having to picture and analyze it.

"Then, I have news!" Camille announced. "The public health authorities found Ferdinand the Baker's cat Angst taking advantage of a rack of unguarded éclairs last night. And, you will not believe the consequences we must now all suffer for it! Ferdinand was caught on video, filling with crème again all the Bastille Day éclairs—after Angst had licked out all their interiors!"

Everyone within hearing, as one, made the universal sound of the sickened cat and guffawed.

"Now, since last night, we have no baker. Ferdinand must live in the Camargue! The Camargue is as far as he must go to live before the rumors about him here will be arrested. He is now to be the specialist supreme of Camargue pastries-- without our own pleasure or applause and with only white horses and bulls to steal a kiss with his fine pastries. It's a cat-astrophe!" Everyone giggled then and groaned.

"And what about the poor little Angst?"

"That fat cat barely escaped without either the life or the death sentences; he remains at my house, with all my pastries under guard. If only I didn't have to go now all the way to St. Y to buy them. Perhaps, as recompense for adopting Angst, I am hoping for a decline in the mouse population."

"But, what about our bakery then!" Pearl asked.

"*C'est fini, c'est tout,* alas. We drive to Y now. But of course!"

Mademoiselle Pearl did begin to laugh and cry at the sound of that, she did not know why. Her favorite little bakery—gone to the Camargue and maybe never coming back again. Another parting.

She turned her tear-streaked face away and pressed her napkin to her sallow cheekbones, hopefully before she could give away her outburst. What a brilliant smile she could fabricate on demand.

Madame Simone adjusted the shoulder pads on her safari shirt and fanned her face with her straw hat. "Oh, don't be stupid, friends; the world is more than butter and rolled oats." They all looked at Pearl, cooed and laughed, forgetting for one moment only why they had been ill at ease.

"As for the nipple," Jean-Luc Redon announced, taking off on one of his tangents for which he was famed. "Here is a fact worth notification to all at an early age. I myself spent most of my life without this thought, *mon Dieu*. In my understanding until just two weeks ago, in man or woman, each one nipple had only just the one hole. And, out it squirts: the mother's milk! Most people perhaps think the very same, I do not know. How many persons here at our festive table think the nipple, men or women's just the same, has one hole?"

"Don't be ridiculous. Is this another of your ruses?" Tomás asked. "How could it have more, Jean-Luc?"

"Be still, foolish one," Mimi admonished her husband, who set to lightly drumming out impatient rhythms on the tablecloth with his fingertips.

"When I had a little procedure," Jean-Luc went on, his angled eyebrows darting about, "for removing one piece of skin that I did not want—no, not the circumcision, rest assured—your distinguished Doctor Malaplate explained it to me, in just such a conversation as this one, perhaps to distract this patient from the ailment. He is good at comforting the patient. 'The nipple has many, many holes, miniscule,' he said, 'but all in the one little knob.'"

"That most excellent Doctor Christian Malaplate! Always something quaint he knows to cheer you up," the sincere Monsieur Pereault spoke up. "I feel better right away knowing the physiognomy of the breast nipple! I don't know why. It changes the entire world view though, does it not?"

"And I also," Madame Crusteau piped up, just as she was raising her baby from her breast and toweling off. She lowered the blue silk top, handing off the infant, the last baby born in St. X since The Great Dearth of Births had begun, to Monsieur Crusteau. "I will prefer now to think of myself as the sprinkler system. It seems to take some of the pressure off, I don't know why."

Camille Desbordes smiled wanly and applied herself to the third course of the day. "*C'est fabuleux!*" she had to admit.

"What did Doctor Christian Malaplate say to you when you were so ill? We heard today that you had *la typhöide,*" Marie-Odile asked the poor Pearl. "He seems to have made you well."

"Oh no," she said. "I hate to think what I must have had. But, not *la typhöide*. I missed everything. I was asleep."

"She slept the sleep of saints," Camille Desbordes said.

"Oh my," Pearl said, trying to make light of it. "From what I hear, everyone in town has given me a bath."

"Not I!" said Marie-Odile. "I brushed your hair."

"But no!" All her other friends who were gathered around denied it. No, they had not even known of her illness until today, they said. Why had no one who truly cared for Pearl not notified them?

Camille Desbordes went red in the face then at the thought. She grew a little angry even, at the insinuation that she had not yet done enough, that she, Camille Desbordes, had had time to go through all of Pearl's wedding records, wherever they were kept, to find out every address and number of her friends. She had decided instead to save Pearl's life, rather than penning and alerting an international telephone book!

Without forethought, just then Pearl looked down hopelessly at her watch; and, in response, everyone else tried not to look at theirs. In the background, the children's orchestra could be heard in a cacophony of tuning up, without Beau.

Just *a* Stone's Throw Home

"There is a place on the third *colline*, that has latitude exact and longitude for making wishes reality," Camille Desbordes said, leaning across the table for the wine. "It is important to have the right place in order for the wish to take effect."

"O, je sais."

"Je sais."

"I am telling this for Pearl," Camille Desbordes said on a pompous note. "I went to that place when Pearl was ill. I made my wish. I thought I would say so now that she is here. To say so before would have been to make my intentions too strong. My wish was for Pearl to eat. But today, it is just the same! She begins to munch, but she can do no more. I am afraid she will die the death of the Karen Carpenter."

"Thank god, she's not starved to death," Madame Simone cried out. "But just the same, you have saved a life—and an albino girl's. It is a wondrous life at that! Who knows at the beginning what strange things you will see and what will happen to you. I know about that."

They clamored to drink a toast to the one called Pearl being alive, before Madame Simone could go on, clinking their glasses together and cheering her in rather too loud a unified voice. All of them could see that Pearl was secretly pleased with their last part of the tribute anyway.

"I have been to your fine wishing hill, Madame Desbordes! And my wish not only did not come true," the slate-haired archaeologist said, as usual putting her wrench into the good intentions of someone close, but stirring up interest just the same— "I have not now been able to stop desiring it. I am become the one obsessed with a foolish notion. A demon has me now, *toute la menu*. But for you the summons worked. How can this be!"

"What was your wish, Madame Simone?" Madame Pereault asked, squeezing her husband's hand and ministering to her row of red-and-blue-frocked little children next to him. "Yes, tell us, please."

Madame Simone smoothed down her bobbed hair. "No, I can not tell."

"Trickster!" Jean-Luc Redon chided, lighting up one Gauloise upon another and handing it on to her. "Pretty and vicious little tease!"

"*Non*, Monsieur Redon, I only offer my little history up to you as the perfect example of what that place might do to you, if you please, not as material for thesis at *université*."

"I recommended *la colline* for Pearl. Not for everyone," Camille Desbordes disdained.

"Have you ever had such *chevre*?" Madame Simone asked evasively.

"Enid the goatherd has been creating a special mold for the celebration all this year. Goat cheese for eight hundred and always a raft of unexpected interlopers, *bien sur*. This year, in the Incredible Year. And, her goats have not been swept away like some in the flood."

"Madame Simone, you wished for goat cheese?" Boswell said, annoyed. "Is that why you made your trip to Madame Desbordes' perplexing hill?"

"*Mais non*! Many times yes, but not on that mountainside. You missed my point. Diversion was my point."

"Diversion?" Camille Desbordes smiled coolly at her, offended.

"*D'accord.*" Madame Simone puffing up like a hen just before laying out the happy egg. She settled about on the bench. "*D'ac, d'ac, d'ac.* Yes, it is a lovely mountain, your mountain, and mine. Although it seems only a hill. It happened, I cannot deny, not too soon after I had become a widow. I had a stone quite exquisite, and it was painted in the earliest centuries, on the cusp of second century and the third—originally in a cave. In Turkey, if you must know, and now you do! You are like flies in the stagecoach; you must hover over everything! *Mon Dieu*! Is there no privacy?" she laughed at herself, although no one else did. "Anyway, the stone was painted by a small man. I imagined the cave stone painter to be not unlike one, an archaeologist, who had loved me very much in my younger days. I would have done anything for that man, such is the experience of the passion of the archaeologist when *l'amour* is taken away and returned again repeatedly. I could picture him quite well. On the stone also was a dog, very large, the Great Pyrenees, great hunter and protector, fighter of wolves and bears, the protector of *les chateaux*, and so forth. You mustn't let me run on so— Well, you know the dog that *la Poste's* wife keeps under the table there. The one who rescued her child whilst Pereault himself was pirouetting in the yellow inflatable, courtesy of the Post between St. G and St. S.? The same kind of dog he was, on the little stone with the little man." She sipped at her wine and forked the apples circumnavigating the custard center of her tart, but the day was so luxuriously hot, no one thought of stopping her tale, not even Jean-Luc, so she went on.

"Also a little boy and a large woman appeared on the bottom half of the stone and another large man," she said. "Pass the *fromage, s'il vous plaît.*"

Goat cheese and individual tarts were consumed by all, and the most excellent coffee served. Mademoiselle Enid and her son passed their table then to fond notice. "*Salut,* Mademoiselle Enid, *bon fête. Bon fromage!*" the diners at the table interjected as they passed by, without once losing thought of Madame Simone's rambling histoire.

Madame Simone was said to be able to say nothing forever, or something in nothing secretly. And, well, as The Beloved, who had a large collection of leaf fossils said, it all came down to infinite darkness and pebbles anyway with Madame Simone.

"So," she said, "making a long *histoire* short again, it was the location of this stone that I asked about while standing at the proper crossing of latitude and longitude. Before I asked, I thought of it unemotionally, as the question of interest only. I had long ago misplaced it, or probably it had been stolen, so I had thought for a very long time. But still I lived in the same beautiful villa just outside of town in the olive groves, to a period after Francois died. And, the stone had never turned up. There was hope for it, yet it was a small hope, still *difficile.* The stone had been gone for several years. And it was perhaps a meter wide—"

"A meter wide!" Camille Desbordes and the little seamstress cried out, and several others. "You said it was small!"

Madame Simone shrugged as though every last one of them had been born and remained ignorant. It was not long, of course, until they shrugged and realized that, relatively, the stone must have been small to such a one as her, to one who had chipped away at underground caves that seemed to run under the entire continent.

"It must have been stolen, that is what I thought. But in the end, I was obsessed with it. I could think of nothing else. The wishing place had only changed my life in compounding my desire, without producing the object of significance!"

Camille's brow furrowed with the rest. There seemed to be no response to such an inference. Pearl herself thought only to make her own life different, now that seemingly everything had been lost. But she did not know how, and could not stop thinking of it. The betrayal she felt was immense.

Jean-Luc Redon turned to Pearl, cutting off the archaeologist in midstream. "What did you think when you were about to die?"

Startled, Pearl looked up and laughed quickly and briefly. "I thought I would soon be eating a big creamy cheese in heaven," she laughed, smiling through her teeth as though she had taken a bite. The wine was poured again.

The sunlight lay heavy and hot, freckling its golden glitter across each face. But, to the Beastly Boswell, it looked as though the shadow of some dark thought lay upon Pearl's hair. He offered up her apricot-colored sunhat to her and leaned in to help her tie the hat on.

"Oh," Boswell interjected knowingly, unable to look away from her lovely face shaded beneath the brim. "Pearl always talks like that when she lies." Pearl looked shocked, but he could not heed. "And as everyone who knows her well will tell you, she only lies when she absolutely must and then only to make others feel comfortable, don't you know."

"All right," Pearl sighed. "I have been looking for my perfect village, since I was a very little girl up-rooted from a town, very much like this one, you see. Well, in size anyway, and layout perhaps, and amiability. And we still do have *fêtes* like this, in the small rural towns. And saints' days, and fairs for blessing the fleet when the fishing boats go out on Lake Michigan. You have no idea what it is like, how lovely some places in America—"

"Halt! *Vite!*" Jean-Luc Redon roared. "Or, you will take up the homesickness and leave us to go home! What do you mean? You are looking for another village?" Almost reflexively he took out his lighter and lit the candles he had brought and put them in the little tin candlesticks and passed them down the table, as the sun was threatening to go down behind the Blue Mother and over all of them. Yes, in those quick moments, the day had turned from hazy sunlight to a misty dusk, or maybe it was a tearful sentimental glaze that had entered upon their eyes.

"But it was this village, exactly this truly perfect, enchanting village in which I have had the good fortune to live, that I thought I would be torn from as if out of an old calendar, if I died. That's what I thought. I was plagued by malaise. And fear, that I will have to leave her, our village. I am not recovered from that fearful feeling even now."

Jean-Luc nodded in relief.

"I understand you. Like my stone—" Madame Simone interrupted, casting one arm like the rim of a tuna net into the air. "It was some magic thing from my inherited past. I have never felt about a person or a village in that way, I am sorry, no. But, to me a small stone, and an old one, is my one true experience. I have come close," she said, "with men, but, no, not since Francois; for me now, it is the obsession with the identity in the past of a stone. Maybe, I did receive the answer to my wish."

No one said a thing to disturb her peaceful love of a stone after her husband was gone, because among them there was no one who had not felt the experience of lost love, even though some had been far less married than Madame Simone had been. There was also one among them under an apricot-colored hat who now was experiencing the tender threshold—in or out of it, who could be sure?

"But it was not the same for me," Pearl said. "In your village, there are persons to love and miss. In my vision of death, there was no longer anyone here, and I missed her still, the village herself."

"In my vision also, with the stone there is no one else!" Madame Simone leaned over to touch Pearl's hand, and Pearl managed not to draw her hand back.

"Not even your husband who was torpedoed in the war?" Mimi ventured to ask.

"*Non!*" Madame Simone said. "Certainly not that one. I have forced myself to forget. Now I feel nothing at all. When I dream now, fortunately there is no one but myself—it gives me great contentment. Perhaps, Pearl, you will come to this contentment. Even security. Sometimes I think I have never felt so well."

"I have sometimes felt the way you long for, in your history," Camille Desbordes considered. "For me, it is the color and texture of bark and leaves—individual trees, the way the knoll opens outward, and the mint leaves unfurl each day in my garden, the petals beneath my window panes, every day of my life where I have lived for thirty years since I was a teenaged girl and left home…"

"For me, it's Ireland to which I will not force myself to return," Jimmy recollected, a little bitterly, the others thought. "My country—so many differences. I ran away young, I worked long, everyone I loved in that history of mine is moved or buried, aren't they now? It is only the silence there that I feel; but, I cannot feel content about it as you do, Madame Simone. I hope I never will."

FORGOTTEN KEYS

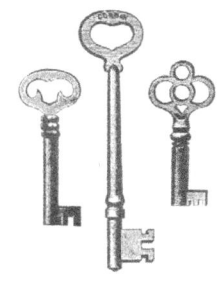 **THE MONTHS PASSED SLOWLY,** and surprisingly, no one called to ask about Beau. Not even the young musicians who worked at their store called to report in on their progress, or to ask advice. One day Pearl felt well enough to drive and set out for their *magasin*. When she got there, she found the music store abandoned and locked and realized that she had forgotten the key. Always her Beau had been there when she'd arrived, but she had not been back since she'd become ill and had to give up teaching school months before. She stared in through the windows at all the familiar shining instruments, the sheet music in sheaves.

Doctor Malaplate had warned her, gently of course, that she would have recurring bouts of illness all her life perhaps, that she would never be completely well, but then she had never been robust anyway. That's what she had said to the doctor. What was good health if you've never had it? But it was a lie. She had had it here and there anyway, for little moments, if not for long stretches like most everyone else.

∞

The night before, she had had a peculiar dream; and now, like a catchy tune, she could not get it out of her head:

Also, you always insist on thinking of me as your brother, Christian Malaplate sighs at last, rolling his eyes and clicking his tongue at her, and then he kisses her on the forehead. I would like to bite you, too, all over, he says finally, if you were not my patient and if you did not absolutely infuriate me while you are in such fevers. Otherwise, perhaps I would resuscitate you!

∞

A note was on the door, declaring that all music lessons were cancelled until Ambrose could return from their world tour. Another message had been scribbled at the bottom stating that a new schedule would be set with new music instructors at *le Maire's* office next week.

Had she fallen asleep again? For here she was with her head on the table, still at the *fête;* Camille Desbordes brushed her arm gently and said her name.

"Pearl. Pearl— Wake up. Look up, someone's here."

The moment she woke she saw relief in the way his one eyebrow jagged up and down over the eye patch, but when he kissed the side of her face and spoke into her ear she heard him say, "I don't know whether I will ever forgive you for your heartlessness—sending me away like that."

Ambrose picked her up from off the bench and held her up, dancing about between the tables like a stringed mannequin. Ebert the drummer, setting up hastily on the stage, feathered one of the drums, calling him. Which was the dream now? She couldn't be sure. There she was sitting at the table again and before her, larger than life, with their friends on the stage, Claud was half-playfully wagging about with his saxophone, ready to knock Ambrose aside while he was strumming his first chords.

"D'accord," Ambrose said into the microphone.

While he played, his face was as impassive as if they had never met. As he stared at her, she felt her own face burning at the sight of his dark hair, his thin-lipped smile and his hazy eye...

With a terrible crash of tin plates, bronze vases, and silverware, his forearm swept everything from the kitchen table onto the floor.

When she woke again, she saw that she was in her bed and her persistent visitor, Jimmy Boswell lay on the floor, wrapped fully clothed in a sheet on the sofa cushions he had carried in from the living room. When she woke again, it was to Boswell's unassailable note: *Off to Paris. Call me, usual number, let me know if he comes home or there's any chance of your wanting me to do the return. B.B.*

LITTLE INSECURITIES

**A VERY REAL, GUTTURAL SCREAM** seemed to commence somewhere near the cavernous cellar. It swept around to rise from the new neighbors' house and burrowed in through the meter-thick common wall. Up the chortling went, seemingly emanating from the other side and moving into the second story where in fact she lay stunned; and then it shimmied by her as if the sound itself had been an eel moving through water, almost undetected, finally to lodge in her side.

The sound rose again then as she grew increasingly conscious. Animal or human? What kind of animal or human had it been? It was not a yammering, though it seemed filled with complaint. It was not crying, though it held a terrible unspeakable pain.

"What was that?" she gasped aloud—to no one at all, mortified and alone.

Her pupils riveted on the one spot in the pale wallpaper from which it seemed the next outcry might come. Now the ululation seemed to emanate from the next room over in the neighbor's house. She lifted up her head and slapped her hand over her own mouth as though somehow that might have some effect. For a time she feared that the new unseen neighbor from Sète was in the act of slowly and pitilessly murdering his wife.

∞

There was then a cringing screech of a tone that must have come from the young woman, so horrifying that it overrode even her own greatest disappointment at having had her mourner's sleep interrupted again. Soon it was high and wailing, followed by a lower yammering and grunting, which she took to be the distant rebuttal of a man. Quickly the higher pitched voice, in some travail, set out to assail him. And then he again gave his utterance, lower but no less sepulchral. Deep, throaty, guttural, thick with a meaning known only to others, someone signaled. But to and for whom? And was it an argument? Or a plea for help? She reached over and turned on the radio to drown out the sounds.

"But what if he's murdering her?" she asked herself. Another bellow and a correspondingly tortured sound threatened to break through the common wall between the two medieval homes.

The mayor had told her to avoid even mentioning the police in the village, unless it was a case of murder—already accomplished would be good.

She sat quickly down again and the wail went up as if triggered by the bedsprings under her. It seemed to spiral from the cellar and ratchet its way around the cornices and whisk out, catching on the irregularity of the terra-cotta roofing tiles. Perhaps an animal was being slain?

"I can't! I won't sit still and listen to a person losing—being killed!"

She looked into her softened, meager face in the gilt-framed mirror across the room. "No matter how afraid. Especially not now, after all of this—"

She got up, pulled on her dress, and slipped into her sandals. If only Beau were there, he would go with her! He would take up his shirt from the back of the little blue chair. "No, I'll go," he would say. "You wait here, Madame, and rest yourself."

Very slowly and curiously she then commenced to sniff the air as she went into the hall. All my senses have perked up! she thought. How unusual! She felt more alive than she could remember feeling for months. Riveted with fear, her jaws clamped together in determination.

Here, she said to herself while passing into her kitchen. I'd better take this along then, if I'm going where I'm not wanted. She snatched up the fruit basket Mimi had brought her that day. For the briefest moment, she looked at the knife expecting to leave it behind and then, thinking better of it, she set it also into the basket.

The berries were especially ripened, a dark purplish as if they were about to burst veins; the plums and pears, too, were mature. The figs were equally ready for tasting, nestled in the powdery blue of the napkin with the one persimmon to its side. They were almost too beautiful for life, she thought. She took one out and laid it into the blue bowl, and set off down the stairs and into the suddenly all-too-quiet night. Was she hurrying or was she hesitating on the cuff of time.

Whatever the new neighbor might like, he would not be ready for visitors carrying baskets of fruit so late. As soon as she was down the steps and out the door, she stood before their entrance, conjuring. His shirt would be hastily and wrongly fastened with perhaps a ruff of brown slipping out around the buttons. Blood. There might be blood.

She pounded on their door until she thought she had begun to feel the correspondent rattling even in the stone cellars below, and even in the street. Impossible! she thought. A late crowd gathered outside the house now on their way home from their own private, after-party fêtes.

"Yes, yes, such a caterwauling! We heard it, too."

"And such a shame when Ambrose's wife has been so recently ill."

"I met her once but they say I wouldn't know her, she is so changed."

"Ah, the poor honeymooners," someone whispered as if she could not hear.

"I have a conference tomorrow. And with this racket I can't sleep or hear myself think any better than a pair of shoes!"

"And, now he's disappeared, so handsome, the pair of them. And now she's to have inconsiderate neighbors like that, *mon Dieu!*"

The desperate sound ripped from the house into the street. Everyone fell silent, horrified and listening. Pearl clung to the doorknocker.

"*Mon Dieu,*" the little seamstress from the other side of the street cried out, appearing beside Pearl at the door. "It sounds as if he's pulling out her nails!"

"Marie-Odile! I wish you hadn't said that!"

"One by one," the short garagiste with the dimpled chin ventured in a hushed voice, as the scream repeated and echoed up the rue.

A small discussion ensued about breaking down their door, but it seemed, after all, that the sounds had stopped while they had been in the grand debate. Finally, out of frustrated good intention or boredom, one by one, the neighbors drifted home. Up and down the streets, a rash of radios roared on at full blast to cover the possibility of a repeated experience. Pearl stood again in the tunnel the street made against the night; she set the basket on the new neighbor's stoop and returned home. "From all your neighbors," she had written. "We wish to welcome you. We wish you many peaceful nights."

ETIQUETTE *on* RUE VIVIENNE

CAMILLE DESBORDES HAD LONG SINCE stopped bringing Pearl food; and so, now, against all her own wishes, Pearl had to come out of her house regularly to shop. One day the neighbor woman and Pearl happened to emerge from their houses at the same moment. Why! How familiar the neighbor looked, standing on the stoop like that with her back to Pearl! And, she did not look even a bit bruised from the back, even in her sleeveless dress!

"Bonjour, Madame," Pearl called, but the woman did not turn around. Off she started down *la rue* without even one civil word. Stunned by her rudeness, Pearl stood staring after her until finally she began to follow. It was the only way to leave their *cul de sac* anyway, in order to arrive upon the center of village life.

On this day Pearl was on her way to important business: to *la Poste*, she was going to inquire whether they had had any word for her of Beau's whereabouts. Perhaps, she hated to admit, he had been so angry with her that he would never speak or return; but she could not imagine that he would not have changed his address or let someone, perhaps one of his sisters, know. If they had had no word of him, she was prepared to call or even to go to Lyon where his sisters and his mother had moved and inquire of them.

When she came to the outlet of the street, she turned in the direction of the *Place*, continuing after the pale yellow dress and ponytail that belonged in her neighbor's house. How pertly the woman moved along, far too jauntily for someone who might have endured such pain on previous nights. Finally, Pearl began to run after her, calling, "Stop, please wait, Madame." But, the young woman turned a corner and ducked inside, behind one of the extravagant bronze doorknockers with the faces and figures she had so often admired. Behind which one could the woman be? The lion's head? The mermaid? Or, the eel?

How rude, she thought. Now, no one wishes to speak to me because of what Beau has done to embarrass the villagers at the most important *fête* of the year. In effect, her groom had silenced the festivities and put a stop to even the dancing! It was he who had first organized the musical aspects of the village, installing a love of performance in even the smallest children at the church and school, and he had abandoned them. To say nothing of how he had abandoned her during and after her illness, on the word of an old friend! How could he blame her for this?

It was a disgrace, she could not help but admit to herself. She would have been angry with him even if she had not known him personally. And now all the little children were disappointed and would have to be rerouted into other musical plans. Some would not be able to make the change. Their enthusiasm would be lost.

More than one village had denounced him, to be sure. In Café Rousseau it was said that he had put fame and money before her, his own wife, whom he had insisted upon marrying without a ceremony, against her will! She had overheard them saying it in Café Rousseau, and beyond, more than once.

In the *boulangerie*, she chose her daily bread and two small quiches, one admittedly just in case of Beau's possible return. She had been buying extra food for him, hopelessly, ever since Bastlle Day. Another chicken was turning to rot in her tiny refrigerator. She would have to throw it out, now that it smelled each time she opened the door. She had been afraid not to prepare for his return, for fear of the bad luck that negativity could bring.

And even worse, on their terrace overlooking the castle, and in their central courtyard, the rain barrels had gone dry and nearly all of Beau's gardening splendors had died. She herself felt too frail to carry the water pitcher back and forth to them. It was enough to get to the *Place* to buy food without collapsing in the street. She felt as though her veins were shaking inside her frame, along with the marrow in her bones.

Certainly it felt shameful to ask anything further of Camille Desbordes, after her speech at the *fête* about the sacrifices she had made for Pearl. Surely she would have appeared if she had wanted to help her again. More than likely, Camille had encompassed herself in the effects of having a new beau.

Now just as she was going into *la Poste*, out came the pony-tailed woman, face to face. Full-mouthed, smiling directly into Pearl's face, the beautiful woman raised her hand in greeting. She smiled radiantly at her, attempted speech, and then passed by. She had seen her after all! Now she knew why the beautiful couple Beau and she had happened upon in the woods had not noticed them when they had stumbled practically right onto their lovemaking. Now the beautiful couple were their new neighbors, and were entirely deaf.

The MAHOGANY DESK *of* LOUIS QUINZE

 **BY DAY, PEARL QUENEAU WORKED** in the music store, organizing the instructors and the children's lessons. She managed to reestablish the children's choir from among her school children. Yet, at night, she was so alone it seemed the very air of their house shimmied within the dust of abandonment.

Time slipped along month by month until one day in the store, three years later, she was recording the purchase of a child's flute in the ledger. She'd come to take pleasure in keeping these records on the beautiful desk set with the enormous paisley-filigreed pad and the matching cup for pencils, the ebony ink well and stand. How carefully she dotted her letters now, and flourished her capitals; how she marked off every franc so accurately.

One flute to the tiniest of Pereault children, Laurent, she wrote down, and in parentheses: (*small blond boy with scar like a scarab above left eyebrow, received in the recent dust storm, his mother said.*) All the children's names came easily now and to which instruments they aspired. Just as she was crossing the seven in her ledger, she heard footsteps and glanced across the room. Up, she looked toward the approaching customer, and nearly fell off the chair where she was perched behind the shining mahogany surface.

There Beau towered, slightly larger through the chest and shoulders, slightly more stooped, with the glimmer in his eye. She practically drove her fountain pen through her papers at the sight. "My Beau!" she cried out loud. The domineering virtuoso, who had disappeared from her life years before, hung his baseball cap on the peg outside the door and marked the building closed that day for business.

∞

It was not long until the townspeople had the story, after he himself told it round Café Rousseau: how Ambrose le Beau had set out with the boys from his French blues band to arrive in Los Angeles. There, in the first weeks, they had been robbed of all their cash and instruments and equipment; and he in the fray had nearly lost a lung and had been sent to hospital. The other band members had drifted off in a haze of good tidings to earn their instruments back. At first he had worked a little as a waiter after he got out of hospital, and then he had been a cook in a hamburger joint making everything but the famous hot dog. and ended up playing solo guitar until, after three months, slowly the rest of the band drifted back to where they had started out and joined him on the stage.

Non, the famous recording contract had not happened easily, but surely that was just bad luck. Now it had really happened.

Les États-Unis were just as he'd suspected. The man who'd stabbed him in the chest had also carried a gun on his hip, he said, or perhaps he would have fought him off a little more seriously. Ah, but what did it matter? *Non,* how could she think he would have been discouraged? It had just taken quite a lot longer than he'd expected. Eventually it had all come to pass, just as he knew it would. After all, he was French!

She asked him why he had not written to tell her all of this, and he looked shocked.

Did no one tell his wife that he had never written a letter in his life but to *le Maire* whom he thought of as his father? It was a matter of pride, he said. Surely someone had thought to tell her that? The Mayor, who had kept the band's forwarding address since before his departure, had written him almost daily about her progress. Had the mayor not told her anything? Ah, perhaps The Beloved had thought it a matter of confidence. Soon perhaps she would be speaking to Ambrose face to face, *le Maire* had been suggesting for the last few years, until that very day when she had followed The Beloved's hints to the music store where Beau had nearly knocked her off her feet with his one-eyed glance.

FLARES

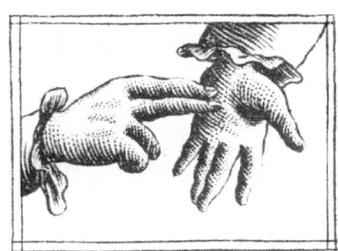

AS IN SOME FOLK STORIES, the returning hero lost no time in regaining lost ground. He tried not to notice how his wife stood back from him in dismay. The *fermé* sign was posted in the window, and the metal shutters were lowered to the pavement. As soon as he had hunched himself into her smaller car and she was safely secured beside him, they sped home to what he hoped would be a noisy reception.

When the wind murmured later on that evening and she lay coiled against his chest under his heavy arm, slicked into peacefulness by his perspiration, a summer storm rose up with such volition that the long curtains at one end of the house lifted straight out horizontally, nearly into the adjacent rooms. Even the draperies at the doors in the long central hallway did the same, swelling through the entire house, mounting with the furious winds and their rich odors of damp vines and rain-slicked pavement. Along the downwind southern side of all the houses, neighborhood laces plunged out the windows above the street into the sudden shower.

∞

Pearl could not know what their neighbors were fighting about, but she tried to consider it one day when Ambrose was not at home. As she said to Camille Desbordes, it might be something as simple as the telephone bill. But Camille Desbordes had seen the deaf man himself with a young red-haired woman at the sports café in the neighboring town. She said they had been signing to one another very intimately.

"Perhaps she is his sister?" Pearl offered. "He has a nice, slightly reddish cast to his hair as well--"

"No," Camille said. "His sisters have normal hearing, or so I heard in the *Bar des Sports*."

"But the sister would still sign to him," Pearl noted. "Everyone he knows must sign to him."

"Oh yes," Camille Desbordes laughed at herself. "Of course, that would be true. Still," she said, "he had his hand on her knee—not that there is anything wrong with it."

"Ah well, that might be entirely innocent," Pearl said. "And, as you say, Who cares? Still, it might solve the mystery."

Yes, Pearl could see that that might make the slender deaf woman next door to them rage rather seriously then—if she knew and if she minded.

"If the deaf woman has the jealous nature—" Camille Desbordes reminded. "We don't know whether she has the jealous nature, Pearl."

"We all have the jealous nature," Pearl contended. "Whether we like it, or claim not."

"That is just too, too American," Camille scoffed.

Camille Desbordes herself did not have it, she claimed. And perhaps she did not. Pearl could see that in Camille Desbordes for one, who had proven herself an extraordinary woman in most all ways, perhaps there were no jealous bones or muscles in her. Still, Camille was the one who had suggested a problem with the red-haired girl.

"Well, one thing is true," Pearl offered. "If those people make noise every night I am going to want to do something. I can't even pound on the wall or go knock on the door to stop them."

"Flares," Camille Desbordes suggested.

"Flares," Pearl said, in slow and delightful dawning. "Oh my goodness! Flares!"

Camille Desbordes had the solution always. "Throw a flare at their window! Then all you have to listen to are the entire village coming out to scream at you along with *les pompiers*, who arrive to stop your village from burning down to stones and soot."

"Oh! I wasn't going to throw it actually in their window! Why did they have to move in right now?"

That night the neighbors began again, just as Pearl was preparing dinner. "I was going to drop a note through their mail slot yesterday," she said to Ambrose, jotting it down, "asking if they needed help, and explaining." After her illness, she could not abide loud noises. She could not seem to stop the shooting pains they caused.

"Pearl!" Ambrose was horrified. "You are going to write to tell them that they are disturbing our silence when all they have is silence? I am disappointed in you. This is not *l'Etats-Unis*, Pearl. We do not attack people here for the special talents God gives to them."

This last barb stung her so deeply that she went in the other room and sat at the end of the sofa where she did not think he could hear. She cried into her hands. When Ambrose came in, she tried to sit up straight and look away from him as though nothing at all had happened. Soon she realized that the sobbing next door had stopped, as if the beautiful couple were now impossibly listening for her. But, in a moment it commenced again. Oh no! she thought. At the sound of such unaided misery, she feared she might grind her own teeth down.

"Perhaps these sounds do not affect you?" she said bitterly, and ridiculously, she realized almost immediately. She could not help crying again at the desperate sounds the woman was making. "What is he doing to her?" she asked again. "How can we just sit and ignore them?"

But Pearl had seen the woman again on the street just that day. She had dyed her hair now and cut it into a short black cap of pixie hair, cut all around her head as if with pinking shears. Her short skirt revealed long, thin, beautifully shaped legs without a bruise on them. Her arms and neck and shoulders, also, were growing tan as the summer progressed. There was not a violent mark to be seen.

"Sounds do affect me," Ambrose said softly. He took hold of her hands; and she thought she might withdraw them. "Of course, sounds affect my every mood. All of your sounds affect me also. Even your most private ones, Pearl, the ones you think I don't hear." He trained his honey-colored eye on her until finally she could look at him. "I live for your sounds," he said. "For the living orchestration of you."

"That's because you are a musician," she snuffled, dabbing again at her thick lashes where the tears were starting to well and glisten again. "And because you are so incredibly kind, and forgiving to everyone— And because you are the kindest man, I ever met--" And then, Madame le Beau was blubbering again, quietly, in the sudden tranquility that met them from next door. "But why, oh why, did they have to move in next door to us? Just when you've come home."

And why did you leave me for so long without sending word that you were okay? she wanted to ask. What kind of man would do that to me?

Ambrose the Bandmaster was having other thoughts as well. How could he have lost such an important start in the world, the very one he'd so desperately sought? How could anyone now respect him? He had almost refused to come home, but for The Beloved's constant and unanswered nagging in postcards and even elongated letters. Once also, *le Maire* had tracked him down by telephone. Ambrose had let the whole village down; he knew that. He had been a great hope and then an embarrassment. About this The Beloved never wrote and had never once admonished him, even when he had at first appeared at *le Maire's* door several days ago.

"Shhh," Ambrose whispered to her. "Be quiet. Shhh! Do you want the whole village to hear?"

SATURDAY BAZAAR

 **IN SPITE OF THE GREAT DEARTH OF BIRTHS** in St. X, which had lasted now for just over three years, they were in a rage of trying then to conceive their Robert or Olivia. Pearl set aside all her qualms and thought perhaps the illness had numbed her. And soon, there was no one who mattered to her but Beau and their would-be family, and the children she'd taught and the children who came to their little store. Every dawn, he bathed in the good fortune of his return and slept a little later, while she lay watching the giant sleeping. His broad pink nipples rose and fell, nestled in the moderate pelt along his chest, his long hefty shanks stirred as he dreamed, his Adam's apple nodding occasionally above the pocket at his collarbone. She lay her cheek against his arm as his breath beat out a gentle wind tune.

"*Mais non!*" Beau cried, slapping his forehead before breakfast.

"What is it?" she returned, sitting up in bed. She had never seen Beau waking in a bad mood.

"It's Saturday!"

"You love Saturdaty."

"All day," he said. "Those neighbors will also be home today. On my Saturday!"

Ambrose loved to lie in bed with her very early Saturday mornings when he didn't have to go to work. The shop kept them going financially between his musical forays, but for the rest of his Saturdays now, each week he had someone else employed. On Saturdays they went to the market and bought their goat cheese and *saucisse*, their pastries, and weekend vegetables. They bought the newspaper and stopped at the hardware store. Then they rushed home, had coffee in bed and made love all Saturday afternoon, before they began their weekend projects on the house, painting and sawing and fixing late into the night.

Now they heard it beginning again next door—the whimpering. It was nothing like they had ever heard anywhere before.

"We could go to the market again!" she cried. "Perhaps they will be gone by dinner. Or we will go on a foray. We will go to Sète. They've come from Sète, we'll go to Sète. For the weekend!" she said.

"*Zut!*" Ambrose pouted. "*Zut! Zut! Zut!* I am going to write them a note myself." The kitchen drawer gave in with a groan and jerked open. Ambrose took out a pen and the scratch pad.

"Now, now," she said. "Silence is all they've got," she reminded him.

"Well, we haven't," he brooded, chewing on the end of the pencil and throwing it to the floor.

She rubbed his arm and reminded him silently of other formerly honorable statements she'd heard.

"Well then, come on." He steered her into the bathroom where the floor tiles were stacked against the wall. It was the only truly interior room in their house. And the bath was nearly Roman, it was so large. They had already finished preparing all its surfaces for the tiles, the week before her long-ago river illness.

Beau pulled the outer heavy door closed and opened it again, listening. The new neighbors were strangely silent.

"God bless them and keep them," she said "for once they've put a cork in it."

"'Put a cork in it.' What an amusing saying."

"I am going to learn sign language," she said, "so I can teach it."

"You are?"

"Yes, and so are you."

"I am?"

"*Bien sur,*" she said, caught in the doorway between coming in and going out.

A Sunday Roman Bath

 **Tea steamed in their cups** as they shifted onto the terrace, staring out through all the flowering plants Ambrose had arranged to hang from the arbor. An old man in a black suit jacket and beret peddled his bicycle through the vineyards toward the castle. Monsieur Pereault's bright yellow *camion de poste* sped down the lane into the far side of the landscape. The sun streamed hot and cozy onto them through the vines.

She thought of the installation attempts they'd already had for the baby. For hours that morning, they had lain luxuriously among the ceramic blue and white scenes of ancient village life. After a time she'd hung her head over the side of the tub, panting for water. Beau turned the shower on her, and soon enough they'd been floating in the bath.

"Now what shall we do?" Beau asked, dropping his dark, wet head back into her arms. Gently she bit the tops of his ears.

"Careful!" he warned. "Or, I will be like the famous alien! The Spock! Careful! Our children will be pointed."

She bit the top of his ear again. "Astro-turf!"

Afterward, they tiled the entire bathroom floor in a flurry of activity that normally would have taken them most of the week.

Later in the day, "I didn't see you two at the market," Camille

Desbordes called up from the street. "I brought you some things. You have to eat plenty of goat's cheeses now, Pearl, if you're trying to put in a baby, especially when the town has the curse of the flood on it. And, here is a chicken. Roast the chicken with this quail inside of it." They heard the lower door opening and Camille's big gypsy basket being left on their lower step.

When Pearl had roasted the supplies, inside the chicken nestled the quail; and inside the quail lay the unfertilized dove's egg. "You!" Beau said, holding up a boiled egg with a plum inside of it and a ripe cherry at its interior. With his mammoth yet delicate hands he drew apart the cherry and found the dab of caviar she had decided to install there. He offered her half of the leftover spread of tiny black eggs, and they ate them together. Their new neighbors could be heard running about like mice in the walls, she observed, but they were not attempting to shout at one another or kill themselves. The village seemed to fade away then. The wind must have changed direction, because the curtains floated back into their chamber, drifting toward the bed and its dreamy canopy.

There was something to be said for extreme heat. How sweetly Pearl slipped over him again and again; how gracefully the body slipped into another's fluids. When they woke, the bells were ringing. Hand in hand they went into the village. They sat together so closely in the *Place*, their hands together, the Blue Mother over them. The air reverberated with the unique languages of birds.

BLUE DOORS

**IN THE CORNER OF THE MIDDLE GARDEN** was an old stone sink set against a concrete wall. Ivy grew there, and the passion flowers. They could see out over the ruins of the ancient castle. Wild boar briskly nuzzled one another in the moonlight beneath its walls. Out there, the vineyards stretched past St. G, and on toward Nice, and beyond through Italy.

At their feet, the lower village lay half asleep, and the town road ran intently toward the neighboring castles and hill-top villages. From down below came the friendly chick-chick-chick of Monsieur Nabot's lips as he encouraged his horse home from Café Rousseau, followed by the horse's snuffling and snorting, then the whirring of the slightly crooked wooden wheels over cobblestones. The little scops owls emitted their electronic honing tones, and the cicadas offered their late summer susurrations.

When they had returned home again, they situated themselves on the balcony terrace to watch a strawberry moon rising over the vineyards. Beau sat down between Pearl's legs. He put his head on her thigh. "Do you think she, or he, is already smiling in there?"

"Yes," she said, stroking his hair. "I think she, or he, is already smiling."

Beau lifted up his head in the shadows and gazed at her. She stroked his haggard forehead. Nothing would ever be able to take his experiences in America from his face. He put his cold glass on her leg and she jumped a little. "Not falling asleep?" he laughed.

"Not I."

Beau sighed contentedly, turning his head on her knee. "Let me see if I can see."

"See?"

"Yes." He stood and began lighting the candles he had strung all over the balcony garden. So many times they had enjoyed sitting outside, concealed from the street, listening to the slight flicking of wicks. "Let me see you." He offered her his hands and pulled her up. He lifted her onto the stone table, then buried himself under her skirt and slipped her panties down over her calves and feet. "Let me look for her—or him," he said holding the flashlight up toward her. "Let me see."

"Stop it, silly," she fussed at him. "You're not completely mad now, are you, Beau?"

"Yes," he laughed, "*sans doubt*. Mad as the hat. Mistral mad!" But then he was all seriousness. "But no, I have given up sniffing such madness. And I will never again! For you, I am reformed!"

The feel of the stone table was quite different from a wooden one, its smoothness and its strength together all at once. The cool surface was such unrelenting relief to the spine in the searing heat of the summer night.

Leaning backward over an ivy-covered wall, held only by one's lover to keep from falling into the street below, one might increase the angle of reception, the chance of a son or daughter. One's hair fell down in sheathes far beyond one's own existence as if one were part of the foliage descending to the turf below. One felt wildly alive as the breasts, too, slipped downward toward the street, the face and arms growing heavy with blood. The weight began at the back of the eyes and in the neck; and even the forehead began to seethe with heat as he burst in upon you again then again and again, from where he stood firmly rooted on the terrace, thinking of nothing else and no one at all.

Only years later, long after Ambrose had passed from their idyllic world, would Pearl realize that he had been peering into her to look for a flush of blue in the door to her cervix that would mark the coming of their little child.

In due time, it was mentioned by many a villager in Café Rousseau that the Deaf Woman of Sète was seen to have stepped out from *la boucherie* with a large package clasped to her swollen belly, there to be seen by her neighbor the Pearl, standing across the way near the village fountain, surrounded by blooming irises, and quite swollen herself. On the other side, the little unwed seamstress was looking very plump. And across the road, also the beaming wife of Pereault de Poste, and there, the new woman baker. Ambrose and all the young fathers could be seen strutting about, not unlike the new Monsieur le Coq after his morning crow above his newly painted sign astride the door between the *boucherie* and the *tabac*. No child coming to reside in the ancient center of that village could have wished for more playmates than the Beautiful Couple of Sète had inadvertently started up.

As it would turn out, of all the oddities of that little orchestra of playmates who had been formed in those years, the most useful would belong to the sunny-haired Quinn Queneau le Beau who wore the slightest scent of garlic near his right ear, and who was lauded, even in his earliest years, for having such exquisite hearing that he could predict the duration and intensity of inclement weather, even before it had begun to venture toward that exquisite little village niche between mountain and Mediterranean: St. X.

About the Author

 **Meredith Steinbach** is the author of *Village with Blue Doors, Beata Rustica: The Tale of the Would-Be Saint, The Charmed Life of Flowers: Field Notes from Provence, The Birth of the World as We Know It; or, Teiresias, Zara, Here Lies The Water, Reliable Light,* one play and numerous short stories.

Prizes and honors have included 2013 Paris Book Festival First Prize/international general fiction category; 2012 New England Book Festival, Honorable Mention/general fiction category; Thomas J. Watson Institute Travel Grant for Research in France and Greece; the Bunting Fellowship of Radcliffe College at Harvard University; O. Henry Award for the Short Story; 100 Distinguished Stories, Best American Short Stories; National Endowment for the Arts Fellowship; Pushcart Prize for the Short Story; Rhode Island State Artists' Grants, and the University of Iowa Fairall Scholarship for a Fiction Writer.

She lives in Rhode Island in a sea captain's cottage with her family and a spin-dancing corgi and a Great Pyrenees mountain dog. She is Professor of Literary Arts at Brown University.

Previous books by Meredith Steinbach:

THE CHARMED LIFE OF FLOWERS: FIELD NOTES FROM PROVENCE

a novel by Meredith Steinbach

 *THE CHARMED LIFE OF FLOWERS* is award-winning novelist Meredith Steinbach's magical tale of camaraderie and delight in the face of adversity. Professor Steinbach reconsiders and reconstructs the components of an old-fashioned fairy tale in this modern day novel set off the beaten path in the vineyards and olive groves of Southern France. When Pearl Queneau, the little albino schoolteacher, seeks refuge in the village of St. X, even the plants and animals transcend their days as textbook entries and come to life for her. Here she falls in love with the proverbial Woodcutter and raises her son in an atmosphere of increasing tolerance and generosity---but for the ill will of a few miscreants who would try to cause them irreparable harm.

REVIEWS & ACCOLADES:

Winner, 2013 Paris Book Festival, international general fiction category

Honorable Mention, 2013 New England Book Festival, general fiction category

CAROL LOEB SHLOSS, Carol Loeb Shloss, author of *Lucia Joyce: To Dance in the Wake*): "This book is as improbable as it is delicious, as dark as it is full of rapture. Above all, it is a meditation on the delightful colors of all growing things: adolescent sons, surviving mothers, and the eels and hedgehogs and plane trees and flowers that inhabit the small villages of our imagination. An amazing read... so scary and yet so incantatory."

JOE W. HALDEMAN: "*The Charmed Life of Flowers* is a love-letter to Provence and to the lives that are intertwined there, animal kingdom and the vegetable one, as well as the charmed and charm-less humans who drift through and observe, and know a little. The writing is evocative and accurate and hard to put down."

THE BIRTH OF THE WORLD AS WE KNOW IT;
OR, TEIRESIAS,
by Meredith Steinbach

"In her fourth book of fiction, award-winning American novelist Meredith Steinbach reimagines the life of the Greek seer Teiresias. Having outlived everyone he ever knew, the seer looks back at the most significant episodes in his life--a visit to the Delphic oracle, mediating arguments between Hera and Zeus, his experiences as both man and woman--as he confronts the traveler Odysseus in the Underworld. Narrated from shifting points of view with tremendous psychological acuity, Steinbach's novel intertwines time, event, and narrative."

Reviews:

Publisher's Weekly: "…a metaphysical tour de force. Steinbach's writing is as elegant as a neoclassical column."

St. Louis Post Dispatch: "Her latest work of fiction, *'The Birth of the World as We Know It,'* [is] a witty cross-breeding of Greek tragedy and contemporary fiction. Think James Joyce and Homer in a running conversation."

MARJORIE GARBER, Harvard University, Vice Versa:
"I take the liberty of quoting at length because Steinbach's work is not as familiar as Eliot's or Joyce's, and also because Steinbach does something they do not. She imagines Teiresias in the moment that will answer the gods' question."

Chicago Tribune: "The source of the considerable strength of *Teiresias* resides not only in the vividness with which Steinbach imagines each event of her narrator's life, but in her willingness to let those episodes collect and cumulatively resonate in her reader's imagination...narrated with an extraordinary and just passion."

Harvard Review: "superbly orchestrated, ornate, convoluted retelling, one in which she has spiced up, ad-libbed, and otherwise domesticated, re-routed, authenticated, and tampered with the archetypes. Steinbach seems to be following no other voice than her own; the result is a shamanistic meditation on the telling of time, the telling of history."

Boston Review: "She is like Joyce, mingling an ironic undertone with sensuous descriptions of vintage cosmetics, sexual sporting, war, and grief. Plot is shiftily dispersed throughout the book, playfully revising the natural sequence of events, so that the novel reads rather like a long, accelerating prose poem borne forward by its rhythms."

ZARA, by Meredith Steinbach

"'Zara Montgomery has not had an easy time of it in this town,' the housekeeper tells us. In moments as close as dreams, as impersonal as newspaper accounts, Meredith Steinbach gives us the life of Zara Montgomery— the precocious only child of a successful Midwestern physician and a failed British lieder singer. In *Zara*, Steinbach has given us fiction as it was meant to be—exacting, compelling, and enduring. The lucidity of this writing, the intricate craft of her structural designs, the richness and humanity of her characters, all point toward Meredith Steinbach as a novelist of exceptional power."

Reviews:

JOHN HAWKES: "Rich, horrific, beautiful, *Zara* is about the life of a woman extraordinary in every way, and is written in prose as strong and fabulous as Zara herself. I could not admire more this profound and exhilarating novel."

HILMA WOLITZER: "Zara is a beautifully realized character whose story is constantly engaging and moving. Ms. Steinbach is gifted and nervy and her book is very accomplished."

BOSTON REVIEW: "She's a critic of myth who also chooses to re-dream and brilliantly reinvent it. In *Zara*, . . . she considers the challenge of heroism in an American setting."

Los Angeles Times Book Review: "Steinbach probes vulnerability, futility in a style interlaced with quality and power."

Chicago Tribune: "The completely written quality of *Zara* marks an author page by page discovering the giddy limits of her talent. . . . I doubt a finer first novel will be published this year."

Chicago Magazine: "A rare, invaluable prize."

Boston Magazine: "A masterpiece."

HERE LIES THE WATER
by Meredith Steinbach

"Steinbach's intense novel of a circle of friends in rural New England addresses the misunderstandings and lies that destroy people by depriving them of 'the human will to love and learn.'"

Reviews:

Hungry Mind Review: "There's far more metaphor in *Here Lies the Water* than plot or character. Let's read it like a poem. The descriptive language is remarkable. . . . We are sustained by loss, memory, and the order and beauty of art. . . . Steinbach's prose is opulent, musical, disconcerting."

The New York Times Book Review: "Meredith Steinbach would probably cringe at the comparison, but her second novel is the spookiest tale of life gone wrong in suburbia since Ira Levin's *Stepford Wives*... As these revelations mount, ... its gorgeous but sometimes soporific prose becomes its strength, for it makes the wallop that's packed at the end even more powerful."

RELIABLE LIGHT by Meredith Steinbach

"In this collection of seven stories, Steinbach again distinguishes herself as a writer of sensitivity and grace. The effect is of real voices and real situations, portrayed with scrupulous fidelity to human nature. In robustly simple and direct prose, Steinbach introduces characters who range from an old woman in a nursing home to a black doctor in a New England village. In 'To Be Sung on the Water,' a woman visiting her mother's grave with her sister and young nephew is dismayed to find it sunken and filled with water. The boy's question, 'Why is your mama sleeping in that little lake?' helps bring the protagonist to a moment of transcendent understanding. 'In Recent History' observes the people whose lives have been profoundly affected by one man's experience in Vietnam, which he is tragically compelled to recreate. In the aftermath, the narrator occasionally glimpses the man and thinks, 'How strange and painful to see his face, as if he had not one terrible secret moment in his heart.' Constructed with a quiet and effective craftsmanship, these tales range in tone from comic to tragic, displaying the diversity of Steinbach's interests and themes."

Reviews:

Publishers' Weekly: "In this collection of seven stories, Steinbach again distinguishes herself as a writer of sensitivity and grace."

The New York Times Book Review: "Meredith Steinbach has won both a Pushcart Prize and an O. Henry Award for short fiction, and it's easy to see why. At her best, she gives us what we want from stories: root emotion recognized through someone else's consciousness.